Praise for
Red Velvet Revenge

"With a rodeo, a road trip, and the delectable title *Red Velvet Revenge*, the Fairy Tale Cupcake bakers are back, lassoed into big trouble this time. You're in for a real treat with Jenn McKinlay's Cupcake Bakery Mystery. I gobbled it right up."

—Julie Hyzy, bestselling author of the Manor House Mysteries and White House Chef Mysteries

"Sure as shootin', *Red Velvet Revenge* pops with fun and great twists. Wrangle up some time to enjoy the atmosphere of a real rodeo as well as family drama. It's better than icing on the tastiest cupcake."

—Avery Aames, author of *Clobbered by Camembert*

Buttercream Bump Off

"A charmingly entertaining story paired with a luscious assortment of cupcake recipes that, when combined, make for a deliciously thrilling mystery." —*Fresh Fiction*

"It is the characters and their interaction and dialogue that make this a standout mystery . . . *Buttercream Bump Off* is another tasty entry, complete with cupcake recipes, into what is sure to grow into a perennial favorite series."

—*The Mystery Reader*

"A hilarious story with smart heroines . . . If this series doesn't leave you hungry for more of Melanie and Angie, ~~es~~, then shame on you!"

~~Romance~~ Readers Connection

Sprinkle with Murder

"A tender cozy full of warm and likable characters and a refreshingly sympathetic murder victim. Readers will look forward to more of McKinlay's tasty concoctions."
— *Publishers Weekly* (starred review)

"McKinlay's debut mystery flows as smoothly as Melanie Cooper's buttercream frosting. Her characters are delicious, and the dash of romance is just the icing on the cake."
— Sheila Connolly, author of *Fire Engine Dead*

"Jenn McKinlay delivers all the ingredients for a winning read. Frost me another!"
— Cleo Coyle, national bestselling author of the Coffeehouse Mysteries

"A delicious new series featuring a spirited heroine, luscious cupcakes, and a clever murder. Jenn McKinlay has baked a sweet read."
— Krista Davis, author of the Domestic Diva Mysteries

Red
Velvet
Revenge

Jenn McKinlay

BERKLEY PRIME CRIME, NEW YORK

THE BERKLEY PUBLISHING GROUP
Published by the Penguin Group
Penguin Group (USA) Inc.
375 Hudson Street, New York, New York 10014, USA

Penguin Group (Canada), 90 Eglinton Avenue East, Suite 700, Toronto, Ontario M4P 2Y3, Canada
(a division of Pearson Penguin Canada Inc.) • Penguin Books Ltd., 80 Strand, London WC2R 0RL,
England • Penguin Group Ireland, 25 St. Stephen's Green, Dublin 2, Ireland (a division of Penguin
Books Ltd.) • Penguin Group (Australia), 250 Camberwell Road, Camberwell, Victoria 3124, Australia
(a division of Pearson Australia Group Pty. Ltd.) • Penguin Books India Pvt. Ltd., 11 Community
Centre, Panchsheel Park, New Delhi—110 017, India • Penguin Group (NZ), 67 Apollo Drive,
Rosedale, Auckland 0632, New Zealand (a division of Pearson New Zealand Ltd.) • Penguin Books
(South Africa) (Pty.) Ltd., 24 Sturdee Avenue, Rosebank, Johannesburg 2196, South Africa

Penguin Books Ltd., Registered Offices: 80 Strand, London WC2R 0RL, England

This is a work of fiction. Names, characters, places, and incidents either are the product of the author's
imagination or are used fictitiously, and any resemblance to actual persons, living or dead, business
establishments, events, or locales is entirely coincidental. The publisher does not have any control over
and does not assume any responsibility for author or third-party websites or their content.

PUBLISHER'S NOTE: The recipes contained in this book are to be followed exactly as written.
The publisher is not responsible for your specific health or allergy needs that may require medical
supervision. The publisher is not responsible for any adverse reactions to the recipes contained in
this book.

RED VELVET REVENGE

A Berkley Prime Crime Book / published by arrangement with the author

PUBLISHING HISTORY
Berkley Prime Crime mass-market edition / July 2012

Copyright © 2012 by Jennifer McKinlay Orf.
Excerpt from *Going, Going, Ganache* by Jenn McKinlay copyright © 2012 by Jennifer McKinlay Orf.
Cover illustration by Jeff Fitz-Maurice.
Cover design by Lesley Worrell.
Interior text design by Laura K. Corless.

ISBN: 978-0-425-25138-6

BERKLEY® PRIME CRIME
Berkley Prime Crime Books are published by The Berkley Publishing Group,
a division of Penguin Group (USA) Inc.,
375 Hudson Street, New York, New York 10014.
BERKLEY® PRIME CRIME and the PRIME CRIME logo are trademarks of
Penguin Group (USA) Inc.

PRINTED IN THE UNITED STATES OF AMERICA

10   9   8   7   6   5   4   3   2

For Lynne and Bob Orf,
the best in-laws a girl could ever have.
I feel very lucky to be a part of your family.

Acknowledgments

First, here's a shout out to Daneen Holcomb, who came up with the fabulous title *Red Velvet Revenge*. Well done! Also, I have to thank the artist, Jeff Fitz-Maurice, who created this spectacular cover. I want to go there now.

As always, I need to thank my fans (best fans ever) for joining in the fun and making the Cupcake Bakery Mysteries national bestsellers! Truly amazing!

For always helping me get to the finish line, I want to thank Jessica Faust, Kate Seaver, and Katherine Pelz.

And lastly, a big thank you to my families, the McKinlays and the Orfs, and to my dudes Beckett, Wyatt, and Chris—this would mean nothing without all of you.

Red Velvet Revenge

One

"What are we going to do about the business?" Angie DeLaura asked. She was sitting across the table from Melanie Cooper, dishing up her 23 Skidoo sundae while Mel sipped on her Camelback soda.

They had escaped their cupcake bakery, leaving it under the supervision of their two employees, and were sitting in the Sugar Bowl, Scottsdale's landmark ice cream shop. Mel always had the Camelback soda, vanilla ice cream scooped into old-fashioned soda with a pitcher of extra soda water on the side; it was her longtime favorite.

She glanced around the pink and chrome interior and noted that the Sugar Bowl hadn't seemed to age a day since it opened in 1958. Not that she had been around then, but her mother, Joyce, had been, and she remembered coming here when she was a little girl just like Mel remembered coming here with her father and her brother when they were kids. There was something about the thick glass ice cream dishes served on paper doilies on the classic white plates that was charmingly nostalgic.

Growing up, the Sugar Bowl had been a favorite hangout of Mel and Angie's along with their other childhood chum Tate. The three of them had practically owned the table by the window, where Mel and Angie now sat enjoying the respite from the scorching-hot July day outside.

Summer in the Valley of the Sun was as mean as an old man with sciatica. The sidewalk was so hot, Mel was sure the bottom of her flip-flops were going to melt. Just walking around the corner from their shop, Fairy Tale Cupcakes, had made both Mel and Angie sweat like marathoners, which they clearly were not, given that the relentless heat had them moving about as fast as a pair of desert tortoises.

"What do you mean what are we going to do about the business?" Mel asked. She was staring out the window, watching the midday heat rise from the street, making everything shimmer as if it actually were melting under the ferocity of the midday sun.

"It's a hundred and fourteen degrees out there," Angie said. "Our tourist business has completely dried up, and the last special order we had was for the Levinsky bar mitzvah two weeks ago."

Mel made a very loud slurp on her straw and reached for the pitcher to add more soda. She looked at Angie and said, "Your point?"

Angie blew out a breath, stirring the dark brown bangs that hung across her forehead. The rest of her long hair was piled up in a clip on the back of her head. She gave Mel a level look as she scooped up another gooey spoonful of her sundae.

"I think we should close for a week or two," Angie said. Mel opened her mouth to protest, but Angie barreled ahead. "Hear me out. It's costing us more money to be open than to close, we can both take a vacation until monsoon season hits, and then when we reopen, our regulars will be back and our tourists will slowly trickle on in again."

"You know, if you want to go to Los Angeles to see Roach, you can just go," Mel said. "We don't have to shut down the bakery so you can go be with your boyfriend."

Mel knew her tone was harsh, but sheesh! Close down the bakery? She couldn't help but think that it would be the kiss of death for their small business.

Angie's eyes narrowed and she plunked down her spoon with a *plop*. She looked like she was winding up to argue, and Mel braced herself, as Angie's fiery temper was hotter than the desert sun and known for leaving scorch marks on the recipient of her ire.

Angie never got the chance to let loose her volley of mad. With a bang and a puff of blue smoke, an ancient, oversized van/truck lurched into a parking spot on their side of the street. Mel and Angie whipped their heads in the direction of the noise.

"Is that . . ." Angie began, but Mel was already rising to her feet.

"Yup, it is," she said. "I'd recognize that shaggy mane and the other bald head anywhere."

Angie began to shovel the last of her sundae into her mouth. She slapped her free hand to her forehead, and Mel knew Angie had just given herself a walloping case of brain freeze.

They hurried to the cashier's window by the exit and paid their tab. Mel rushed back to leave their waiter's tip tucked under her soda pitcher.

"But Oz and Marty are supposed to be watching the bakery," Angie said as she followed Mel out the door.

Mel was pretty sure the blast of heat that smacked her full in the face as she stepped outside singed her eyebrows. She tried to look on the upside—as in, no waxing or plucking—but people without eyebrows just looked odd.

She ran her fingers over her brow bone just to reassure herself that they were still there and then felt positive that the acrid smell that was assaulting her nose wasn't burnt hair but rather the noxious blue smoke coming out of the tailpipe of the decrepit van in front of her.

"Oz," she called to her young intern. "What are you doing here?"

The young man who had been the bakery's paid intern since last spring turned to look at her from where he had his head under the hood of the van.

"Hey, Mel," he said. He stepped back and opened his arms wide. "Check it out. Isn't she a beauty?"

"That depends. Is she a contestant in a demolition derby?" Angie asked. She was fanning the back of her neck with one of the thick paper napkins from the Sugar Bowl.

"Heck no," Marty said, stepping forward. He was a dapper older gentleman who had come to work in the bakery several months before, when Mel and Angie had discovered that if they were to have any sort of personal life, they needed backup.

Oz and Marty exchanged excited glances and then spoke together. "She's your new cupcake van."

Mel looked at Angie and assumed her dumbfounded expression mirrored her own, and then looked back at the van. She took in the oversized white behemoth, which reminded her of an old bread truck. It was covered in faded Good Humor and Blue Bunny ice cream stickers, and she felt her powers of speech evaporate as she tried to form a response.

"I know it isn't much to look at now," Marty said. "But we could trick this baby out and it would be sweet."

"Where did it come from?" Angie asked.

"*Mi tío* Nacho—er, my uncle Ignacio left it to me when he died last year," Oz said. "It's been in my cousin's garage down in Tucson, and they finally drove it up."

"That's great, Oz," Mel said. "I'm so happy that you're going to have some wheels."

"No, it's not just for me," Oz said. "You two gave me my first job at the bakery and I want to give back. Marty and I are thinking we can motor around the hood and sell cupcakes."

"In that?" Mel asked. She had visions of her carefully cultivated image for the bakery going up, well, in a puff of blue smoke.

"Come on," Marty said. He took Mel's and Angie's elbows and half guided, half dragged them toward the back of the van. "You just need to go for a ride and you'll see the potential."

"All right, I'm going," Angie said, and she shook Marty off. Oz hefted up the rolling door in the back and Mel and Angie climbed aboard. Vintage steel freezers lined both sides, and Mel took in the scratched sliding window on the left side of the truck that appeared to have been retrofitted.

There was no seating. Angie plopped down on the floor, and Mel sat beside her while Marty and Oz scrambled into the front. Mel wrinkled her nose. Something smelled bad, like an expired dairy product. She suspected the smell lingered in the beige shag carpet but she didn't want to get close enough to verify her suspicion.

It took three turns of the key and a punch to the top of the dashboard to get it going, but the van finally coughed itself back to life, and Oz backed out of the parking spot, using the overly large side mirrors to guide his way.

The polyester shag carpet that covered the narrow strip of floor between the banks of freezers stuck to Mel's sweaty legs and itched. She sat with her knees drawn up and noticed that Angie did the same.

They puttered around Old Town Scottsdale, and then Oz headed out to the open road.

"Let me show you what she can do," he said, as slick as any used-car salesman.

"Really not necessary," Angie said. "Around the block will do."

But it was too late. Oz took Indian School Road out toward the highway. They were idling at the on-ramp traffic light when a big pink van pulled up beside them. Mel got a bad feeling in the pit of her stomach.

Marty and Oz had their windows down, because, in addition to the sour milk smell, blue exhaust, and itchy shag carpet, the van's air conditioner didn't seem capable of cooling the van to a temperature of less than one hundred.

Mel peered out the window over Marty's shoulder and groaned.

"What is it?" Angie asked. She rose and moved to kneel beside her.

"Olivia Puckett from Confections Bakery just pulled up beside us."

Two

As if sensing their stare, Olivia's head swiveled on her thick neck in their direction. Her nose wrinkled as if, from several feet away, she were getting a whiff of eau de stink from the truck, but then her eyes met Mel's and her expression cleared. The corners of her mouth turned up in a humorless smile.

"What is *that*?" she shouted.

"It's a van. What does it look like?" Marty shouted back. He'd had a few run-ins with Olivia in the past, and she was not on his short list of favorite people.

"It looks like a piece of sh—" she shouted back, but Oz revved the engine, drowning out whatever she had been about to say.

"Don't you listen to her, baby girl," Oz said as he patted the dashboard. "She's evil."

But Olivia had misconstrued his attempt to keep the truck running as an invitation to race.

She leaned out of her window and yelled, "You want a piece of me? Come get it!"

"She did not just say that," Angie said to Mel.

"Oh, yeah, she did," Mel said.

Olivia was revving her engine, and she cackled, looking at them like they were no more than bug guts smashed on her windshield. They both turned to lean over Oz's seat.

"You heard her!" Angie said.

"Punch it!" Mel ordered.

Oz revved his engine. Marty checked his seat belt. Mel and Angie braced themselves against the backs of the front seats. The light turned green and Olivia shot out of her lane, turning onto the two-lane on-ramp that led up to the highway.

Oz stomped on the gas, and the truck lurched forward as if it really wanted to give chase. Then it began to make a horrible grinding noise.

"I'm giving her all she's got, Captain!" Oz yelled over the noise in a terrible Scottish accent.

"All she's got isn't good enough!" Angie quoted back to him.

Marty glowered at the two of them. "*Star Trek*? You're quoting *Star Trek* now?"

As the former ice cream truck lumbered into the middle of the intersection and Olivia's sweet pink van was nothing but a memory and a flash of mocking taillights, Oz's new baby gave a deep, shuddering heave, knocking both Mel and Angie to the floor. It made a deafening *BANG*. Then it stopped dead.

Mel and Angie picked themselves up off of the nasty carpet. Cars zipped around them to get to the on-ramp before
the light changed. A line of cars formed behind the truck,
however, inciting honks and a few one-fingered salutes
when drivers unable to get around them missed the light and
were forced to wait for the next green.

"What are they so mad about?" Angie snapped as she
and Mel climbed out of the back of the truck. "We're the
ones who broke down."

She looked like she was going to charge the middle-aged
man in the Mustang, who had honked and flipped the bird
at them.

In an attempt to avoid Angie being carted off to jail, Mel
said, "Angie, you're the lightest. You steer us to the side.
Oz, Marty, and I will push."

Angie gave the man in the car one more blast of stink
eye before she climbed up into the driver's seat.

Oz joined Mel and Marty at the back of the van. Mel was
about to tell Marty not to strain himself, but as if he knew
what she was about to say before she opened her mouth, he
held up his hand to stop her.

"I'm old, not dead," he said. "I think I can manage not
to stroke out on you from a little exertion."

"Got to give it to him," Oz said with a shrug.

"Fine, but be careful, both of you," Mel said.

Marty and Oz exchanged put-out looks, and Mel wondered if this was what the mothers of teenage boys felt like.

They had to wait for a break in the traffic, and as soon as
it was clear, Angie yelled, "Push!"

It took every ounce of strength Mel possessed to help get
the van in motion, and she was pretty sure the only thing

more painful would be trying to push out a baby. The van was like a great beached whale being encouraged back into the ocean.

They were covered in sweat before they'd gone ten feet. The sun beat down on their backs, and Mel could feel her short blond hair become soaked and matted to her head as she pushed. Angie had the van in neutral and managed to crank the steering wheel in a sharp U-turn.

They crossed two lanes of oncoming traffic, and Angie hit the brakes as they slowed beneath the highway underpass, bringing them to a stop in the shade.

Mel, Oz, and Marty slumped against the back of the former ice cream truck in relief. Angie popped out of the driver's side door and took a look at the three of them.

"Everyone okay?" she asked.

The collective huffing and puffing kept them from answering, but since no one was supine on the curb, Angie seemed satisfied.

A large, cream-colored Cadillac Escalade pulled up and parked behind them. The driver's side door popped open, and out stepped an older gentleman wearing a white straw cowboy hat. Mel suddenly felt like she was in an old Western movie and the good guy was coming to the rescue.

" 'Don't say it's a fine morning or I'll shoot ya,' " Angie whispered in a low drawl.

"John Wayne in *McLintock!*," Mel whispered back. They exchanged heat-weary high fives.

"You folks look like you could use a hand," the man in the hat said.

Mel would have hugged him, but given that she was beginning to offend herself with the amount of sweat pouring off of her, she refrained.

"We sure could," Marty said as he wiped his hand on the side of his leg and held it out to the stranger.

"Marty Zelaznik."

"Slim Hazard, at your service," he said as he clasped Marty's hand in return. He was tall, and it wasn't just the cowboy boots that he wore that made him so. He was wearing a cotton Western-style shirt with an embroidered yoke and jeans that sported a belt buckle as big as Mel's head.

"This is Melanie, Angie, and young Oz," Marty said as he gestured at the rest of them. Mel wasn't positive but she thought she heard a note of admiration in Marty's voice. She knew it wasn't for them, so he had to be impressed by the cowboy in front of them. His next words confirmed it.

"You wouldn't be Slim Hazard from Juniper Pass, would you?"

Slim pushed his hat back on his head and put his hand on the back of his neck, as if he were embarrassed that Marty had heard of him.

"Yep, I'm afraid that's me," he said. "Here, son, let me have a look."

Slim ambled over to where Oz crouched, looking under the van to assess the damage from below.

"Wow, it's really him." Marty looked gobsmacked. He glanced at Mel and Angie to see if they were as impressed as he was. When they both shrugged, he frowned. "You two are lacking in your rodeo lore."

"Clearly." Angie wiped the sweat off of her forehead with her forearm. "So who is the bronco buster?"

"Only one of the greatest cowboys who ever lived,"

Marty said. "His family hosts the Juniper Pass Rodeo every year."

At Mel's and Angie's blank looks, he gave a *tsk* of disgust.

"It's the biggest rodeo in the country!"

Mel shrugged. Marty looked as if he'd continue, but just then Slim and Oz joined them.

"Now, don't you worry," Slim was saying to Oz. "I've seen worse than this. Why, with a little elbow grease, you'll have her up and running in no time."

He gave Oz a solid pat on the back and looked at the group as if seeking back up.

"Yeah, absolutely, good as new," Mel said, and Slim smiled at her.

Oz still looked ill at ease, but less like he was going to throw up. She was pretty sure she heard him mutter some soothing words to the defunct truck. Poor kid. It was a rough break getting wheels, only to lose them on the very first day.

"Can I offer you folks a lift?" Slim asked. "It's a mite too hot to be standing out in this heat waiting for a tow truck."

"We would love one," Angie answered for them all. Without waiting for assistance, or maybe afraid that Slim would change his mind, she headed toward the Escalade.

"Thank you, sir," Marty said. "You're being very kind."

"Not at all, and call me Slim," he said. "Come on, youngster. Your van isn't going anywhere; you may as well let her rest."

Oz gave the van a one-armed pat that looked to Mel like a surreptitious hug before he followed them into the Escalade.

Angie was already buckled into the middle seat and chatting to the petite blonde in the passenger's seat, when the others climbed in.

"Everyone, this is Tammy Hazard, Slim's wife," Angie said.

"Hi, y'all," Tammy said. She turned in her seat and gave them a well-manicured wave.

Mel's first impression of Tammy was that she had very big hair. Big and blond, it puffed up on her head like a meringue and then settled on her shoulders in a controlled wave. The next thing she noticed was that Tammy wasn't as young as she first appeared. She was very well maintained, with just the right amount of makeup, She had a neat figure but she wasn't skeletally skinny or going to pudge. If Mel had to guess, she'd have put Tammy solidly in her fifties, which she thought complemented Slim nicely, who looked to be somewhere in his sixties.

"It's hot enough to fry an egg out there," Tammy said. "You poor things. I'm so glad we came by when we did."

Both Oz and Marty gave her dazzled smiles. Mel wasn't sure if it was heat exhaustion or being in the presence of a female who wasn't dripping her body weight in sweat, but they both looked smitten and climbed into the far back.

Mel took the seat next to Angie. She felt bad that she was perspiring on the butter soft leather, but unless Slim and Tammy had a towel tucked in the vehicle, there wasn't much she could do about it.

She turned back once she was buckled in, and Slim shifted the vehicle into drive. "Now, where can I take you folks?"

"Could you drop us off at our bakery?" Mel asked. "It's just down the road a few miles."

"Absolutely," he said.

He pulled out into traffic, and Mel turned to check on Marty and Oz. As they pulled away, Oz heaved a broken-hearted sigh.

"It'll be okay, Oz," Mel said. "We can call a tow truck from the bakery and get it to a garage."

He didn't seem consoled.

"A garage?" Angie asked. "That thing needs to go to the great junkyard in the sky."

"Angie!" Mel hushed her.

"I can't afford a garage," Oz said. "I need someone to fix it on the cheap."

Angie studied him over her shoulder. Then she pulled her cell phone out of her pocket and made a call.

"Sal, it's Angie," she said. "Yeah, I'm fine."

There was a pause.

"No, Sal, I haven't broken up with Roach yet."

She looked at Mel and rolled her eyes. Angie was the youngest and the only girl out of the eight DeLaura children. The brothers did not like her current boyfriend, a drummer in a rock band who went by the name Roach. Literally, every time she talked to any of the brothers, they managed to work her breaking up with her boyfriend into the conversation.

"Sal, listen," Angie said. "I have a situation."

There was another pause, and Mel could hear Sal's raised voice.

"No, not that kind of situation!" Angie snapped. "What kind of girl do you think I am?"

There was another pause, and Mel was pretty sure she heard groveling on Sal's end.

"Listen, we have a van that's broken down under the 101 underpass off of Indian School Road," she said. "Do you think you could have your tow truck come and get it?"

Angie spun around in her seat and gave Oz a thumbs-up.

"Do me a favor and have one of your mechanics take a look at it," Angie said. "We'd like to know how much work needs to be done to make it street legal."

Angie continued her chat while Mel leaned forward to give Slim directions through Old Town to the front of the bakery. Slim stopped in one of the many empty parking spots directly in front of Fairy Tale Cupcakes.

"Is that your bakery?" Tammy asked.

"It is," Mel said. She knew she sounded proud, and she couldn't help it. She loved her shop right down to the last paper cupcake liner. "Come on in, and I'll give you a tour and some cupcakes."

"Did you say cupcakes?" Slim hopped out of the driver's side and hustled around to open the door for his wife.

Tammy grinned. "Slim has a terrible sweet tooth."

"Well, he has come to the right place," Mel said.

Slim opened both of their doors, and they all climbed out. Mel led the way into the bakery to find Tate Harper, the financial backer of their baking venture, sitting in one of the booths.

He rose at the sight of them and took a step closer to Mel to hug her, but then stopped with a frown.

"You're all wet," he said. "And the place was locked up and no one was here when I arrived. What happened?"

"First, introductions," Mel said. "Slim and Tammy Hazard, this is our business partner, Tate Harper."

They all shook, and Mel said, "Marty, why don't you show Slim and Tammy the cupcakes on display and load them up with a six-pack of their choice."

"Oh, no, we couldn't," Tammy protested.

Mel shook her head. "I insist. You saved us all from heatstroke. It's the least we can do."

"You heard her, darlin', she insists," Slim said, and he winked at Mel. He looked delighted and rubbed his hands together as he took in the display case. Mel suspected Tammy had not undersold his love of sweets.

"All right. Bye." Angie ended her call.

"Sal is going to collect the van?" Mel asked.

"And he's going to have a look at it," she said.

"What van?" Tate asked.

"My van," Oz said, and he slumped into one of the padded booths by the window.

"You have a van?" Tate asked.

"Had a van," Mel said.

"Yeah, until it went *boom* in a drag race against Olivia," Angie added.

"Boom?" Tate asked faintly.

"Eh, more like *bang*," Mel said.

"Did Olivia go *bang*?" Tate asked. He was turning pale and looked like he needed to sit.

"No, she went—" Angie was about to replicate Olivia's obscene hand gesture, but Mel smacked her hand down.

"He gets the idea," she said.

Angie shrugged.

"Is there anything else I should know about?" Tate asked. Mel had known Tate since they were twelve years old. He was tugging on his left ear, something he always did when he was feeling stressed.

"Let go of your ear, Tate," she said. "Everything is cool."

"Then it's settled," Slim said.

Mel spun around to see Slim and Marty shaking hands. Marty still had the worshipful gaze of an adolescent boy in his eyes, and Mel realized he was in the throes of a full-on man crush.

"Oh, this is wonderful," Tammy said. "Selling cupcakes at our rodeo is just the kind of hip twist it needs."

"Uh . . . what was that?" Mel asked.

"Isn't it great?" Marty asked. He was so happy even his bald head was glowing. "We're going to sell cupcakes at the Juniper Pass Rodeo."

Three

Mel, Angie, and Tate stared at Marty as if he'd suddenly overdosed on his blood pressure medication.

"Marty, Juniper Pass is way up north," Angie said. "We're talking hours away. How are we supposed to sell cupcakes up there?"

"The truck," Marty said. He looked to Oz for backup. "It'll be a great dry run for our bakery on wheels."

Oz perked up from where he'd been slouching. His eyes lit up and he looked at Angie.

"When do you think you'll hear from Sal?" he asked.

"Probably in a couple of hours," she said.

Mel looked at Slim and Tammy, who were watching the exchange in bemusement. As the chief baker and the person who lived above the bakery, Mel was supposed to be in charge of the business. But as she looked at her crew, she couldn't help but note that it looked as if the lunatics were running the asylum.

She knew it was time to get control of the situation or invest in a wholesale order of straitjackets.

"Slim, the rodeo sounds like so much fun," she said. "But other than deliveries, we've never taken cupcakes on the road before."

"Well, there's no time like the present," he said cheerfully. "Your business looks as dried up as a grape in the sun."

Marty was nodding like a bobblehead doll, and Mel glared at him.

"And it would be good for us, too," Tammy said. "The rodeo could use a contemporary punch, and what is more happening than cupcakes?"

"Apparently, whoopie pies are the pastry of the future," Tate said.

Angie looked like she wanted to kick him. "Well, that's just stupid."

He shrugged. "I just report the trends. I don't make them up."

Mel felt her stomach twist with anxiety. She loved her cupcake bakery. Yes, she made special-order cakes, too, but she really just loved the compact size and perfection of the cupcake. She didn't want to turn Fairy Tale Cupcakes into Fairy Tale Whoopie Pies.

"Well, the invite is wide-open," Slim said. "The rodeo is in two weeks. If you folks want in, you just give me a holler and I'll make room for you."

"Oh, we want in," Marty said.

"Marty!" Mel and Angie said at the same time. "We need to discuss this."

Marty stuck out his lower lip in a full-on pout, and Mel frowned at him.

"That's not going to work," she said.

He huffed and slouched into the booth across from Oz.

Mel rolled her eyes. Honestly, why was it that all of the men in her life had the emotional maturity of twelve-year-olds?

Tammy checked the delicate gold watch encrusted with diamonds on her wrist. "Oh, Slim, we have to get going. We have that meeting with the Chamber of Commerce."

"Oh, right," he said. He smiled at the others. "She keeps me on task. I don't think I could function without her."

Tammy gave him an adoring smile, and Mel decided that the Hazards were one of the nicest couples she'd ever met.

"Thanks for the ride," Mel said. "You really saved our bacon."

Slim grinned. "Are you kidding? For cupcakes, I'd have driven you all the way down to Tucson."

They left with a wave, and Mel realized they had been the only visitors in the bakery all day. The afternoon stretched out before her, and she thought of the stack of bills sitting on the desk in her office.

"Oh, Mel," Slim called to her from the door. "Just so you know, the rodeo draws about twenty-five thousand visitors."

The door shut behind him with a thud that masked the sound of Mel's jaw hitting the black-and-white tile floor.

Twenty-five *thousand*?

She spun around to face the others, and she was pretty sure she had dollar signs shining in her eyes.

"Angie, get Sal on the phone. We need an update on the van, stat."

Mel spent the afternoon planning for the cupcakepalooza that would be the rodeo if they could manage to pull it off. Marty was giddy, Oz was just happy to have his van being worked on, Tate was dubious, and Angie was oddly quiet.

"So, this whole plan is dependent upon Oz's van being functional," Tate said.

"Yeah, and Sal says it's doable," Mel said.

They were sitting at the steel worktable in her kitchen. She had a notebook out and was making a list of the bakery's most popular cupcakes. She figured the best way to manage the rodeo crowd was to keep it simple with just four varieties of cupcake that hit everyone's sweet spot.

"So, you're just going to close the shop for the week and take off," Tate said.

"Tate, we are in a lull of epic proportions. The mercury has hovered around a hundred and fourteen for the past week, and there's no break in sight," Mel said. "No one wants to eat a cupcake right now. They only want frozen foods."

"Maybe you should freeze your cupcakes," he said.

"Angie, back me up," Mel said. "You were just saying that we should close for a week or two."

Tate turned from Mel to study Angie. "You wanted to close? Any special reason?"

Mel could have kicked her own behind. Tate and Angie had been her best friends since junior high school. The three of them had bonded over a love of old movies and junk food. Unbeknownst to Mel, Angie had carried a torch for Tate for years.

Like Mel, Tate had been completely oblivious right up

until Angie landed herself a rock-star boyfriend. Now he stood pining on the sidelines while she tried to figure out whether she was going to move to Los Angeles to live with Roach or not. He had never managed to gather up the courage to tell her how he felt, and it had become painful for Mel to watch the two of them, knowing that they loved each other but were too chicken to do anything about it.

"Well, with business being so slow and all," Angie said, "I just thought we could take the time to . . ."

"Go to California?" Tate supplied.

"Or Canada," Angie said. "Or Nepal. You know, there's a whole great big world out there."

"Uh-huh," Mel and Tate said together.

"Look, if we're going to do the rodeo, I need to know if you're in, Angie," Mel said. "I figure we'll need to bring Oz, since it's his truck, but space is limited, so we're looking at just the three of us."

"What?" a voice barked from the swinging door. "You can't go without me."

Marty stood, staring at them, looking outraged with his hands planted on his hips.

"We only have so much room, Marty," Mel said.

"But I brokered the deal," he said. "I'm the one who talked Slim into hiring you."

"And I really appreciate it," Mel said. "But you and Tate are going to have to stay behind. There's just not enough room."

"What?" Tate asked in an equally put-out voice. "But I'm a partner in this bakery. I demand to go."

Mel looked at Angie. "Well, if you want to bag out, it looks like I'll have plenty of help."

23

"Oh, no, I'm totally going," Angie said. "I've never been to a rodeo before." Mel grinned. She knew it was selfish, but she was delighted that Angie had chosen the bakery and her over Roach.

"Well, that settles it, then," Mel said. "You, me, and Oz. We just have to get the okay from his parents."

Tate and Marty exchanged indignant looks. Tate pointed to the kitchen door behind Marty, then hooked his thumb at the back door and Marty gave a nod. Before Mel could figure out what they were up to, they were both lying on the floor of the kitchen, blocking the exits.

"What is this? Occupy Fairy Tale Cupcakes?!" Angie asked. "What do you think you're doing?"

"We're in protest mode," Tate said. "We're going limp and we're going to lie here until you agree to let us come along."

"Are you kidding me?" Mel asked. "What if I don't give in? Are you going to hold your breath until you turn blue?"

She watched Tate lift his head and look at Marty. He raised his eyebrows in silent question, and Marty gave him a small nod.

"Thanks for the idea," Marty said.

The kitchen door slammed into his side, and Marty grunted but held his ground. The kitchen door didn't budge.

"Hey, the door is stuck," Oz yelled from the other side.

"Yeah, we know. There's a one-hundred-and-seventy-pound dust bunny blocking it," Angie shouted back.

"One hundred and sixty-four pounds," Marty corrected her.

"Whatever," Angie said, making her hands into the shape of a *W*.

"*Clueless.*" Tate identified the movie quote from his supine position.

Mel and Angie looked at each other and the two men on the floor. This was a losing battle if ever there was one.

"All right, you can come," Mel said. "But you may be riding on the roof to make room for the cupcakes, you have to take a shift selling cupcakes out of the van, and I don't want to hear any whining. Deal?"

Marty and Tate sat up with matching grins and said, "Deal."

"Why do I get the feeling I'm going to regret this?" Mel asked.

Four

"Are you sure Sal can have the van fixed in time for you to go?" Joe DeLaura asked.

Mel looked up from where she was squatting on the floor of her apartment's tiny kitchenette, pouring milk into a saucer for her cat, Captain Jack.

Captain Jack was all white with a couple of black patches, one of which covered his left eye. He looked like quite the pirate and had a rogue's temperament, so when they had rescued him from a Dumpster a few months ago and Angie had dubbed him Captain Jack, Mel hadn't bothered to change it.

His purring, which sounded remarkably like an idling V8 engine getting ready for a drag race, increased as Mel stood and put the milk away in the fridge and the saucer was officially his.

"I don't know," Mel said. "I called Slim Hazard to tell—What?"

"Nothing," Joe said with a grin. "I just really like his name."

Mel smiled. Joe was sitting at the counter, watching her. He was in casual attire for a change, a fitted T-shirt and shorts. Being an assistant district attorney, he rocked the suit thing pretty much 24-7, and Mel always felt like she got the "real Joe" when he had the time to dress down and just be with her.

Given that it was still brutally hot outside, they were bunkered in her apartment, which was a snug eight hundred square feet, so it cooled easily.

She glanced out the window, noting that the sun hadn't set yet and it was undoubtedly still turkey-roasting hot. Once the sun set, things would cool down—not much, but enough to make the idea of venturing outside seem less like being caught in an inferno's back draft.

"I wish you could have seen Marty with him," Mel said. "I haven't seen a case of hero worship like that since my nephews saw the man in the giant rat suit walking around the Chuck E. Cheese."

"I think Chuck E. is a mouse."

"Either way," she said. "I think Captain Jack could take him."

They both looked down at the feline, whose purrs had turned into noisy slurps of joy.

"No question," Joe agreed.

Mel circled the counter and sat down at the breakfast bar beside Joe. She reached for her glass of ice water and took a long sip, aware that Joe was watching her.

"Anyway, I told Slim we had to get the van fixed up, and he said not to worry and that they would make room for us no matter what. I noticed when we gave him a six-pack as a thank-you for giving us a lift that he has a sweet tooth and a weakness for my Death by Chocolates," Mel said.

"I like him already," Joe said.

He reached over and laced his fingers with hers. Despite the coolness of the apartment, it was still July in Arizona, and hugging was kept to a minimum.

"Angie has been badgering Sal about the van, while Oz has been spending his days at the dealership helping out," Mel said.

"I didn't know Oz knew anything about cars," he said.

"He doesn't," she said. "I think he's just watching over his baby chick."

"Oz as mama hen. I like that." Joe gave her his patent-worthy amused grin.

He absently ran his thumb over the inside of her wrist, and Mel felt her pulse kick up a notch. Honestly, all the man had to do was walk into a room and smile at her and she was as useless as a puddle on the floor. It had been like that since the first time she'd been flattened by his grin when she was in middle school and he was in high school.

Joe was the middle of Angie's seven older brothers and had spent his life as the peacemaker of the rambunctious DeLaura clan. Mel had worshipped him from afar, never thinking he would see her as anything but his little sister's pesky best friend.

But one day, he'd come to the bakery, upon Angie's request, to offer Mel some legal advice, and just like that the grin that had always made her knees turn to jelly had come to belong just to her.

For Mel, he had become her compass point. Whenever the self-doubt of adolescence snuck up behind her and her former chubby self tried to kick her in the pants and shatter her confidence, all she had to do was have Joe gaze at her through his lashes and give her his slow grin, that special look that she knew belonged just to her, and all of her insecurities melted like butter in the sun.

"I'm a little worried about how it's going to shake out," she confessed. "I mean, the van looked deader than dead when we left it."

"Sal knows his cars," Joe said. "If he thinks he can fix it, he probably can."

"Yeah, but it had faded ice cream stickers on it and it reeked of sour milk," Mel said. "When I asked Sal if there was any way we could clean out the interior or slap a fresh coat of paint on it, he said, 'Don't worry. I know a guy.'"

Mel looked warily at Joe. A few of the DeLaura brothers were well-known to Mel's uncle Stan, who was a detective on the Scottsdale police force. They were known to him not because they had careers in law enforcement, but rather because they tended to operate on the fringes of the law. It was not something that made Joe happy.

"A guy, huh?" he asked.

"Yeah, so now I'm baking my behind off, trying to freeze several thousand cupcakes and make tubs of frosting, when I may have no place to store all of these cupcakes, and I could find myself selling cupcakes out of my nephews' red rider wagon."

"I'd buy one from your wagon."

Mel laughed. Per usual he knew just what to say. Joe pulled her close, and for the moment all thoughts of the rodeo, the van, and the mountain of cupcakes that needed to be baked were forgotten.

〝〟〝〟

Mel and Angie spent the following week baking until they dropped. The plan was to bake as much as they could, freeze the cupcakes, and then defrost them once they were up at the rodeo.

Mel tried to maintain her optimism. Angie checked in with Sal daily, and in his usual car-salesman suave, he assured them that the van would be ready and tricked out in ways they couldn't imagine. Somehow, Mel did not find this as reassuring as Sal might think.

It was the day before they were to leave for the rodeo, and Mel and Angie surveyed their walk-in cooler at the bakery. There was a staggering amount of cupcakes in it. In fact, Mel was quite sure she had never seen so many cupcakes—not even at the annual Cupcake Love-In, a charity event held in Scottsdale every year.

"If Sal doesn't come through . . ." Mel didn't want to think about it.

"He'll come through," Angie said. "It may be with a king cab pickup truck and a refrigerator trailer, but he'll come through."

"Mel! Angie! Get out here!"

Mel and Angie exchanged a look and backed out of the walk-in.

"What is it?" Angie yelled back.

"Just hurry up!" Marty said.

"Maybe we have customers," Mel suggested.

"Well, his yelling is going to put them off their cupcakes," Angie said.

They sped up and pushed through the swinging kitchen door as one.

"What is it?" Mel asked.

But Marty wasn't behind the counter where he was supposed to be; instead, he was at the front door.

Oz poked his head around the doorframe. He looked hot and sweaty, and the thick curtain of bangs that usually covered his eyes had been secured back by a blue bandanna. He caught sight of Mel and Angie and beamed.

"Are you ready for the big reveal?"

"You mean it's done?" Mel asked. She felt her ribs compress into her chest with a nervous squeeze.

Oz nodded.

"He looks happy," Angie said. "That's a good sign, right?"

"He's seventeen; it has four wheels and an engine. Of course he's happy," Marty said.

The three of them stepped out of the bakery into the midday heat. Mel had expected to see the van parked in front of the shop, since presently there was plenty of parking to be had.

Outside, however, there was a large coal gray lump with Angie's brother Sal and a guy in a blue mechanic's uniform, with the name Lou stitched onto the front of his shirt, standing beside it.

"Baby sister," Sal said with a warm note of affection as he gave his sister a squeeze. "Didn't I tell you I'd come through?"

Angie laughed as she squeezed him in return. "Yeah, you did."

"This is Lou. He's my guy," Sal said.

"Nice to meet you." Lou shook hands with Angie, Mel, and Marty.

"Thanks for helping with this, Lou," Mel said. "We really appreciate it."

"Oh, you have no idea," Sal said. "Are you ready?"

Marty had wandered over to the van and was trying to lift the huge car cover to sneak a peek under it. Without turning away from them, Lou reached over and smacked Marty's hand.

"No peeking," he said.

Marty gave him a sour look but went and stood with the others.

"Are you ready?" Sal asked.

"Yes," Angie and Mel said together, but then Angie added, "No, wait!" Sal's face fell like a meringue on a humid day.

"Why?" he asked.

"Shouldn't Tate be here?" Angie asked. "He's our partner and he'd want to see this."

"Oh, he's already seen it," Sal said. Then he clapped a hand over his mouth.

"Explain." Angie frowned at him.

Sal spread his hands wide in his attempt at sincere. "Well, business being what it is, and costs—"

"You did not!" Angie snapped and stomped her foot.

"Did not what?" Mel asked. "I'm not following."

"Have Tate pay for the renovations," Angie said. Then she whirled on Oz. "Did you know about this?"

All six foot three of him squirmed under Angie's glare, and he said, "Kind of."

"Kind of?" Angie asked. "Like, I'm *kind of* going to kick all of your butts?"

"Calm down, baby sis," Sal began. "Tate came around to the shop and saw what we were dealing with—seriously, a dropped transmission and a bad stink that made even my nose hair curl—and he agreed that if this was really going to be a part of your business venture, then some capital had to be channeled into it."

"How much?" Angie asked.

"I'm not sure," Sal said. "I'm a little fuzzy on the numbers."

"Oh, please. You can sniff out the change in a person's pocket at twenty paces," Angie said. "How much?"

"You may as well tell her, Sal," Mel said. "You know we'll get it out of Tate anyway."

"Twenty K," he said.

Angie staggered. Mel would have caught her, but she got dizzy as the sidewalk tipped a bit.

"Whoa, we're going to have to sell over eight thousand cupcakes to pay him back," Mel said, doing some quick mental math.

"Pay who back?" a voice asked from behind them.

Mel and Angie turned to see Tate standing there.

"Thanks for the text, Oz," he said, and they exchanged some complicated handshake thing that to Mel looked like two birds humping. "I didn't want to miss the big reveal."

Angie took a swing at him, but Tate hadn't been Angie's BFF for more than twenty years for nothing. He ducked and caught her around the middle, hoisting her up over his shoulder.

"Angie, it's too hot for this much exertion," he said. "What are you thinking?"

"I'm thinking I'm going to stomp on you!"

Tate turned to Mel and said, "Well, that's gratitude."

Five

"Tate, we can't borrow any more money for the business," Mel said. "I thought we were pretty clear on that."

Tate shrugged. "It was an opportunity."

Mel gave him a hard stare while Angie grumbled behind them, "Hey, I think all of the blood has run to my head."

"Good. Then you won't be able to do any damage," Tate said, and he slowly lowered her to her feet.

Sal looked at the three of them. "Are we good now? Because I am sweating like a hairy monkey in a polyester suit and I need to get back to work."

"We're good," Mel said as she steadied Angie with a hand on her elbow. Then she glanced at Tate. "We'll discuss this later."

He gave a put-upon sigh but didn't argue.

"All right, then," Sal said. "Lou, if you don't mind."

He gestured for the other man to grab a corner of the gray car cover, and together they lifted it like a preschool parachute up and over the van.

Mel felt her eyes get wide as she tried to take it in.

The faded ice cream stickers were gone, and in their place was the coolest thing on four wheels Mel had ever seen.

Its big rectangular shape had a fresh coat of white paint. *Fairy Tale Cupcakes* was spelled out in their signature cursive font, and Sal and Lou had put an enormous atomic cupcake symbol, the one Mel and Angie used for all of their packaging, which featured an aqua and pink cupcake with the swirls of an atom going around it, on both sides and the back. There could be no doubt in anyone's mind that this was a cupcake truck.

"Squeee!" Angie and Mel grabbed each other's hands and made a girly noise heretofore never heard from either of them before.

"It's awesome," Angie gushed. All four men flushed with pleasure.

"Truly spectacular," Mel agreed. "I am so impressed."

"Oh, you haven't seen anything," Lou the mechanic said. "If you'll follow me, please."

Mel and Angie stepped off of the curb and followed him around the back. He hauled the roll door up to its full height and stepped out of the way.

"Oh, wow, it's like a mini-me version of the bakery," Mel said.

Gone was the nasty shag carpet. In its place was black-and-white tile flooring just like the bakery's. The interior had been painted pink, and the freezers had been polished up until their steel exteriors positively gleamed.

"And check this out," Sal said. He moved over to the side that used to have the scratched sliding window. There were new windows there now. He slid them open and then un-latched the side cover, which rose up to form a metal aw-ning, giving shade to both the window and the people waiting at the window.

Angie leaned forward and popped her head out. Tate was standing there, smiling at her. Mel leaned out the window beside her, trying to decide if it was the right height. It was perfect.

"May I take your order, sir?" Angie asked in her best server's voice.

Tate gazed at her with such a fierce look of longing that Mel had to look away. She heard Angie hiss a breath in between her teeth, and she was sure Angie had seen the look, too.

"That depends," Tate said, his voice gruff. "Are you on the menu?"

Angie stared at him for a heart-pounding second and then jerked back into the truck and spun around. "Well, I guess that answers that. We obviously need a menu board."

Mel was rooting around in the freezers, trying to decide if there was enough room in them for all of the cupcakes she had made. It was going to be a tight squeeze, but she thought they'd make it.

She glanced out the window at Tate, who was looking inordinately pleased with himself. Honestly, just because he could make Angie blush, he thought he stood a chance with her. Idiot.

Mel shook her head. She was so not getting involved in this. Instead she took in the overhead storage and the built-in mini–display rack that Sal had obviously had custom-fit to sit in front of the window. She had to admit, this truck was a work of art. The only question now was how did it run?

"So, Oz, how about a test drive?" she asked.

He looked as if he'd been waiting for her to ask, and he wrestled his keys out of his pocket and jumped in the driver's seat.

Tate took the passenger's seat while Marty climbed in back with Mel and Angie.

"Wait!" Sal yelled. "Lou, show them the jump seats."

Mel and Angie exchanged a look while Lou climbed into the back. Built into the wall behind the driver's seat and the passenger's seat were four jump seats that folded out of the wall just like the type flight attendants used on airplanes.

"I can't have baby sister and brother's girlfriend driving around in this unless they're buckled in," Sal said.

"Oh, Sal, that's so sweet," Angie said.

She and Mel took the seats behind Oz, and Marty took one of the two on the other side. Their legs were wedged up against the freezer, but it was better than squatting on the floor. Lou put down the awning and closed the window. Then he hopped out of the back of the truck and pulled the roll door down.

Sal stuck his head in Tate's window and said, "Call me if you have any trouble."

"They won't have trouble," Lou said with a confidence Mel really appreciated hearing from a mechanic.

They took a winding tour of Old Town Scottsdale and then cruised up Hayden Road along the greenbelt.

There were no ominous grinding noises or puffs of blue

smoke, and for the first time Mel actually believed they were going to pull this off. She thought of a few days spent in the cooler elevation of northern Arizona, and twenty-five thousand rodeo fans eating her cupcakes. She grinned.

"Promise you'll feed him and play with him every day," Mel said. "He likes to be rubbed just below his chin."

She held Captain Jack in one arm and rubbed his chin with her free hand. He purred and pushed his triangular little face against her.

"I promise," Joyce Cooper said. "Surely, if I handled your brother's iguana, Figaro, for all of those years, I can manage a wee little kitten."

"I don't know, Mom," Mel said. "He has the ability to slip into another dimension, I swear. One minute he's there, and the next second he's gone and you can't find him anywhere. It's very disconcerting."

"Oh, don't be silly," Joyce said. She held out her arms, and Mel reluctantly handed him over. She knew her mother would take excellent care of her little man, but oh, she was going to miss him.

"Be a good boy," Mel said. She kissed Captain Jack's head and he batted playfully at her nose. She felt her throat constrict, but she swallowed hard and gave her mother a hug. "I'll have my phone with me at all times, so call me if you have any questions or concerns."

"I will, sweetie—don't you worry."

Mel noted that her mother was talking to her in the same calm and reassuring voice she used on her sister-in-law when she and Mel's brother left their sons with Joyce so that they could get away.

"Is dear Joe going with you?" Joyce asked. She always called him *dear Joe*, leaving Mel no doubt as to how she felt about him. Mel sincerely hoped she and Joe never broke up, because she knew her mother would undoubtedly take it the hardest.

"No, he has to work, and with Tate, Marty, and Oz going, we're pretty much at capacity," Mel said.

"Well, be careful," Joyce said. "Don't get trampled by a bull or anything."

"I'm not going to get trampled by a bull," Mel said. She turned away to hide the smile that was threatening to bust out. Only her mother, the worrier, could think of something as crazy as death by bull trampling.

Six

In the end, no one had to sit on the roof, but it was a tight squeeze for all of them in the back with the cupcakes and tubs of frosting and their luggage. Angie made a footrest out of her carry-on, and Mel watched as she texted furiously when they pulled onto the highway and headed north.

The way her thumbs were flying across the QWERTY keyboard, Mel had no doubt that whoever was on the receiving end of her message was not getting a lot of smiley faces or LOLs.

"Problem?" she asked.

"Nothing a swift kick in the leather pants wouldn't fix," Angie said.

Mel knew only one person who wore leather pants. "So, it's Roach, huh?"

Angie slammed her phone shut and glowered at it before dropping it in her lap.

"He's all mad because I'm going to the rodeo, instead of coming to California to be with him," she said. "I tried to explain that this is my business and I have to be there, but he's not listening."

Mel was quiet for a minute. Because she had such strong feelings about Angie leaving, she had really tried over the past few months not to say anything but to let Angie figure this out herself. But now she felt obligated to point out the obvious.

"But, Ange," she said. "We have enough people to work the rodeo; you could go to California."

Angie gave her an annoyed look. She glanced over Mel's shoulder to where Tate sat in the front of the truck with Oz. They were chatting about the band the Ramones and the punk rock movement of the late 1970s. Then she glanced across at Marty, who had his head tipped back against the wall, cushioned by his travel pillow, with his mouth slightly ajar as he dozed.

"Here's the thing," Angie whispered, and Mel had to lean forward to hear her over the drone of the engine and the chatter in the front seat. "Roach's scene, well, it gets exhausting."

"Meaning?" Mel asked.

"Out every night all night, playing gigs or recording or just showing up at an event because the PR machine wants to keep his name busy." Angie let out a big sigh. "There's very little peace in his world."

"Have you told him this?" Mel asked.

"Yeah, and then I fly out and he promises it will be different and maybe for one or two nights it is. We sit in his huge house on the hill in Laurel Canyon, and then Jimbo, his manager, calls and we're off to a ball game or a celebrity golf tournament or a movie premiere."

"My heart is breaking for you," Mel said. "Really, I'm shattered. Didn't you get to meet Liam Neeson and Bradley Cooper the last time you were there?"

"Yeah, and I didn't faint. I thought that spoke well of me. They were very nice," Angie said. "But that's not my world. Whenever I'm there, I just feel like Roach's accessory. I might as well be one of his drumsticks, you know?"

"No, I can't say that I do," Mel said.

"Well, how about the lawyerly functions you have to attend with Joe?" Angie asked.

Oz swerved sharply to the right, and Angie fell over into Mel's lap.

"Sorry!" Oz yelled. "There's a lunatic out here in a BMW, and I think he's trying to run me off the road."

"BMW?" Angie asked. "What's it look like?"

"Black with orange flames coming up the hood," he said. "He's waving at us. Do you think there's something wrong with the truck?"

The BMW pulled up alongside them and started honking. Angie stared at the phone in her hands and then out the window at the car.

"Oz, pull over!" she ordered.

"What?" Oz shouted back. "We're on the Beeline Highway in the middle of nowhere."

"Just do it," Angie said.

"What's going on?" Tate asked. "Angie, if this is a road-rage thing, the last thing we should do is stop."

"There's no rage . . . yet," she said.

Tate sent Mel a confused look, and Mel mouthed the name *Roach*. Tate's eyebrows rose, but she said nothing more. This was Angie's situation; Mel would let her explain it or not, as she chose.

Marty grunted and rolled over, his nap undisturbed even as Oz pulled over onto the shoulder of the highway and slowed the van to a stop.

In seconds, Angie was out of her seat and lifting the rolling back door. Mel felt the blast of heat hit her from the scorching air outside.

She debated waiting in the truck but decided the only polite thing to do would be to go and say hello, even though she had a feeling this was going to be intensely awkward.

Tate climbed out of his seat and met Mel on the side of the van.

"Tate, we might want to hang back," Mel said.

He wasn't listening. As the door to the BMW opened, Tate strode forward and stood beside Angie. Mel hurried to catch up.

Roach, in all of his tattooed, long black hair and rock-star glory, climbed out of the BMW and opened his arms wide. Angie seemed to hesitate but then hurried forward to hug him.

Roach planted a kiss on her that caused Tate to look away at the saguaro cactus, creosote bushes, and large boulders that filled the landscape on this stretch of road.

When Roach and Angie broke apart, Roach glanced over her head at them and nodded. "Hi, Mel, Todd."

"It's Tate," Tate said through gritted teeth.

"Good to see you, Roach," Mel said. She glanced at Angie, who looked troubled. "We'll just be over there if you need us."

Mel looped her arm through Tate's and forcibly dragged him to the back of the van. They sat in the shade on the floor of the van while they waited.

"What's he doing here?" Tate hissed.

"No idea," Mel said.

"Has Angie said anything to you about moving to Los Angeles with him?"

"No, but I haven't asked because I don't want to pressure her," she said. "What about you? Have you said anything?"

Tate looked miserable. "No."

Mel rose up on her knees and glanced through the front window of the truck. Angie and Roach were talking, and it looked to be heated, as there was a lot of arm waving and head shaking going on.

Marty was still asleep, lulled no doubt by the drone of the engine, as Oz had kept the truck idling while they waited.

"Oz," Mel said. "You'd better cut the engine. We don't want the van to overheat."

Oz was staring out the window at Roach. Mel had to repeat herself twice before he could pull himself out of his trance. Once the engine was off, he climbed over Marty, who napped on, and squeezed himself onto the floor with Tate and Mel.

"He's got his own magnetic field, man," Oz said. "I wish he could teach me that."

"Huh," Tate said. "I don't think he's all that."

Mel had to agree with Oz on this one. Roach did have

the electric rock-star thing. The man pulsed energy like other people sweat.

The three of them were silent listening to Marty snort and snuffle in his sleep. Mel could feel a trickle of sweat run down the side of her neck over her collarbone and down into her shirt. She didn't want to rush Angie, but this was rapidly becoming unbearable.

"It's time, babe!"

Mel squirmed as she recognized Roach's voice. He was shouting, but it didn't sound as if he was angry; more that he was just determined.

"I can't keep chasing you. You have to make a decision, once and for all."

Mel heard Angie mumble something back. Tate looked as if he was straining to hear what was being said. There was a long silence, and then the sound of squealing tires kicking up gravel broke the quiet and Angie appeared at the back of the truck, looking sweaty and upset.

"Well, what are you all waiting for?" she snapped. "Let's go!"

Marty grunted in his sleep and adjusted himself while the rest of them scurried back to their places.

Once they were all buckled up and Oz had turned on the engine and cool air started to pour out of the vents, Mel wiped the sweat off of her forehead with the bottom of her T-shirt and glanced at Angie.

She looked preoccupied, and Mel didn't want to pry, but she couldn't ignore what had just happened, either.

"Are you all right?" she asked.

Angie nodded. "You heard him?"

"Yeah," Mel said. "Did you know he was in town?"

"No, he flew in this morning, hoping to surprise me. Surprise!" she said.

"Well, I'm shocked that you didn't go with him," Mel said. "It's kind of a big deal for a guy to track you down like he did. Some might even say romantic."

"Not really. I had texted him earlier that we were on the Beeline Highway headed north," Angie said. "And you know, that's another part of his whole rock-star life that makes me crazy. He's so used to getting everything he wants when he wants it—he figured if he just showed up in his sports car, I'd ditch my business, my friends, and my life to go off with him. You'd have thought I was speaking a foreign language when I told him no. He just didn't get it."

"So, that's why he gave you the ultimatum?" Mel guessed.

"Yeah, when I get back from the rodeo, I have to tell him whether I'm moving to LA or not."

"Wow." Mel didn't know what else to say.

"Yeah."

They were silent for a long stretch of road. Finally, Angie returned to their earlier conversation.

"So the lawyer functions with Joe," Angie said. "How do you like those?"

"I don't, particularly," Mel said. "But it's an important part of Joe's life, and Joe is important to me."

Mel felt what she could swear was a knuckle digging into her lower back. She didn't need to turn around to know that it was Tate registering his disapproval at her comments. Too bad. She was just being honest with Angie, and she wasn't going to skew her opinions his way when he didn't even have the courage to tell Angie how he felt.

"I suppose," Angie said. "I do care for Roach, and when it's just the two of us, he makes me feel like I'm somebody, like I'm the most important person in the world. But with all that comes with him, I just don't know if that's the life for me."

"Have you told him this?" Mel asked. "He might be willing to make some changes for you."

Now the nudging in her lower back turned into an insistent pinch. Ouch! Thankfully, Angie's phone began to chime. Mel reached behind her and caught Tate's fingers in hers, crunching them as hard as she could.

"It's a text from Sal," Angie said, looking relieved, probably because it wasn't Roach continuing their argument. "He says good luck."

"Oh, that's nice," Mel said. She released Tate's fingers and made her face a mask of pleasant.

"I think you're right, Mel," Angie said. "I need to talk to Roach about his lifestyle. Maybe we can reach a compromise."

She popped out her keyboard and began firing off another text.

Meanwhile, Mel felt Tate try to pinch her again, and she smacked his hand away.

Angie looked up at the noise. "You okay?"

"Yep, it was just a fly," Mel said. "I think I killed the pesky little bugger."

"Oh." Angie went back to her text while Mel gave Tate her most fearsome "quit it" look.

He glowered back at her and turned away. Mel rolled her eyes. What was it going to take for Tate to tell Angie how he felt? She had almost died a few months back in an accidental poisoning, and Tate had been beside himself—or, more accurately, beside Angie, maintaining a constant vigil until she pulled through. If her near-death experience couldn't get him to profess his feelings, what could? With Roach putting the pressure on Angie to make a decision once and for all, it was do-or-die time for Tate. Mel hoped that, for his sake, he didn't blow it.

Mel shook her head and opened the cozy mystery she was reading. The Poisoned Pen, a mystery bookstore down the street from the bakery, had had a Fourth of July Firecracker sale. All paperbacks were 50 percent off. Needless to say, she had stocked up; naturally, the foodie mysteries were her favorites. She hoped to have this one finished before they landed in Juniper Pass, because she doubted she'd have time once they got there. She had a feeling, with twenty-five thousand people in attendance, there was not going to be a lot of downtime at the rodeo.

〰️

They took a quick break for lunch when they were halfway to Juniper Pass. Mel was happy to get out and stretch her legs. The air was already cooler this far north of the Valley, and she was looking forward to it being downright chilly at night in the pines of northern Arizona.

They topped up the gas, and everyone resumed their seats in the truck, only this time Tate drove, giving Oz a break.

"Now, you don't want to stomp on the gas pedal," Oz was lecturing. "You want to be nice and gentle."

"Oz, I was driving when you were just a twinkle in your mother's eye," Tate said. "I think I can handle it."

Oz looked nervous. Tate put the truck in drive and stepped on the gas. The truck lurched and then evened out.

"I told you so," Oz said with a shrug.

"So you did," Tate conceded. "Anything else I need to know?"

"That's it," Oz said. They were silent for a moment; then Oz added, "I'm pretty sure."

Tate followed an old two-lane route through the winding hills of red earth covered with scrubby green juniper trees that led up onto a long stretch of grassland.

Mel handed her book to Angie, who had been cursing since the battery in her phone died. The rocking motion of the van made Mel woozy, and with fifty pages of the mystery to go, she gave up the fight, tipped her head back, and dozed.

A high-pitched whimper roused Mel from her slumber, and she opened her eyes to find they'd left the grassland behind and were now winding their way up a steep mountain. A glance out the window made her light-headed as she took in the sheer drop, the only barrier between them and certain death being a metal guardrail.

Oz was making strange, strangled noises in his throat, giving away the identity of the whimperer, as Tate hugged the curves of the two-lane road.

"Dead Man's Curve," Angie said. She was studying the map. "That's what they call this stretch. See all of the white crosses along the roadside? That's where people have driven off the edge and died."

"Thanks for sharing that," Marty snapped. He was awake and looked tense and pale.

Mel reopened her book and refused to look up. Even

when a sports car passed them on the left, pushing them even farther toward the treacherous edge as the van wobbled ominously, she refused to look up or acknowledge the sweaty palm prints she was getting on her book. She read the same page three times before the van finally left the deadly stretch of road behind.

By the time they pulled into Juniper Pass, Mel was ready to leap out of the truck and run alongside it. The five-and-a-half-hour trip had left her numb in the bum, and her legs were twitching with the need to stretch.

Tate followed the old route into town and worked his way along the side streets until he reached the center. The Juniper Pass town green took up one square block. A large stone courthouse sat on one end, and the rest of it unrolled into a lush lawn of green inhabited by huge, shade-making American elm trees.

The buildings that surrounded the square were old-fashioned Western-style brick buildings with squared-off roofs and upper stories with long rectangular windows that seemed to peer down on the town, keeping watch. The fronts of the shops boasted porches with railings that looked as if they were just waiting for a horse or two to be tied up.

"Is it just me or have we fallen back in time a year or two or one hundred?" Angie asked.

Seven

"Whoa," Oz said as he came to stand beside Mel on the curb.

Music blared from a saloon across the street, and as they watched, two men in full Western dress, from their boots to their hats, pushed through the swinging doors, making the music sound even louder.

The saloon also had a restaurant, and Mel could smell something smoky and delicious wafting on the air.

"Anyone else hungry?" she asked.

"We need to check in and move the truck first," Tate said. He handed out the luggage.

"Where are we staying?" Marty asked.

"Well, I had a hard time getting any rooms," Tate said. "Because of the rodeo, most of the town is booked months in advance, but I happened to call right after a cancellation."

Mel felt her sensors go off. She didn't like the way Tate was talking up the answer. It was the sort of voice people used to tell you that they were out of your favorite ice cream or that those jeans you just spent a fortune on *do* make your butt look as big as Texas.

"Tate, don't try to candy-coat it," she said. "Give it to us straight."

"Okay," he sighed. "That's where we're staying."

He pointed across the street at the saloon.

As one, they all looked at the saloon where the two men had just disappeared. A swinging iron signpost proclaimed it the LAST CHANCE SALOON.

"Last chance for what?" Angie asked.

"Probably best not to dwell on that," Marty said.

"Here's the thing," Tate said. "This is an old hotel and they only had two rooms left."

"That's okay; we can bunk up," Angie said.

"Okay, why don't we check in," Mel said. "Then we need to get the van down to the rodeo grounds. There is a big kickoff parade around the town square tonight that I don't want to miss."

Oz opted to stay with the truck. Mel had a feeling he wasn't ready to let his baby out of his sight. Tate took Oz's bag and his own and led the way across the street to the saloon. The music became louder and mingled with the roar of voices and the sound of glasses being plunked down on the thick wooden tables.

Mel felt something crunch beneath her sandal and looked down to find the floor was covered in a thick coating of peanut shells.

"I'm glad none of us are allergic," she hollered to Angie.

"No kidding," Angie yelled back.

A live band was playing a Toby Keith song about loving this bar, and the crowd was singing along with them for all they were worth.

Tate stopped at the bar, and an older man wearing a black leather vest over a crisp white shirt with a bolo tie gestured to a small door on the other side of the bar. Mel noticed that the man had a salt-and-pepper mustache that was waxed on the ends into curls. With the matching salt-and-pepper fringe around his head, he looked the picture of an Old West bartender.

Mel scanned the room to see if there were saloon girls present, but no. She found herself oddly disappointed that there was no Miss Kitty in attendance.

They followed Tate through the door nestled in the wall and found themselves in a small parlor with lace curtains over a picture window that overlooked the town green. A tall wooden counter stood on one side of the dark-paneled room. It had a service bell that Tate gave a quick tap.

Just seconds after the bell rang, a woman appeared from a door behind the counter. She was dressed in a floral West-ern blouse and jean skirt. Her impossibly red hair was piled up on top of her head in a mass of curls, making her appear younger than she was. If Mel had to guess, she'd put the woman squarely in her late fifties. She looked like she'd put some miles on her tires, but she wore it well. Maybe Miss Kitty existed, after all.

"Good afternoon. Welcome to the Last Chance Saloon," she said. "My name is Delia. How can I help you all?"

"Hi, Delia. I'm Tate Harper. I have some rooms re-served."

"Indeed, you do," Delia said. "I am so glad you could make it, Mr. Harper."

She batted her long eyelashes at him, and Mel could see that Delia had known how to work it in her youth. In fact, she was doing a pretty good job of working it right now.

"Ahem," Marty coughed. Tate looked at him and then caught on.

"This is my associate, Marty Zelaznik," he said.

"How do you do, Mr. Zelaznik?" Delia said.

She gave Marty a coquettish look, and Marty looked 100 percent, grade-A smitten.

"Oh, good grief," Angie said. "Isn't he dating Beatriz?"

"I thought he was," Mel said. "Come to think of it, I haven't seen much of her lately. You?"

"Hmm, no," Angie said. "Has he been holding out on us?"

"Well, if he has, it's game over."

Delia handed Tate the keys while he signed some papers. Mel and Angie each sidled up to Marty and took a firm grasp of his elbows.

"Something you care to share, Marty?" Angie asked.

He looked between the two of them and paled. Then he caught Delia watching, and he went for suave.

"Ladies, can I escort you to your room?"

Delia gave him an approving smile and turned back to Tate.

"Unless you want to suffer a full-on DeLaura-style atomic wedgie, you'd better start talking," Angie hissed.

Marty looked pleadingly at Mel.

"Don't look at me," she said. "I'm her backup."

"All right, I'll tell you upstairs," he said. When they didn't let go of him, he added, "I promise."

"Check his fingers," Angie said to Mel. "No crossed fingers?"

Mel looked at Marty's hands. "No, he's good."

"Now, you just head up the stairs and yours are the first two doors on the right. Your rooms overlook the street. You even have a small balcony, so you can watch the parade from up there."

Mel and Angie exchanged a look. It sounded promising. They grabbed their bags and hurried up the stairs.

The stairs were narrow but opened up into a wide hallway that was half–white wainscoting, and above it the walls were painted butter yellow with an old-fashioned wall sconce every ten feet.

Tate was bringing up the rear, so Mel and Angie turned around on the top step and boxed Marty in before he could get away.

"Spill," Mel ordered.

Marty gave a sigh. "There's nothing to tell."

"What's going on with you and Beatriz?"

Marty pressed his lips together.

"You may as well give them the details, Marty," Tate said. "I can tell you right now, you'll never get one toe past them without full disclosure."

"But it's personal," Marty balked.

"We're family," Angie said. "There's no such thing as personal within a family."

"You have serious boundary issues—you know that?" Marty asked.

"Still not moving," Mel said.

"Oh, all right, I give up," Marty exclaimed. "She dumped

me. Happy now? She cut me loose for a double-jointed yogi freak."

"Well, that blows," Angie said.

"Completely," Mel agreed. "I liked her."

"Me, too," Marty said. His voice was suspiciously low, and both Mel and Angie reached to give him a hug.

"Well, don't you worry," Angie said. She stepped back and studied him. "You're a fine catch, and some other lucky babe is going to be happy to know that you're on the market."

"That's right," Mel agreed. "I think Ms. Delia downstairs was checking you out."

"You think?" Marty asked hopefully. "I kind of got that vibe, but I didn't want to come across too strong."

"She's definitely interested . . ." Angie began, but Tate cut her off.

"Are we done here?" Tate asked from behind Marty. "Now that you two have given his personal life a thorough physical, can we see our rooms?"

"Oh, yeah, you bet." Mel and Angie scooted out of the way, letting Marty and Tate join them in the hall.

"We're right here," Tate said. He paused in front of the first door and used the old-fashioned key to open the lock beneath the glass doorknob.

Mel glanced at the door. It had a brass number 8 on the front. Tate swung the thick wooden door open, and Mel and Angie stepped in. This room had two queen-sized beds made up in matching 1950s-era white chenille bedspreads.

A vintage walnut wardrobe took up one corner of the

room, while a matching walnut dresser with a large mirror stood against the wall opposite the beds.

"I feel like I'm in Nonni's bedroom in her house on Long Island," Angie said. She lovingly put her hand on the dresser on which sat an antique pitcher and basin. "It even smells of lemon furniture polish just like hers."

Mel crossed the wooden floor to the French doors. A sheer curtain hung over it, but she noticed there were heavy drapes pushed to the side that would cover the doors when closed. Probably, they'd been installed to block out the early-morning desert sun so that visitors could sleep. For now, she left them drawn and moved aside the sheer curtain to unlatch the door and pull it open. The narrow balcony was only about three feet wide but had a small wrought-iron table and chairs and connected to the balcony next door, which made it run the length of the building.

Mel could see Oz waiting beside the truck. She waved, but he wasn't looking up. She looked over the town and decided that this was definitely going to be the place to watch the parade.

She ducked back inside to see Angie open another door that led into a small bathroom. While they checked out the double sinks, a door on the other side opened, and in walked Marty and Tate.

"Did I mention that these two rooms are generally rented out as a suite?" Tate asked.

"So, one bathroom?" Mel asked.

"Looks like we're sharing," Tate said.

Mel and Angie peeked into the boys' room to find that it was the same as theirs but also had a trundle bed. All four of them looked at the bed Marty had pulled out from under his bed, and as one they said, "Oz."

"Speaking of, we should get back to him," Mel said.

The four of them trooped down the staircase and left their room keys with the lovely Ms. Delia.

"We keep the keys here at the desk," she said. "Someone is always on duty, so don't worry about coming in late."

They ducked back through the bar, and now that she had stretched the tired out of her bones, Mel could feel the festive atmosphere of the place filling her up, making her want to shoot a game of pool and chug down a frosty beer at the bar.

She looked longingly around her, and Angie looped her arm through hers.

"Later," she said. "We need to get to the rodeo grounds first."

They strode out into the afternoon sun and climbed into the truck. Mel's entire body protested being forced back into the jump seat, but she made herself buckle up.

Oz took the wheel while Tate navigated. Juniper Pass was a small town and pretty much survived on the revenue the rodeo generated each year. The rodeo grounds were strategically located close to the center of town to keep the tourist dollars flowing in and out of the local businesses.

They turned onto a wide dirt road, and Oz slammed on the brakes.

"What the h—?" Angie began, but Mel cut her off. "Oz, what are you doing?"

They both turned around to see what had happened. A small group of people were standing in the road with their arms linked, as if in protest, and Mel wasn't sure but it looked like they were dressed for Halloween with bloody smears on their shirts and ripped and torn clothing.

" 'Come and get it! It's a running buffet!' " Oz said.

"*Shaun of the Dead*," Angie identified the movie. "Do you think they're supposed to be zombies? Mel, did Slim say this was a zombie rodeo?"

"That would be so cool," Oz said.

"Stop animal cruelty!" a gorgeous woman, despite the bloody outfit, shouted.

She was standing in the middle of the group, so Mel assumed she was in charge.

"Oz, roll down your window," Mel said.

Oz did, and the woman rushed forward with her followers behind her. "Rodeos are barbaric! Stop the abuse now!"

"Uh," Oz stammered as she tossed her long, strawberry blond hair in his direction.

"Are you a news van?" the woman asked, looking over all of them and focusing on Tate, as if hoping he was a reporter looking to give her a close-up.

"No," he said. "We're a vendor."

"So, you're for animal cruelty," the woman spat. "Killers! Murderers!"

"Hey!" Angie took that personally. "Take that back!"

"Make me," the blonde taunted.

Before anyone in the van could react, Angie unbuckled her seat belt and leapt over the back of Oz's seat and was half out the window, trying to connect her fist to the blonde's face.

"Marty, a little help here," Mel said. They each grabbed Angie's legs and held on.

The blonde, sensing that she was in danger, gave a squeak of fright and jumped off of the road to the curb. Her entourage followed, and Oz punched the gas, leaving the group of protesters behind in a cloud of dirt.

Mel and Marty gave a heave and dragged Angie back over Oz's seat.

"You okay?" Mel asked.

"Yeah," Angie said. "Sorry, about that. She hit my hot button and I'm already in a bit of a mood."

Marty gave Mel a look that said "no kidding," but he wisely did not say this out loud.

They followed the road's jutted path until they came to a wooden booth built on the side of the road. Tate handed Oz their vendor permit, and the cowboy monitoring the entrance in his ten-gallon straw hat waved them through.

"You want to head over to the food area," he said. "When the road splits, go to the right."

They passed several outdoor pavilions and some outbuildings that Mel imagined were for the contestants.

Oz turned right and they found themselves bumping along a grassy path. There were several food vendors already in place, and a woman with a clipboard, who appeared to be in charge, signaled them into a vacant spot.

They climbed out and the woman hurried over.

"Hi, I'm Estelle. You must be the Scottsdale cupcake people that Slim told me about," she said. "We're so excited to have you here."

Tate stepped forward and made the introductions. Estelle stared at Oz's lip ring for an extra beat, but she quickly glanced away with a nervous smile.

"I just know you're going to be a huge hit here at the

rodeo," she said. "Now, I put you in between the barbecue pit and the beverage cart. I know I like something sweet after some pulled pork, and I think it'll make you an even bigger draw."

A billow of smoke plumed toward them, and Angie coughed. They all glanced over at their neighbors and saw a sign that read BILLY BOB'S BBQ with a cartoon pig in a chef's hat grinning at them.

"That's just wrong," Oz said. "All around wrong."

Eight

"Why are they firing up the grill now?" Mel asked. "I thought we weren't open for business until the rodeo started tomorrow."

"Oh, that's just their smoker," Estelle said. "They'll smoke the meat all night to make sure it's nice and tasty tomorrow."

Estelle hurried over to show Oz where to plug in the truck so that they could run the truck's refrigerator and freezers on an alternate power source.

Mel and Angie made sure the truck was parked with the service window facing out.

"We need some tables and chairs on the side," Mel said to Tate and Marty. "People need a place to sit when they're eating."

"We'll go scout some," Tate said.

He and Marty disappeared while Mel and Angie opened the back of the van and dragged out the sandwich board they used in front of the shop in Scottsdale to advertise the special of the day. Angie was the more artistic of the two of them, and she had drawn a luscious cupcake on the board and then listed the prices below it.

"We should put this out where people walking by can see it," Mel said.

Together they hauled the sign out to the dirt road and opened it up.

"Cupcakes?" a voice asked. "Someone please tell me that's a joke—a bad one."

Mel turned around to see two men standing in front of the barbecue pit with their arms folded over their chests, frowning at her. One was tall and thin, clean-shaven, with thick brown hair and bright blue eyes. He was wearing jeans and a fitted white T-shirt with barbecue sauce stains on it. At least, they looked like barbecue sauce stains. It could have been blood, but she didn't think so.

The shorter of the two was built sturdy and wore a Harley Davidson T-shirt and a long chain that presumably kept his wallet in his back pocket. She certainly hoped it was attached to a wallet and not something more nefarious, such as a Bowie knife. He had long wiry hair held back in a ponytail, and his chin was covered with a thick long beard. Mel could admit that she would be afraid to meet him in a dark alley, and she figured he probably chose to look like this on purpose, obviously compensating for his lack of height by being flat-out scary.

"It's no joke," Mel said. She was pleased that her voice sounded calm. "We own a bakery called Fairy Tale Cupcakes, and Slim invited us to come up and work the rodeo."

"Darlin', who do you think is going to buy a cupcake when you are situated next to a booth full of meat?" the taller one asked.

Mel felt Angie stomp around the sign to stand beside her. She glanced at Angie's face. It was set in lines of seriously unhappy.

"Look, Billy Bob," Angie snapped, but the short one interrupted.

"I'm Billy," he said. Then he jerked a thumb at his tall companion. "He's Bob."

Mel frowned. She wasn't sure if he was messing with them or not. The tall one didn't move, so she assumed he wasn't. Billy and Bob and barbecue—how original.

"Fairy Tale Cupcakes?" Billy laughed and pranced around in a circle, his chain swinging on his hip. In a voice raised high to sound like a woman's, he said, "Oh, cupcakes are so cute!"

He then clapped his hands together under his chin and simpered at them, obviously mocking them.

"Why, I ought to . . ." Angie began, but Mel pinched her right above the elbow. "Ow!"

Mel knew Angie was getting ready to unleash her can of whup-ass, and that would make for a very shaky start to the rodeo. No, it was best to beat these two at their own game.

"I propose a little wager," Mel said. "If you two are so sure that barbecue beats the cupcake, then why don't you put your reputation where your mouth is?"

The two men exchanged a look. "What do you mean, like a bet?"

"Total sales," Mel said. "Whoever racks up the most in

total sales at the end of the rodeo wins—and no price goug-
ing allowed."

"This is gonna be like shooting fish in a barrel!" Billy
laughed.

"What does the loser have to do?" Bob asked.

Mel thought about it for a moment. She turned to Angie.
"I think I'd really like to see these two handing out cupcakes at the closing ceremonies, wouldn't you?"

Angie grinned. "In our pink Fairy Tale Cupcake aprons,
no less."

The two men exchanged a look, and Mel thought she
saw a tiny bit of fear register in Billy's eyes, although it was
hard to tell through all of his facial hair.

"Okay, but if we win, then you two work the closing
ceremonies pulling a shift in the pit, wearing our girls' uni-
forms," Bob said.

Mel glanced over his shoulder to see three young women
in Daisy Duke shorts and red plaid halter tops, helping set
up the barbecue pit. Oh, good grief!

Bob gave her a slow smile, as if sensing she was too ap-
palled to take the bet. Huh!

"Deal," she said. She and Bob shook while Angie and
Billy tried to out–junkyard dog each other with matching
sneers.

Billy and Bob pounded knuckles while they walked
away, laughing at Mel and Angie over their shoulders as
they went.

"The liberated woman inside of me will shrivel up and
die if we have to do that," Angie warned.

"Tell me about it," Mel said. She glanced down at her
underwhelming frontal anatomy. At least Angie could fill

out the uniform. Mel was going to look as buxom as a celery stalk. "We have to win."

"Win what?" Tate asked as he and Marty hauled a large plastic table with chairs on top over to the truck.

Mel and Angie exchanged a look. Angie screwed up her face and shook her head, signaling that the bet should be kept on the down-low from Tate. He rarely approved of that sort of thing.

"We have to win . . . that hole," Mel said.

"*Caddyshack*?" Tate plopped his end of the table down, and Marty did the same. "Why are you quoting *Caddyshack*?"

"Angie thought she saw a gopher," Mel said. "It kind of started a whole thing."

"Oh." Tate raised one eyebrow and studied her face. Mel opened her eyes wide and smiled back. He frowned. He knew her too well. He wasn't buying the innocent act.

"Hey, look over there," Marty said. He pointed over at the barbecue joint. "I'm not positive, but I think those guys are mocking us."

Mel glanced over to see Billy and Bob making rude gestures at them. They were miming the curvy outlines of a woman with their hands, laughing, then pointing at Mel and making straight lines like a flight attendant demonstrating the aisle in an airplane. She felt her face burn.

"So mature," Angie huffed in disgust. "I'm going to barbecue the chubby one's backside, I swear."

"I'll go have a little chat with them," Tate said. "There's really no call for that."

"Um, let's just let it lie," Mel said. She grabbed his arm, stopping him in his tracks. "Probably they're not cupcake guys, but once the rodeo opens, we'll all be too busy to heckle one another. Right, Angie?"

Angie was too busy glowering at Billy, who was pointing to his buxom waitress and then pointing to Angie, slapping his knee, and laughing.

"Right, Angie?" Mel repeated.

"What? Huh, yeah, I guess," she said.

Tate frowned. "Well, okay for now, but if the yahoos don't settle down, I'm going to have two words for them—ker pow."

"Yahoos?" Angie asked.

"The other name I had in mind wasn't very nice," he explained.

Angie grinned at him, and Tate looked momentarily stunned. Marty gave a grunt of disgust, looking at Tate like he was too stupid to live.

He moved to stand beside Mel and asked under his breath, "How much longer till Dopey screws up the courage to tell her how he feels?"

"Your guess is as good as mine," Mel said. "Come on. Let's lock up the truck and head back to town. I'm hungry and the parade is going to start soon."

Oz was very reluctant to leave his baby behind. Mel had to promise him that it would be okay, and Estelle, bless her, gave him a solid pep talk about rodeo security. Finally, they all began to walk the dirt road back to town.

By the time they arrived at the Last Chance, they were hot, thirsty, and hungry. The Last Chance bar served food, so Oz was allowed to go in with them and order dinner, which would be delivered upstairs to their rooms.

As soon as the food and drink arrived, Mel took it out on

the balcony and sat at one of the little tables. Angie shared her table while the boys all sat at the table outside their room, with Oz sitting on the floor, since they were short one seat.

There was a hum of excitement in the air as people who had staked out their spots on the square earlier in the day began to position themselves for the parade. The crowd circled the block and was about ten people thick on both sides, with loads of little kids hoisted up onto grown-ups' shoulders so they could see over people's heads.

Vendors pushing carts with balloons and stuffed animals worked the crowd, while parents emptied their pockets to maximize the parade experience for their kids. A red, white, and blue balloon drifted up in front of the balcony, followed by a child's wail of upset. Tate, to his credit, tried to grab it, but it was too far away.

Mel watched it drift up over the town center and out into the surrounding neighborhood until it was no more than a dot. A glance over the rail and she saw the mother of the child tying a new balloon onto the kid's wrist. The girl's tears dried up, and her parade experience was saved.

"How big is this parade?" Angie asked through a bite of her burger.

"I don't know," Mel said. "Since it kicks off the rodeo, which is the town's big moneymaker, I'm betting it's substantial."

A dull roar from the crowd below caused them all to look down. A float carrying a bevy of beauties was leading the parade. The banner strung across it pronounced it to be for the contestants for the Juniper Pass Rodeo Queen 2012.

Mel and Angie watched as the wannabe queens tossed

out beads and candies to the kids in the crowd. The pretty girls waved, and the kids waved back. All of the girls wore poufy meringue-type gowns with tiaras and elbow-length gloves.

"It's the tiara," Angie said to Mel. "It just sucks a girl right into the crazy. I mean, who doesn't want to wear a tiara?"

"Too true," Mel agreed. "I know I'd humiliate myself for some bling on my head."

After the queens came the cowboys from one of the local ranches; then the rodeo clowns arrived in full dress. They pranked the crowd, throwing buckets of confetti and squirting one another with water before zipping off in their tiny car.

A convertible appeared, and sitting on the back of it and waving to the crowd was one of the most handsome men Mel had ever seen.

"Who is *that*?" Mel asked.

She glanced down the balcony to see if anyone knew and noticed that the men were as riveted as Angie.

Marty squinted and then nodded. "Yep, that's him. Ty Stokes, the greatest bull rider ever to hit the circuit."

Nine

Mel and Angie both rose from their seats and leaned on the rail to get a better look at the man sitting in the back of the convertible waving to the fans.

From what Mel could see, he was average in height but built strong. As he tipped his head back, she saw that he had rugged features: a nose that appeared to have been broken, a square jaw, and eyebrows that rode low on his brow, making him look like a man who had something to prove.

As the crowd began to chant his name, he lifted his black hat and waved it over his head. Mel caught a glimpse of neatly trimmed black hair and then he smiled. It was as if someone had ignited a sparkler. Ty Stokes's face lit up when he smiled, and the crowd went crazy in response.

"Oh, my," Angie breathed from beside Mel.

"Indeed," Mel agreed.

71

She glanced down the balcony, but the men didn't seem as impressed with Ty. Not even Marty, who was the biggest rodeo fan—well, the only rodeo fan—amongst them.

"Look at his clothes," Marty said. "That boy is bought and paid for. There is not one stitch upon him without a label, and you can bet your fanny those labels paid dearly to be there."

"That's good business," Tate said, although he didn't sound overly impressed.

"Huh," Marty scoffed. "Everyone's a sellout."

"I imagine in this sport, you have to make as much money as you can while you can, because life in the saddle belongs to the young," Tate said.

They all watched as Ty's car passed. He had an entourage of three men sitting with him, and, just as Marty had said, his car was draped with rodeo promoters' logos.

A high school marching band was next, and then the local veteran's group came by, drawing huge cheers of appreciation from the crowd for their service to the country. Angie stood up to give her loudest two-fingered whistle, causing the soldiers to laugh and wave up at the balcony.

The local 4-H club went by on their float, which was shaped like a giant cow, and then a few more marching bands passed.

Lastly, a big powder blue Cadillac convertible brought up the rear. Sitting high on the back and waving to the crowd were Slim and Tammy Hazard. Slim wore a dove gray Stetson on his head with a white Western shirt embroidered with black roses on the yoke and the sleeves. Tammy wore a pretty ruffled sundress in matching gray and black.

She was tossing candy out of the convertible, much like the bevy of beauties who had gone before her.

"She must have been a rodeo queen at some point, don't you think?" Angie asked. "Look at that wrist motion she's got going. She can huck that candy fifty feet out, making it look effortless."

"And the wave," Mel agreed. "She's got the beauty-queen wave down, like Cinderella at Disneyland."

"Hey, Slim!" Marty hollered. "Up here! We're up here!"

Marty was hanging over the railing, trying to get his hero's attention. Mel caught Tate's eye, and he grinned. Although neither of them would ever say as much to him, it was cute to see Marty so enthusiastic.

Slim was just passing below them when he happened to glance up. He had to lean back to see them, and as he did a horrific *bang* sounded. Slim fell sideways onto the back of the car, pulling Tammy with him.

From her vantage point on the balcony, Mel could see a red stain mar the black roses on Slim's shirt. He'd been shot! The crowd was silent for a beat, and then the screaming started. Panic ensued below as people snatched their kids and began to run.

Slim's driver was forced to stop or risk running over the fleeing mass of people. He climbed over the seat and manually lifted the convertible's roof, hauling Slim and Tammy down into the seat while pulling the roof over them to block them from view. One of the women from the rodeo queen float was racing through the crowd, trying to get to the convertible.

"Daddy!" she was screaming. "Daddy!"

Mel realized she must be Slim's daughter. The sheriff

and several officers arrived and began to move the crowd to the side. The mass of people quickly thinned, and the convertible began to move. Honking incessantly, it cleared a path, then hopped the curb to go around a balloon vendor whose cart had tipped and was blocking the street.

The young rodeo queen caught up to the convertible and jumped in through the front window, hauling her big ball gown behind her, not even waiting for the car to stop.

"What the hell just happened?" Marty asked, looking dumbfounded.

"Someone shot Slim," Mel said. She was trying to process it as she said it, but it seemed so unreal. Even having just witnessed it, it was unbelievable.

A wail of sirens broke through the sound of the panicked crowd. Two squad cars worked their way into the chaos. One stopped and began to manage the flow of people while the other went after the convertible. Mel hoped it was to give it an escort to the hospital.

She glanced at her friends and noted that they all wore the same slack-jawed expression of shock. Then it occurred to her that although they hadn't heard any more gunshots, that didn't mean the shooter wasn't still out there—and didn't they make some tasty targets sitting up here on the side of a building.

"Everyone inside," she ordered. "Now!"

Her shout knocked them out of their stupor, and they clambered back into their rooms. Mel latched the door behind them and drew the drapes shut while Angie hurried across the room and opened their door. The men met them in the hall.

"I can't believe someone shot Mr. Hazard," Oz said. He sounded wheezy, as if he wasn't getting enough air into his lungs. "I've never seen anyone get shot before."

His bangs were hanging over his eyes in their usual thick curtain, and Mel was worried that he might be going into shock.

"Don't freak out, Oz," she said. "But I need to get a look at you and make sure you're okay."

"I'm okay," he said. He sounded anything but.

"Be that as it may," she said. She reached up and gently brushed the hair out of his eyes with her fingers.

Oz blinked. She wasn't sure if it was because of the sudden light or because he had someone's fingers near his eyes. She stared at his pupils until she was sure they weren't dilated or rolling back into his head.

"You have pretty eyes, Oz," Angie said from behind Mel. "You should show them off more often. I mean, look at the length of your eyelashes. It's a crime for a dude to have lashes like that."

"And they curl on the ends," Mel said. "Totally unfair."

Oz stepped back from Mel and began to frantically smooth his fringe back over his face.

"Now that we've established that Oz is not going to faint, maybe we should think about what we saw right before the shooting," Tate said. "I'm sure the police will want to know if any of us noticed anything suspicious."

"I was looking at Slim," Mel said.

"Me, too," Angie agreed.

"I was eating," Oz said. "The last thing I remember was looking at my burger before I took a bite."

Marty cleared his throat. "Yeah, that sounds about right."

"About right?" Mel asked. "What were you looking at, Marty?"

"The parade," he said, but he didn't make eye contact.

Angie planted herself right in front of him with her hands on her hips. "What part of the parade?"

"Oh, fine. If you must know, I was looking at the rodeo queen float," he said. "Those girls have a nice way about them."

Angie snorted and turned to Tate, looking as if she was going to say, "Can you believe this," but he was actively studying the pattern in the carpet beneath his feet. It was too bad for him, because he didn't see the shot to his upper arm coming.

"Ouch!" He jerked his head up and rubbed his arm where Angie had slugged him. "What'd you do that for?"

"For not having your eyes where they belong," she snapped.

Mel suspected it had more to do with him ogling other women, but she wisely said nothing.

"How was I supposed to know that Slim was going to get shot?" he asked.

"Listen, other than Oz, we were all watching the parade," Mel said. "It doesn't matter where you were looking"—she paused to give Angie a quelling glance—"but whether you saw anything out of the ordinary or not. Now, everyone think. Do you remember anything unusual or out of place?"

They were quiet for a moment as they each tried to recall the events as they'd seen them right before the *bang* of gunfire. One by one they shook their heads. With such a large crowd, Mel had a feeling it would have been extraordinary for any of them to have noted anything odd, but still, they had to try.

"Do you think he's going to be okay?" Angie asked. She sounded worried, and Mel knew exactly how she felt. They hadn't known Slim very long, but he seemed like a nice man, not someone with an enemy who would shoot him.

"Let's go see what we can find out," Tate said. He led the way down the narrow stairs to the small lobby below. They entered the Last Chance through the small side door provided and found the place unusually subdued in the aftermath of the shooting.

Delia from the front desk was there, and she looked wide-eyed and worried. Ever the gracious hostess, she hurried over.

"Are you folks all right?" she asked. "Is there anything I can get you?"

"No, we're fine," Marty said. He gave her a concerned look. "Are you all right?"

And just like that Delia crumpled into a heap of sobs and tears. Mel knew how she felt. After her father died, she had fought to maintain her composure, and usually she was fine, right up until someone asked how she was, and then she fell apart.

Marty gently took Delia into his arms and let her cry all over his shirt.

Mel and the others left him to comfort her and made their way to the bar to see if the bartender knew anything more about what happened.

With his salt-and-pepper mustache still waxed into curls, the bartender was wiping down the bar in a compulsive sort of way, leading Mel to think he was doing it more to comfort himself than because it needed cleaning.

Tate leaned on the bar and asked, "Excuse me, sir. We were wondering if there's been any word about Mr. Hazard yet?"

The bartender looked up and offered his hand. "Folks call me Henry," he said. He and Tate shook. "We heard on the scanner a few minutes ago that they're almost at the hospital, but we've heard nothing since."

A pall settled over the group.

"Did anyone see anything?" Mel asked Henry.

He shook his head. "Not that I know of. I assume the police will be questioning folks, but I haven't heard anyone say they saw the shooter."

"Who would want to shoot Slim?" Angie asked.

Henry shook his head. "Can't say. He's the heart and soul of Juniper Pass; without him there's no rodeo. Without the rodeo, we're a ghost town."

A customer signaled Henry from down the bar, and he gave their group a nod before he went back to work.

"Is it just me," Oz asked, "or are the rest of you getting a bad feeling about this?"

Ten

"What do you mean?" Angie asked.

"I mean, someone tried to kill Mr. Hazard," Oz said. His voice was high, and although Mel couldn't see them through the fringe of bangs over his face, she was sure his eyes were bugging.

"We don't know that," Tate said.

"Tate's right. It could have been an accident," Mel said. "Maybe someone just got overexcited about the parade."

"And what—tried to let the air out of Slim's tires?" Angie asked. "I'm with Oz on this. There is definitely a bad vibe about this."

A commotion at the front door stopped their conversation as they all turned to see what the ruckus was about. In strolled Ty Stokes, the famous rodeo star. He had his entourage of three cowboys with him, and they kept close to him as if they were a moving wall, separating him from the riff-raff.

Even from across the room, Mel could feel the energy pour off of the guy like he was a movie star or a demigod. Ty made straight for the bar and took an empty seat where his handlers could circle him. While waiting for Henry to serve him, Ty glanced over the bottles along the back of the bar to check himself out in the mirrored wall. Obviously, Ty was his own number one fan.

"Hey, how about a little service here." Ty smacked his hand on the bar.

He grinned his five-hundred-watt smile as Henry hustled over. He certainly didn't seem at all concerned about Slim being shot; quite the opposite, in fact. He was laughing as he ordered a round of drinks for his group. It almost looked as if they were celebrating.

"Come on," Angie said. "Let's go. All of a sudden, it feels crowded in here."

Mel glanced back at Marty. He was still talking to Delia, and it looked as if he'd be occupied for some time. She followed the others out into the street, which was eerily quiet after the noise of the parade and the ensuing mayhem. There were several police officers in the street, and it seemed to Mel they were trying to gauge the trajectory of the shot.

One of them glanced up and saw the four of them. He strode over, looking as if he meant business.

"I'm sorry, folks; we're trying to keep the street clear while we investigate."

"No problem," Tate said. "We'll get out of the way."

"Do you know who did the shooting?" Angie asked.

The officer pushed back his wide-brimmed hat, and Mel noted that he looked young, probably in his mid-twenties. She glanced at the name badge on the left pocket of his tan uniform. It read, *Deputy Justice.* Good name, she thought.

"No, ma'am, we don't have any information yet," he said. He sounded regretful.

They all nodded and headed down the sidewalk and around the corner. A diner was on the adjacent street, and Tate suggested they go get coffee.

The rounded chrome and glass building looked like it was a spaceship that had landed in the fifties and decided not to leave. The aqua and yellow sign above it, that proclaimed it the Stardust Diner, was faded from long years in the desert sun, but it was shaped in a retro fifties sunburst that Mel found charming. They walked into the small but clean restaurant and took the empty corner booth.

A waitress came by with menus, but they all shook their heads. Coffee would do.

"Just four coffees, thanks." Tate smiled at her.

The waitress glanced over the four of them, and Mel got the feeling she could read her customers at fifty paces.

"Did you all just come from the parade?" she asked.

Tate nodded on behalf of all of them.

"Slim's a tough old bird," she said. "He'll be all right."

The waitress said it as if there weren't any ands, ifs, or buts about it. She was plump and wore her gray hair tucked into an old-fashioned hairnet that hung off the crown of her head. Her white waitress shoes were spotless, as were her pink polyester dress and white apron.

"Pie," she said. "That's what you folks need. Luckily, we have a special today on coconut custard pie."

"No, thanks. I don't . . ." Tate began, but Angie nudged him in the ribs.

"We'll take four slices of pie and four coffees." Angie paused to read the name embroidered on the waitress's uniform. "Thanks, Ruth."

The older woman nodded in approval. "Coming right up."

"I don't want pie," Tate protested. "How can you possibly eat after what's happened?"

"Are you kidding?" Angie asked. "I can always make room for pie, and if you don't eat yours, I will."

"I heard mini pies are going to take over the cupcake market," Tate said.

Mel snorted. "Yeah, not likely."

Tate raised an eyebrow at her. "Aren't you the overconfident one?"

"Please, it's not overconfidence. Piecrust is one of the most difficult tasks a pâtissier learns. Frankly, it was the dividing line in cooking school. Those that mastered the piecrust and those that didn't."

"So, you're saying there aren't that many good pie makers?" Tate asked.

Mel shrugged. In her experience there weren't, but she didn't want to sound like too much of a know-it-all.

Ruth was back in moments with their coffees. Thick ceramic mugs steamed with the hot, dark brew, and Mel grabbed the sugar shaker while Angie reached for the small silver pitcher of half-and-half.

"Do you think they'll cancel the rodeo?" Oz asked. He was staring morosely into his mug. Leave it to the young one to voice the question weighing on all of their minds. Mel was worried about Slim, but the proprietor in her was terrified that she was going to end up with a van full of use-less frozen cupcakes.

Ruth had just reached the table with their pie. She off-loaded each one from her tray before saying, "Don't worry. They won't cancel the rodeo."

"But doesn't Mr. Hazard own it?" Oz asked.

"He does. And the rodeo grounds are on his property, so it's big business for the Hazards. This one rodeo is what they live off of all year. So, believe me, they won't cancel. His daughter Lily is his right hand," Ruth said. "She'll take over—if need be."

Ruth looked sad, and Mel got the feeling that Slim was more than just the financial backer of the town; he seemed genuinely liked as well.

"Give me a holler if you need anything else," she said.

Mel picked up her fork and tucked into the slice of pie in front of her. The custard was thick and creamy, and the coconut made it taste exotic. Then she got to the piecrust. It was buttery and flaky and melt-in-your-mouth delicious. No one at the table said a word until their forks had scraped the last of the crumbs off of their plates.

"That was awesome," Oz said. He took a big sip from his thick ceramic mug and heaved a contented sigh. Mel, Angie, and Tate followed suit.

Mel waited until Ruth returned to warm up their coffees before she asked who baked their pies. Ruth gave her a big smile.

"I do," she said. "Did you like it?"

"Sour cream in the crust," Mel said. "Very nice."

"And I roll it out between two pieces of wax paper," Ruth said. "Much easier to transfer to the dish that way."

"Did you go to cooking school?"

"Only if you count learning at my meemaw's elbow and ducking when the rolling pin came a-swinging if I messed it up," Ruth said.

Mel laughed. "I had a few teachers like that."

"You should come back tomorrow," Ruth said. "I'm baking strawberry rhubarb tonight."

"Oh, I'll be back," Mel said.

The door to the diner swung open, and an older man in a sheriff's uniform strode in. He looked a bit haggard and took a stool at the counter.

"Excuse me; that's my husband," Ruth said, and she hurried over to the counter with the coffeepot.

Mel glanced at her companions in the booth and at the customers surrounding them. Everyone sat completely still as they watched the sheriff. Mel could tell they were all hoping to hear some news about Slim.

"Is there any word?" Ruth asked. She rested her hand on his arm, and the sheriff gave her a small smile. He removed his hat and patted her hand with his own.

The sheriff, as if sensing the eyes of all of the customers upon him, spun slightly to address the room.

"Slim's going to be fine," he said. "He took a bullet in the shoulder, but it passed clear through."

Cheers erupted in the small restaurant, and Mel sagged with relief against the cushioned back of the booth.

"Hey, Hadley," a man from across the room yelled at the sheriff, "who shot him?"

"No idea." The sheriff shook his head. "We think it was most likely some yahoo, shooting off his gun to celebrate.

Obviously someone who forgot that what goes up must come down."

There were nods of agreement all around the room, and the clatter of utensils and plates resumed as everyone turned back to their food.

"That's stupid," Angie said. "What kind of a moron shoots a bullet up into the air when there is a crowd like the one at the parade?"

" 'Stupid is as stupid does,' " Tate said.

"*Forrest Gump*," Mel and Oz cited the movie together.

"That's more than stupid," Angie said. "It's criminally negligent."

"Maybe you should have to pass an IQ test to own a gun," Oz suggested.

"Well, that would certainly cut down on ownership," Mel said.

Mel thought of her uncle Stan, a detective with the Scottsdale police department, and the one thing she had learned from him over the years was that by and large criminals were dumb, and most of them were armed and dumb, a deadly combination no matter how you looked at it.

"We'd better get to bed," Angie said. "If Ruth is right and the rodeo is still happening, we have a big day tomorrow. I'm going to order a slice of pie to go for Marty."

Tate followed Angie to the counter, swiping the check from Ruth before Angie could pay for it, which caused a small dustup between them.

Mel and Oz watched as they climbed out of the booth.

"Mel, can I ask you something?"

"Anything, Oz," she said.

"Exactly how rich is Tate?"

Mel blew out a breath.

"I know that's rude," Oz said. "But the T-man seems to have everything a dude could want, so he's got to be loaded, right?"

"Well, yeah," Mel said. "If you're asking for a dollar amount, I really can't say, but yeah, it's a lot."

They both looked back at the counter where Tate was watching Angie while she ordered another slice of pie.

"But you're wrong," Mel said. "He may be rich, but he doesn't have everything he wants."

Eleven

"Cupcakes for breakfast? No, I don't think so." A woman grabbed her two daughters by the hands and led them away from the cupcake truck.

Mel sighed. The rodeo's opening ceremony had just concluded, and although she and Angie had hustled back to the van to open for business, so far they'd had no takers.

"Oh, sure, say no to a cupcake, but I bet she lets them eat doughnuts for breakfast," Angie griped.

They were leaning out of the service window and smiling at anyone who walked by, but it was no use. They may as well have been trying to sell umbrellas on this cloudless day.

"Maybe it will pick up closer to lunch," Tate suggested hopefully.

A guffaw carried across the way from Billy Bob's barbecue pit, and Mel looked up to see Billy and Bob, obviously having some deep belly yuks at their expense.

"Mel, you have to do something," Angie hissed in a low voice so that Tate couldn't hear her. "I refuse to lose our bet to those morons."

Mel looked at the line the barbecue pit already had. Sure enough, they had put a scrambled-egg-and-barbecued-beef burrito on their menu, and they were cleaning up the breakfast business. Well, if folks wanted breakfast, she could do that.

"Angie, go get the message board," she said. "We have a new cupcake to add."

Angie took one look at her face and hurried out of the truck.

"Tate, I need you to get some supplies for me," Mel said. Tate had taken a seat at their plastic table and was thumbing through the paper. He was not moving as fast as she would like, so she growled, "Now!"

Tate dropped the paper and hurried forward. "Sheesh, no need to get snippy."

Mel scratched a short list onto a napkin and handed it to him through the window. He scanned the list and gave her a confused look.

"Just do it." She shooed him away.

When Angie came back with the message board, Mel told her what to write. Then she set to work, pulling a fresh batch of vanilla cupcakes out of the freezer to thaw along with one of her tubs of buttercream.

This had to work. The rodeo had been open for only half an hour, but she could already see that the barbecue boys were thumping them. She needed to come up with a way to cut into their business, and fast.

Slim had kicked off the opening ceremonies with his arm in a sling. The crowd had gone crazy when he took the stage in the arena to announce the rodeo was open. He had been sandwiched by his daughter Lily on one side and Tammy on the other. He looked exhausted but determined. Mel and the others couldn't help but admire his grit.

Everyone attending the rodeo seemed to think the gunshot was a freak accident from an overzealous parade attendee, but Mel noticed that Jake Morgan, the man who had been driving Slim's convertible, stayed close to him during the opening ceremony and kept a vigilant eye on the crowd. It may have been an accident, but they were all a bit twitchy.

Angie finished with her drawing just as Tate handed Mel's requested ingredients through the open window of the van. Mel quickly set to work remixing her buttercream with Tate's purchases. In fifteen minutes, she had her new offering, and she gave Tate and Angie the go-ahead to move the signboard out to the walkway.

In less than five minutes, she had a line of twenty people at the van.

"Can I have four of them French Toast cupcakes?" a man asked. "They look deeeelicious."

"Absolutely," Angie said with a grin. And she hurried to fill his order.

Mel kept busy loading her vanilla cupcakes with her newly mixed maple-buttercream frosting and artistically sprinkling chopped bacon on top.

Tate climbed in the van to help Angie at the window, and Mel asked over her shoulder, "Where did you get the bacon?"

"I bought it off of the barbecue guys next door," he said.

Mel had to stifle a laugh. That was perfect.

"And the syrup?" she asked.

"I ran into Lily Hazard—you know, Slim's daughter—and she lent me some out of the ranch's kitchen," he said.

"Well-done," Mel said.

"I got lucky." Tate shrugged. "She's a really nice lady."

Mel saw Angie give Tate a quick frown, but the customers at the window commanded her attention, so anything she might have said was lost in the crowd.

Mel glanced over the two of them toward the barbecue pit. Neither Billy nor Bob looked particularly happy to see the ever-increasing line at Mel's cupcake van.

She wanted to yell, "Who's laughing now?" but she restrained herself. With several days to go, the bet was far from over.

Mercifully, there was enough of a lull after the breakfast crowd for Mel to stock the cooler with freshly frosted offerings. She had decided to carry only four types of cupcakes at the rodeo, and they were the bakery's most popular: the Red Velvet, the Vanilla Vixen, the Death by Chocolate, and the Tinkerbell, a lemon cupcake with a raspberry buttercream. Thankfully, she had made enough vanilla cupcakes to get them through their new breakfast offering.

Marty and Oz arrived just before lunch to take their shift selling cupcakes. When Oz stepped into the van, Mel looked at him with a frown. On his shirt was a cartoon drawing of a cow with a big smile on its face and its arms held out wide as if for a hug. She had seen this T-shirt before, but last time it had fake blood on it.

"What does your shirt say?" she asked.

Oz looked down as if he'd forgotten and had to check, but beneath his fringe of bangs, she saw his cheeks get suspiciously red.

"Nothing." He shrugged. He quickly went to pull an apron over his head.

"Oh, no, you don't," Mel said. She grabbed the apron before he pulled it on and studied his shirt. "Are you crazy?"

This brought the attention of everyone in the very crowded van around to Oz, making him flush an even deeper shade of red.

"What?" he asked. "It's just a shirt."

"Dude," Angie said, and shook her head. "You are going to have your butt handed to you in a to-go bag."

"I have to agree, my man," Tate said. "Bad idea."

Oz snatched the apron out of Mel's hands. "I can handle it."

"Oz, you're wearing a shirt that says, *Cow Hugger*, at a rodeo," Mel said. "Why don't you just wear a shirt that says, *Please kick my a—*"

"I get the idea," Oz interrupted. "But it's not just me. There's a whole group of us here."

"You mean that wacko we met at the gate the first night we got here?" Mel asked. "Marty, you were with him this morning. How could you let him wear this?"

"Oh, please, you've seen the hottie who asked him to put it on. How was he supposed to say no?" Marty said. "I'd have worn one, too, but she didn't ask me."

"Are you telling me that you're wearing this because of that blond girl?" Angie asked. "I should have punched her."

Oz tied the strings around his waist. "No! It's not because of her. I happen to believe in the cause. Besides, that wacko is Slim's other daughter, Shelby. I was trying to be polite."

Marty gave a derisive snort and Mel blew out a breath. "If she asked you to dress up like chicken and squawk, would you?"

"No . . ." he protested.

No one believed him.

"Shelby is organizing an animal-rights demonstration," Oz said. "And I said I'd help."

"Are you insane?" Mel asked.

"I happen to believe in the sentiment," Oz said. "I'm thinking of becoming a vegetarian."

They were at a stalemate. Mel didn't think she had the right to tell him what to do, but she couldn't let his fascination for a girl disrupt the business.

"Look, you're a big boy," she said. "I can't tell you what to wear, but there had better not be any protests anywhere near the van—got it?"

"Agreed," Oz said, looking relieved.

Marty and Oz moved to take Tate and Angie's place at the window, and Mel hopped out of the back of the van, with Tate and Angie right behind her.

"So, where to?" Angie asked. "I'm so hungry I could even eat the Bubbas' barbecue."

"Uh, I have plans," Tate said. "I told Lily I'd meet her for lunch."

Mel and Angie both glanced at him. "Well, when I was

looking for syrup, she was really helpful, and then we got to talking and she said she'd show me around."

Mel wondered if he was aware of how lame he sounded.

"Well, don't let us keep you," Angie said. "Your beauty queen awaits."

"She's not a beauty queen," Tate protested.

"Oh, please," Angie snapped. "I saw her in the big, poufy dress on the rodeo queen float. If that's not a beauty queen, I'll eat my apron."

"Start chewing," Tate said, leaning over her as he spoke. "Because she happens to be the best barrel rider in the country, and she's competing tonight, and I for one am going to watch her."

"All righty, then," Mel said. She stepped between them and spun Tate around. "You'd better get going. Angie, let's go find something to eat."

Angie stood glaring at Tate's back. Mel started to walk in the other direction, knowing that Angie would follow when she was ready.

"Barrel rider," Angie scoffed. "Like that's so tough."

Mel clamped her lips together, refusing to get drawn into the spat between her friends, especially since she thought barrel riding really did look hard and not a little dangerous.

"Where are we going?" Angie grumbled behind her.

"Taco stand," Mel said. "I have a hankering for some carne asada tacos, and then I'm going to hunt down this Shelby Hazard and see what we're dealing with. I don't have a good feeling about her being Slim's daughter and staging an animal-rights protest. That seems a wee bit conflicted to me, and I don't want Oz getting sucked into something dangerous."

Angie fell into step with her, and Mel glanced over to see Angie fingering the end of the long braid that hung over her shoulder. Her normally soft brown eyes had a low-banked fire in them, and Mel fervently hoped that they didn't run into Lily and Tate.

She did not want to be kicked out of the rodeo until the only thing they had left was crumbs from all of the cupcakes they'd sold.

"Come on—you'll feel better after you eat," Mel said.

The throng of people seemed to be heading in the opposite direction, and Mel felt a bit like a salmon headed upstream. Luckily they had only a few booths left until they got to the taco stand. Once there, the line moved swiftly and Mel was delighted to park herself at a nearby picnic table and take a bite of the shredded beef taco with lettuce, cheese, and a squirt of hot sauce.

It was more restorative than a nap, so much so that she had three. She and Angie didn't speak while they ate, and Mel was relieved. She didn't know what to say to Angie about Tate and the rancher's daughter.

She washed the tacos down with a frosty cold *horchata*, rice milk flavored with cinnamon and almonds, which was also sold at the taco stand and which complemented the spicy Mexican food perfectly.

"Okay, I think I'm functional again," she said.

Angie finished her *horchata* with a slurp and asked, "Where to next?"

"We look for Shelby," Mel said.

"Maybe she's with the barrel riders," Angie said.

"Nice try, but I think you should steer clear of Lily," Mel said.

"Why?"

Mel looked at her friend. Did she really need to spell it out for her? Angie met her gaze with one eyebrow raised, as if daring Mel to accuse her of being jealous of Tate and Lily. Mel shook her head. She was not going there.

"Come on. We need to do some damage control before this woman sinks her claws any deeper into Oz."

Twelve

While they walked the grounds, Mel took a moment to enjoy the warm sun and the cool breeze. It was a perfect day, and she wished Joe were here to share it with her.

She had called him late the night before to report in about their arrival. He'd not been happy to hear about the shooting but seemed to think that the sheriff was probably right and that an overzealous parade attendee had gotten carried away.

Mel was not sure she agreed, but she knew better than to say anything. She didn't want Joe to worry. But she couldn't help but remember watching the bloodstain appear on Slim's shirt. If the bullet had come from above as everyone speculated, then why was it the front of Slim's shoulder that had been shot? Shouldn't it have been the top? And would it have gone clean through if it came from above? It seemed more likely that it would have lodged in his shoulder.

As they left the food area behind, they cut across a crowded path and entered the large tent that housed the vendors of Western wear. Jeans, boots, and cowboy hats filled the space along with saddles, gloves, and lassos.

Angie glanced around the tent and looked at Mel and said, "Maybe I should buy Roach some chaps. Then maybe he'd forgive me."

"Because you came here instead of going to LA?" Mel asked.

"Yeah, he's pretty unhappy," Angie said.

"I guess he has a right to be mad," Mel said, trying to be fair to Roach.

"He's not mad; he's disappointed," Angie said. "Which is infinitely worse."

Mel patted her shoulder. She had to agree. It was always better to make someone mad at you than to disappoint them. At least if they were mad, you could be mad back, but disappointment really left you with nothing but a grovel option, and who needed that?

"Hey, look at that." Angie pointed across the room. "Talk about being mad—that's a fight in the making if I ever saw one."

Mel glanced up to see Slim, without his usual hat, standing nose to nose and arguing with the woman from the protest, the one who had gotten Oz to wear his cow T-shirt.

"I'm thinking we've found Shelby," she said, and began to walk across the tented area, knowing Angie would follow.

"Young lady, you will take your protest out of this facility and stop disrespecting our vendors." Slim's voice was harsh, and Mel drew up short.

"It's inhumane, Daddy, and I for one won't stand for it," said the young woman facing him. She was about six inches shorter than he was, and now that Mel could see her up close, she had to appreciate the woman's long strawberry blond hair, startlingly pretty face, and generous curves. No wonder she'd managed to charm Oz.

Slim's arm was still in a sling, and he looked pale as he ran his free hand over his face.

"Shelby, you know this is a bunch of malarkey. Why, Juniper Pass was the first rodeo in the country to stop steer roping, and we don't allow the calves to be yanked backward during the calf roping. That was your own mother's idea. We have never allowed the use of electric shock on any of our animals to get them to buck. You know your own grandfather beat the tar out of a rodeo competitor for doing just that."

Shelby sniffed and looked away, refusing to acknowledge his argument.

"The Juniper Pass Rodeo is about more than a bunch of cowboys showcasing their ranching skills," Slim said. "It's what keeps this town alive every year. Without the rodeo, Juniper Pass would cease to exist."

"Who cares?" Shelby snapped. "I hate this dump full of rednecks and losers."

"Does that make us rednecks or losers?" Angie whispered to Mel, who shushed her.

"Is that so?" Slim asked. "Well, it seems to me that you owe all these redneck losers a thank-you. Just where do you think we got the money to pay for that fancy college of yours, anyway?"

"Blood money," Shelby cried, sounding shrill.

Slim gritted his teeth, and Mel could tell he was losing his patience.

"And where do you think the money came from for your swank apartment in Los Angeles, your convertible, the head shots you needed for all of those auditions you've been going on, hmm?"

The handful of protesters behind Shelby began to mutter amongst themselves. Mel noted that the two women looked remarkably like Shelby, with big hair and big boobs and vacuous expressions, while the man looked impeccably groomed but also thoughtful.

"I didn't know," Shelby cried. She glanced at her fellow protesters with wide, innocent eyes. As if sensing she was losing them, Shelby went for the big drama.

"I didn't know. As God is my witness, I didn't know," she cried, and put the back of her wrist to her forehead.

"Wow, her acting is so bad, it's going to leave an odor," Angie said.

"Major stinko," Mel agreed.

"Shelby, stop it," Slim said. His voice was weary. "You grew up on this ranch. You know how it works. You know that we make our living from cattle. Now, stop being such a brat. You're not too big to turn over my knee, you know."

The hat vendor nearby let loose with a snicker of muffled laughter, and Shelby glowered at him.

"You know something, Daddy," she spat. "I'm only sorry that bullet didn't hit you in the heart, but then, you'd have to have one, wouldn't you?"

She spun on her heel and stormed out of the tent with her entourage on her heels. The only one who looked reluctant to follow was the man. Mel met his gaze for just a moment, and he gave her a shrug as he turned to follow Shelby.

"Dad!" a young woman cried as she raced across the room. "Are you all right?"

She had the same lovely features as Shelby, but her hair was a deep, dark brown. Mel recognized her from the parade as the one who had thrown herself into Slim's car. This had to be Lily. She glanced around, and sure enough Tate was following behind her with a lasso in his hands. Mel did a double take. A lasso?

Not only that; he was outfitted as if he were the poster boy for Wrangler. He wore a Western shirt, jeans, and boots. Buttoned-down Armani Tate was gone, and in his place was a smoking-hot cowboy.

Mel turned and saw that Angie had locked in on him as well. In fact, her mouth was hanging slightly open, and she looked stunned.

"Let me go after her," Lily said. "I'll talk some sense into her, or better yet, I'll kick some sense into her."

Mel turned back to Lily and Slim. Lily was holding her father's good arm, and she looked worried.

"No, there's no point," Slim said. "You know how Shelby gets when she's mad. She says hurtful things, but she doesn't mean it."

"She's twenty-four years old, Dad," Lily said. Her voice had a hard edge of anger to it. "When is she going to grow up?"

Slim sighed and looped an arm about her shoulders and pulled her close.

"You're an old soul like me, kiddo," he said, and placed

a kiss on her head. "We can't expect everyone to be as stodgy as us."

"But . . ." Lily protested.

"Let it go, honey," he said. "I think I'll go back to the house to rest. I'll see you in the barrel-racing finals tonight."

"I'll come with you," she said.

"I've got it," he said. "You stay here with your greenhorn and see if you can get him to lasso more than a fence post."

Slim winked at his daughter, and she blushed. Mel felt Angie stiffen beside her. She turned to look at her and found Angie as taut as a banjo string and vibrating as if she'd just been plucked.

"Are you okay?" she asked.

Angie spun on her heel. "I'm going back to the van."

"But, Angie . . ." Mel's voice trailed off as Angie stomped back the way they'd come without once glancing over her shoulder.

Suddenly a loop of rope dropped around Mel's shoulders and was pulled tight.

" 'Hi, Curly. Killed anyone today?' " Tate asked.

Mel couldn't help but grin. " 'The day ain't over yet.' "

"*City Slickers*," they said together, and exchanged a knuckle bump.

"Now, get this off of me," Mel said as she wiggled within the rope.

As Tate lifted the lasso off of her, Lily joined them.

"Lily, this is my friend Mel. Mel, this is Slim's daughter Lily," he said.

Mel and Lily shook. Mel liked that Lily had a warm, firm grip.

"Is Slim okay?" she asked.

"He's been better." Lily sighed. She met Mel's gaze with a direct one of her own. "And he'd be better if my crazy sister would stop her shenanigans. Honestly."

Lily shook her head, and Mel decided she liked Lily Hazard. She seemed like a no-nonsense, down-to-earth kind of person. Tate was watching the brunette with a small smile, and she got the feeling he liked her, too. Oh, dear.

"Lily," a man called out as he strode toward them.

He wore broken-in jeans over scuffed boots, a wide leather belt with a big buckle, a Western shirt that was molded to his broad shoulders, and a hat that looked as if it had survived a stampede and was now conformed to his head. The newcomer made Tate look like a newly minted, shiny penny while he was the worn-down, scuffed penny that had traveled the world picking up a nice patina.

"Hi, Jake," Lily said, and then she gestured to them. "Jake Morgan, this is Tate and Mel. They're food vendors for the rodeo."

"Pleasure to meet you." Jake shook Tate's hand and tipped his hat at Mel, which she found utterly charming.

"Jake is my father's right-hand man," Lily said.

"Nah, that's you, except you're a woman," Jake said. "I'm more like his left hand."

Lily grinned. "And he's humble."

"Aw, shucks," Jake teased.

Jake was not handsome in a movie-star or underwear-model sense. Rather, he was good-looking in a rough-and-tumble, badly-in-need-of-a-shave sort of way. Under his hat, Mel could see dark brown hair that wanted a trim. His eyes were light brown and sported crow's-feet in the corners that deepened when he smiled, but he also had deep dimples that bracketed his smile, which made it impossible not to smile in return.

"How is Slim?" Jake asked. "I heard he was in here having words with Shelby."

"He looks tired," Lily said.

"He should be resting," Jake said. He frowned. "Didn't the doc say bed rest?"

"He did," Lily agreed. "I guess I can thank Shelby for wearing him out enough to send him back to bed."

"Don't worry," Jake said. He squeezed her shoulder. "I'll go check on him."

"Thanks," she said. "He'll listen to you."

Jake tipped his hat to Mel and Tate as he left, and again Mel felt utterly boggled.

"Jake was driving the car when Dad was shot," Lily said. "I'm worried that he blames himself for Dad's injury, as if there was anything he could have done to prevent it."

"Well, that's ridiculous," Tate said. "I mean, it was a freak accident, right?"

"That's what Dad says." Lily frowned at the doorway, as if her thoughts were elsewhere.

"But you don't believe it?" Mel asked.

Lily turned back to her and forced a smile.

"Oh, I'm just being silly," she said with a shake of her head.

Mel wanted to question her further about the shooting, but Lily reached out and squeezed Tate's arm in a familiar way that Mel found alarming.

"I'm going to go make sure Shelby steers clear of the rodeo for the rest of the day," Lily said. "I'll see you later at the barrel-riding competition?"

She was polite enough to pose her question as if she were asking both of them, but Mel got the feeling it was really just for Tate.

"Count on it," Tate said.

"Yeah," Mel agreed. "I wouldn't miss it."

They watched as Lily walked away.

"We should get you one of these hats," Tate said as they made their way out of the tent and back toward the cupcake truck.

"I think yours is too tight," Mel said. "It's obviously squeezing off the blood flow to your brain."

"What? No, it isn't. It feels . . . Oh, wait—that was an insult, right?"

"You think?" Mel stepped out of the tent and back into the sunshine. She took a deep breath and got hit with the rich, peaty scent of horse dung.

"So, a guy from Scottsdale can't dress the part at a rodeo?" he asked.

"Of course he can," Mel said. "But I was under the impression that he was pining for the love of his life, not jollying it up with the rancher's daughter."

"Lily?" he asked. He shook his head. "No, it's not like that."

"Oh, please," Mel said. "It's obvious she adores you."

"Well, I happen to be very adorable," Tate said with a shrug.

"Is this just a joke to you?" Mel asked. "You know Roach is putting the pressure on Angie to move to LA, and if you don't get up the nerve to say something to her soon, she may actually go. What are you going to do then, smartypants?"

Tate blew out a breath. "Look, I can't say anything to Angie."

"Why not?"

"Because I had my chance, and I blew it," he said. "It's not fair to Angie to make her choose between us. What if she only picks me because she *thinks* she loves me, or she confuses friendship love with relationship love and then she loses him, too. No, I can't do that to her."

Mel stopped walking and stood gaping at him. When her power of speech returned, she said, "You are a moron!"

"Hey!" Tate said. He pushed his hat back so he could give her his full glare. "I'm trying to do the right thing here."

"No, you're not."

He huffed out a breath, looking outraged, but Mel held up her hand to ward off any tirade he might offer up.

"Tate, you're my best friend," she said. "I've known you even longer than I've known Angie, so I want you to take what I'm about to say in the spirit that it's being given."

Tate gave her a wary look, as if he was afraid she was going to put him in a headlock and stomp on him.

"Tate, you are a complete and total wuss bag."

"Excuse me?"

"You heard me," she said.

"I am not," he protested.

"Oh, please. Yes, you are," Mel insisted. "You've never had to work for anything in your entire life. You've never had to take a risk, and it's turned you into a ginormous chicken."

"How can you say that?" he asked. He looked hurt, and Mel felt bad about that, but honestly the boy needed to face some facts.

"Tate, you are the only son of parents who have more money than they can possibly spend in this lifetime. You coasted into Princeton as a legacy, and when you graduated, you took a job at your father's firm. Did you even have to interview?"

Tate opened his mouth to protest but then shut it.

"Yeah, I didn't think so," Mel said. "You've never had to ask a girl out, because with a wallet as fat as yours, they hunt you down."

"I think some of them actually like me," he said.

"Of course they do," Mel agreed. "You're rich, cute, and charming. Who wouldn't like you?"

"So, what's your point?" he asked.

"My point is that you're not going after Angie not because you're trying to be fair to her, but because she's a challenge, and you're running scared."

Mel paused to see how he was taking it. His brows were lowered over his eyes, and he was tugging on his ear, which always indicated that he was feeling stressed.

"You've never had to take a risk before, and going after Angie is the biggest risk of your life. I'm sorry, Tate, but if you want Angie, you're going to have to man up, and you're going to have to do it soon or you're going to lose her forever."

Thirteen

"This is my horse, Cocoa Bar," Lily said.

It was evening when Mel walked down to the stables with Tate to wish Lily good luck. After their talk that afternoon, Tate had been quiet and a bit withdrawn. Mel wondered if he'd been thinking over what she'd said. He hadn't seemed mad at her for her candor, and for that, she was relieved.

When invited to come watch the barrel-racing finals with them, Angie had sniffed and declined. Big surprise.

Cocoa Bar was beautiful. He had a shiny dark brown coat with a black mane and tail. He bucked his head at Mel as if inviting her to pat his neck.

"Go ahead," Lily said. "He's very sweet."

"Hey there, big fella," Mel said. She patted his neck and marveled at how soft he was, given that she could feel the rock-hard muscle beneath the smooth coat.

"I can't believe you're participating in this barbarity," a voice snapped.

Lily and the others spun around to find Shelby and her trio of friends standing behind them. Mel noted that they were not, however, wearing their T-shirts tonight.

"Shelby, I appreciate your opinion, I do, but given that the rodeo keeps the town of Juniper Pass alive, not to mention provides the glitz-and-glam lifestyle you've become accustomed to, I should think you'd be more respectful," Lily said.

"Always Daddy's little girl, aren't you?" Shelby hissed.

Mel felt her teeth clench. She admired Lily's restraint, because if anyone ever spoke to her in that snotty tone, she was pretty sure she'd pop them in the kisser.

"Someone has to be," Lily said. "Clearly, you're not there for him anymore."

"Whatever," Shelby snapped. She stormed out of the stable with her crew, and again Mel met the gaze of the man with Shelby and wondered what he really thought of all this.

Lily pinched the bridge of her nose and closed her eyes as if trying to ward off a bout of tears.

"Shelby wasn't always like this," she said. "In fact, she was a champion barrel rider. The best I've ever seen."

"What happened?" Tate asked.

"She wanted to be a movie star, so she moved to Hollywood," Lily said. "Suddenly she wanted plastic surgery and she refused to eat meat. You notice those shoes she had on were leather, so I guess it's okay to wear animals but not eat them."

"It must be tough," Mel said.

She wondered what would happen if her brother Charlie suddenly took a dislike to cupcakes and was hurtfully vocal about it. She didn't imagine things would go well between them.

"Lily, you're up next," a man called from the end of the stable.

"We'll let you get ready," Tate said. "Good luck."

He squeezed Lily's arm, and she gave him a faint smile.

Mel patted Cocoa Bar one more time and whispered, "Good luck."

He bobbed his head, and Mel was sure he'd understood her. She couldn't help but hope he'd win.

Tate and Mel walked the length of the stables and then through a wide tunnel to the stands. It was dimly lit, and Mel squinted to see where she was going. They were half-way through when she bumped into a man in a hat.

She stumbled back and muttered, "Sorry."

"Damn it, you should be," the man cursed. "These are my new boots, you stupid cow."

Mel felt her face flame hot. Even in the dim light, she recognized the formidable figure of Ty Stokes. He had two men with him, and Mel grimaced when the smell of stale beer rolled off of him and assaulted her nose with a one-two punch of PU.

"Mel, are you all right?" Tate asked.

"She's fine. What's it to you, poser?" Ty asked. His voice was slurred, and he wobbled where he stood.

"Come on, Tate, let's go," Mel said.

She took Tate's arm and tried to lead him out of the tunnel, but he was glaring at Ty like he wanted to split his head like a coconut. Oh, dear.

"What are you looking at, pretty boy?" Ty growled. "Didn't you hear the crack of your woman's whip?"

Mel huffed a breath and wished she'd hit him with a knee to his sensitive parts instead of just stepping on his foot. Still, she didn't want Tate to get thumped because of a stupid misunderstanding.

"Listen, Mr. Stokes," she said in her most placating tone. "We don't want any trouble. We're just here to enjoy the rodeo and sell some cupcakes."

"You're the cupcake people," he said. Then he tipped his hat back and laughed. "Excellent. Then you can just trot your behind over to my trailer with a box of cupcakes, and we'll consider this matter done."

"I don't think so," Tate growled. Mel could see that his fists were clenched and he'd set his feet apart in a fighter stance. Uh-oh. As far as she knew, Tate had had only one fight in his entire life.

When they were freshmen in high school, a nasty bully named Dwight Smith had teased Mel, who had been a bit portly at the time, calling her "Melephant."

It got so bad she started hiding in the girls' bathroom to avoid him and was chronically late to class. Until, one day, he did it in front of Tate, who hauled off and clobbered him, making Dwight cry. Dwight got a shiner and a new nickname— "Dwight No Fight"—and Tate got two weeks' detention.

Mel was pretty sure he hadn't had a fight since, and if she remembered right, he'd spent the hour after the fight puking up his breakfast in the boys' bathroom. She didn't think Ty was going to go down quite as swiftly as Dwight had, however.

"What do you mean, you don't think so, Cupcake Boy?"

Ty asked. "In case you haven't noticed, I am the star of this rodeo. Why, without me, it would be nothing."

"Ty!" a voice barked, and Mel spun around to see Slim and his wife, Tammy, headed their way. "I think you need to apologize to Mel and Tate."

"What for?" he asked. He glared at Slim and wobbled on his feet. "Aren't they here for me?"

Even in the dim light, Mel could see the red creep up Slim's neck and settle in his cheeks. A vein throbbed in his temple as he strived to keep his voice even.

"No, they're not," he said. "They're here to make money, same as anyone else."

"Pfff." Ty waved a dismissive hand at Slim and turned back to Mel. "A dozen chocolate at my trailer—got it?"

Slim moved so fast, Mel didn't even see him coming until he had Ty up against the wall with his slinged arm pressing against his neck. Ty's goons looked to be stepping forward, and Tate moved to stand between them and Slim, blocking their way.

"I said apologize, and I meant it," Slim said.

Tammy pressed her fingers over her lips as if trying to keep from crying out. Mel was with her. The tension in the air crackled like lightning as the two men stared each other down.

"You're making a mistake, old man," Ty said.

"You're right," Slim said. "I should have done this years ago when you started getting too big for your britches. Now apologize."

Ty looked like he would refuse, but Slim pushed his arm against Ty's neck and his arms flapped at his sides as his airway was cut off.

"Sorry," Ty choked out. Slim released him and he sagged to the ground.

Slim looked at Ty's goons. "Take him to his trailer to sleep it off."

The men stepped forward, and they each grabbed an elbow and hauled Ty up to his feet. They half carried, half dragged him out of the stable.

Slim looked at Mel and Tate. "I'm sorry about that. Ty's become . . . Well, a horse's ass would be about the best description."

"I don't know," Mel said. "I think I'd rather hang out with a horse's behind than with him."

Tammy broke out in a nervous laugh that busted the tension and made them all stand down from high alert.

"Hey, Lily is about to ride. You all are going to miss it." Jake Morgan appeared at the end of the tunnel.

"Come with us," Tammy said to Mel and Tate. "We have room in our box."

Mel and Tate followed the Hazards up into the arena. The stands were full, and there was a strong smell of popcorn in the air. Big overhead lights were on, illuminating the entire arena.

The Hazards had a box right behind the judges' booth, and they hurriedly sat down with Mel taking the seat between Tate and Jake.

"Is everything okay?" Jake asked. "Slim looks tense. What happened down there?"

"We had a run-in with Ty Stokes," Mel said. "He was drunk."

"Oh, that's not good. From what I've seen, Ty's a mean drunk," Jake said with a shake of his head.

"What's the deal between him and Slim?" Mel asked. "There seemed to be an awful lot of hostility between them."

"Slim was Ty's mentor," Jake said. "It was way before I started working here, so I don't know firsthand, but according to most everyone, they were very close."

"So, what happened?"

"As far as I can figure, stardom got to Ty," Jake said. "He started believing his own press. He thinks he's the only reason the Juniper Pass Rodeo has survived for the past ten years. He's been after Slim for a while to give him partial ownership of the rodeo. So far, Slim has said no."

"Is it true?" she asked. "Is he the only reason the rodeo has survived?"

Jake looked uncomfortable, and he was reluctant when he said, "He does draw a big crowd."

"So Ty thinks the rodeo owes him, and he's pretty mad," Mel guessed.

"Like a rattler about to strike," Jake said.

Mel didn't much like that metaphor. She had a small phobia about snakes.

"Contestant number four, Lily Hazard!" the announcer called out, and Mel turned her gaze to the arena. She could see Lily atop Cocoa Bar just above the gate. The horse looked eager, dancing from foot to foot. The gate shot open, and Lily and Cocoa Bar streaked forward.

Jake leaned close to Mel. "She has to get around those three barrels, making a clover pattern." Then he leaned back to yell, "Woo-hoo, look at her go!"

Mel held her breath as Lily and Cocoa Bar cut close around the second barrel. Cocoa Bar was practically sideways, he was going so fast in the tight turn, before opening it up to dash to the third. Then it was a flat-out run to the finish line. Mel jumped to her feet to applaud with the others. Lily and Cocoa Bar were breathtaking together, and the crowd went wild.

Mel stayed to watch the next two contestants, but they didn't hold a candle to the time Lily and Cocoa Bar had posted. She glanced at her watch and knew she had to get back to the van to help close up for the night. She rose to her feet, and Tate and Jake stood with her.

"Thank you," she said to Slim and Tammy. "That was amazing."

"Don't go yet," Slim said. "It's not over."

"I have to," she said regretfully. "But do tell Lily I thought she was magnificent."

"I'll go with you," Tate said.

"No, you stay and watch," Mel said. She looked him up and down in his Western wear. He was enjoying this too much for her to take him away; besides, she still felt a bit guilty for letting him have it earlier. "You can represent us."

Jake tipped his hat at her, and Mel grinned. She decided she could get used to that.

She slipped out of the arena and headed back to the truck. It was full dark now, and the evening air was cool with the scents of pine and campfires. When she passed the barbecue pit, both Billy and Bob gave her smarmy waves. She ignored them, and they hooted with laughter.

She was pleased to see a line at the truck. Marty and Angie were dishing out cupcakes and chatting up their customers with a nice dose of friendly.

Mel climbed into the back and asked, "Okay, who wants a break?"

"You go," Angie said to Marty. "Delia has paced by the van fifteen times; she's going to wear a trench in the ground waiting for you."

"Really?" Marty poked his head out the window and scouted left and right. "I never saw her."

"That's because you're a man," Angie said with a shake of her head. "You can't manage to do more than one thing at a time."

"Hey, that's not true," Marty said. He looked down at the ten-dollar bill in his hand. "Where'd this come from?"

"The customer standing in front of you waiting for change," Mel said.

"Oh, yeah." Marty opened up the cashbox, dropped the ten in, and counted out the person's change. He handed the bills through the window, and then he stripped off his blue apron. "Well, if you're sure you're okay with me going . . . see ya."

"No grass growing under his feet," Angie said.

Mel pulled on her pink apron and joined her friend in the window.

"So, how was the barrel riding?" Angie asked.

Fourteen

Mel gave Angie a sideways glance as she handed out one chocolate cupcake and one vanilla cupcake to two little boys, whose heads barely reached the service window.

Their mother took two Red Velvets for herself and put the change in the tip jar. Mel glanced up to see the line remaining steady. She had to admit, despite this morning's rocky start, Oz and Marty had been right. The cupcake van was a brilliant idea.

"Well? How was it? Did Little Miss Wrangler win?" Angie asked. She looked miffy, and Mel wondered how much to say.

"It was . . . exciting," Mel said.

Angie's face darkened, and Mel realized she had definitely picked the wrong adjective.

"What I mean is we had this altercation with Ty Stokes in the stable that got my heart pounding quite a bit."

"What happened?" Angie was immediately diverted from the Tate-Lily thing, whatever that was, thank goodness.

Mel gave her the down-and-dirty version, skipping the part where Ty called Tate a poser and her a cow. Angie never handled insults to her friends well.

"I kind of feel like it was my fault," Mel said.

"Because you bumped into him in the dark? That's ridiculous."

"Well, no, but it escalated so fast. I think if I'd just agreed to bring over some cupcakes, then Slim wouldn't have gotten so mad at him."

"It wasn't you," Angie said as she dished out three Tinkerbells to a group of teenage girls. "He sounds like a real jerk."

"Yeah, but I was thinking I should drop off a box of cupcakes at his trailer as a peace offering."

"No," Angie said. "You need to stay out of it."

"But . . ."

"Look, just because we're called Fairy Tale Cupcakes does not mean we can guarantee a happy-ever-after."

"I suppose, but still, from what Jake Morgan told me, the rodeo needs Ty more than Ty needs the rodeo."

"Financial trouble?" Angie asked.

"He wasn't specific, but it sounded like it," Mel said.

"Man, Slim is having a bad week," Angie said. "First he's shot, then his flaky daughter starts a protest, and now his star is making trouble for everyone. I think he needs a box of cupcakes more than the jackass."

"True, but if we can get Ty to calm down, then maybe things will go better for Slim," Mel said.

Angie heaved a huge sigh. "Fine, but I'm going with you. I don't trust that guy to behave."

"With any luck, he'll be passed out and we can just leave the cupcakes and go," Mel said.

It was thirty minutes later when Mel and Angie locked up the truck for the night, making sure the remaining unfrosted cupcakes were in the freezers, the tubs of frosting were in the fridge, and the cashbox was locked up in the mini-safe Sal had installed.

Mel had boxed up some leftover chocolate cupcakes, and they were on their way to Ty's trailer when Billy and Bob stepped out from their barbecue pit.

"Evenin', ladies," Bob said.

"Oh, look the Bubbas got out of their pen," Angie said. "We'd better get the pig handlers over here to corral them."

"Funny," Billy said in a tone that indicated it was not. "So, like, we'd better call out the . . . the . . . dog warden, so he can catch some strays."

They were all silent for a beat.

"Lame," Angie said.

Billy looked at Bob, who gave him a headshake that clearly indicated he should back away from the repartee.

"We had a line all day," Angie said. "Why, I can't even count how many cupcakes we sold. I noticed things weren't quite that busy over at the BBQ."

Billy and Bob exchanged chagrined looks.

"It's not over yet," Bob said.

Angie tipped her head and studied him. "Oh, don't worry. I bet you look pretty in pink."

Mel balanced the box of cupcakes in one hand and grabbed Angie's arm with the other. "Come on, before you tease yourself into a pair of Daisy Dukes. Night, boys!"

Billy and Bob glowered at them as they passed, and as soon as they were out of earshot, Mel turned on Angie. "Are you nuts? This is supposed to be a friendly wager. Do not turn it ugly."

"Puleeze, as if those two need any help in the ugly department," Angie said. She sounded crankier than ever.

"That's not what I meant," Mel said. "And you know it. Now, I get that you and Roach—"

Angie held up her hand. "Not open for discussion."

"Fine," Mel said. "But if you're concerned about Lily and Tate, you don't—"

"It's none of my business," Angie interrupted. "Tate's a free man. He can do whatever he wants."

Mel heaved a sigh. Fine. If Angie didn't want to talk about it, that was just dandy with her. She was fed up with the Tate and Angie show—honestly, just like that Fonzi on water skis episode on *Happy Days*, it had jumped the shark.

"Let's do this, then," she said.

It wasn't hard to find Ty's trailer. It was big and black with flames shooting up the side, tricked out like it belonged to a rock star. Mel briefly wondered if her idea was a good one.

She shifted the box of cupcakes in her arms and knocked on the trailer door.

She could hear the sound of someone moving inside, and one of the men she recognized as having been around

Ty earlier poked his head out. The sound of Brad Paisley singing in the background about mud on the tires got louder when he opened the door.

"Can I help you?" the man asked.

He was big and built solid, and Mel felt Angie stiffen beside her as if she was readying herself for a fight.

"Is Ty around?" Mel asked. The man stared at her. She continued, "I brought him some cupcakes to make up for bumping into him earlier."

The man looked her up and down, but Mel got the feeling he was taking her measure as a person, not undressing her with his eyes.

"You don't have to do this, you know," he said. "Ty was . . . Well, he wasn't himself."

Mel nodded, appreciating the man's straight talk.

"All the same," she said. "I don't want there to be any trouble on account of me. Can you tell him I'm here?"

"I would, but he's out. He took off with Shelby about a half hour ago," the man said with a frown. "You could leave those with us, but I doubt there'd be any left when Ty got back."

Mel smiled. This cowboy was okay.

"Any idea where he went?"

"Not for sure," he said. "But they were headed in the direction of the bull pens, which are in the last outbuilding past the arena."

"Thanks," Mel said. She felt Angie relax beside her.

As they turned to leave, Angie made to head back toward the van, but Mel struck out for the field building, where they housed the bulls used for competition in the rodeo. She was hoping to find Ty and Shelby together, as it would give her a good chance to make a cupcake peace offering to Ty and warn Shelby away from Oz.

"Oh, fine," Angie muttered and turned to follow her.

Judging by the cheers coming from the arena, the barrel-riding competition was still going strong. This part of the rodeo looked deserted. Only the sound of the large animals stomping and snorting broke the quiet.

Angie opened the door to the large outbuilding, and Mel led the way in. The place reeked of musty straw and manure, and she wondered if bringing cupcakes into an area with large animals was a good idea.

A few lights illuminated the gloom, and Mel glanced around, hoping to spot Ty or Shelby before they saw her. She strolled farther across the concrete floor. No one appeared to be there.

"Hello?" she called out. There was no answer.

"Maybe they left already," Angie said.

"Ty! Shelby!" Mel raised her voice.

A heavy hoof stomping on the floor was the only response.

"Mel, I think we need to call it," Angie said. "Let's go back to the trailer and leave the cupcakes with Ty's guys. I'll make sure they understand to save one for him."

Mel had no doubt that Angie would put the fear into the grown men, but still, she had been hoping to talk to Ty to make sure everything was cool.

"Let me just double-check," Mel said. She began to walk the length of the pens, feeling the long-lashed gaze of the bulls watching her progress down the aisle.

The door to the second-to-last pen was open, and she glanced in as she passed. The narrow toes of a pair of cowboy boots pointed up. She stopped.

Angie, who was right behind her, plowed into her back, making her drop her cupcakes.

"What the—" Angie began, but cut off with, "Oh!"

They had found Ty Stokes.

Fifteen

"Do you have your phone?" Mel asked. "Call Tate."

Mel scrambled forward while Angie fumbled with her phone.

It was the blood that made her trip. It had a bitter, metallic smell that was even stronger than the pungent odor of manure. One glance told Mel that the straw surrounding Ty Stokes's body was saturated with blood. His hat was in the corner of the pen, as if it had rolled off of his head and tried to hide. His body was slumped against the wooden wall as if all that was left of him were the remnants of a balloon that had been pricked by a pin. One glance at his chest, however, and Mel knew no pin had done this damage.

Several large holes were gouged into his chest through the fabric of his plaid shirt. The sight made bile rise up into the back of Mel's throat. She didn't know what to do. She couldn't even process what she was seeing. She could hear Angie's voice in the background, but it was a dull murmur like the wind in the trees.

"Help is coming. Is he breathing?" Angie asked as she slipped her phone into her pocket and crept forward to the edge of the pen.

Mel looked at Ty's chest. She saw no rise and fall, nothing to indicate the intake of breath. She had to get closer. She crept forward and reached for his wrist. Her fingers pressed against the spot where his pulse would be. There was nothing, not even the suggestion of blood flow.

"I don't think so. I don't feel a heartbeat," Mel said. Her voice quavered. When she met Angie's eyes, she saw the same horror that she felt reflected in their brown depths.

Angie spun around and shouted, "Help! Somebody help!"

Only the nervous shuffle of the large animals surrounding them could be heard.

"Hello?" someone called, and then they heard footsteps moving swiftly in their direction.

"Thank God," Angie moaned. "We're here. Over here."

"What's the trouble? What are you doing . . ." A man in a denim shirt appeared, but as he took in the sight before him his words seemed to lodge in his throat. He sucked in a breath at the sight of Ty and Mel on the ground. "I'm the veterinarian, Dr. Elway. What happened?"

Mel sagged with relief. "We don't know. We just found him like this. I couldn't find his pulse, and I'm not sure he's breathing."

The doctor hurried forward and began to examine Ty. He lowered Ty's body so that he was flat on the ground. He checked his vitals and put his head to his chest, disregarding the blood-soaked fabric. In only moments, he sat back on his heels and frowned.

"What happened?"

"Angie! Mel!"

A chorus of shouts sounded in the building, causing the bulls to shuffle restlessly.

Mel backed out of the pen, feeling guilty that she was relieved to put some distance between her and the gruesome scene before her.

Slim, Tammy, and Tate arrived. Mel glanced at Slim's face. The horror that passed over his features as he took in the sight of Ty Stokes wrenched her heart, and she stumbled toward the comforting strength of Tate, who immediately looped an arm around both her and Angie.

"Is he . . . ?" Tammy's voice trailed off as if she just couldn't make herself say the words.

"I'm afraid so," Dr. Elway said.

"Was it the bull?" Slim asked. "What the hell was he doing in the bull's pen? What could he have been thinking?"

"Shh, Slim. I know you're upset," Tammy soothed. "But we need to let Dr. Elway talk."

Slim gulped in a big breath and nodded.

"I don't know why he was in here," Dr. Elway said. "All I know is that he bled to death, and if the bull did this to him, then we need to find that bull."

"Excuse me, please. Let me through."

Mel turned and saw the sheriff making his way toward them. She remembered seeing him at the diner the night of Slim's shooting. He pushed past them to join the veterinarian in the stall. He took one look at Ty and muttered, "Aw, hell."

Tate pulled Angie and Mel away from the group by their elbows. When they were out of earshot, he asked, "What were you two thinking?"

Angie raised her hands in innocence. "Don't look at me. I tried to talk her out of it."

"Hey!" Mel frowned. "Way to throw me under the bus."

"Beep, beep," Angie said.

"Mel, honestly, when Angie called to tell me you'd found Ty Stokes's body *because you were bringing him cupcakes*? After how nasty he was, I couldn't believe it. I still can't believe it! What were you thinking?" Tate looked mystified.

"I just wanted to see if I could smooth things over," Mel said. "If I hadn't plowed into him—"

"He would have found some other reason to go off on Slim," Tate interrupted. "You really need to work on keeping healthy boundaries."

Mel frowned at him. She opened her mouth to argue, but the sheriff was making his way over to them, and she forced herself to hold her words.

"Excuse me. I'm Sheriff Hadley Dolan," he said. "Are you the two ladies who found him?"

Mel and Angie nodded. Mel shook his hand first and then Angie did.

"I'm Melanie Cooper, and these are my partners, Angie DeLaura and Tate Harper."

"Slim tells me you have the cupcake van over in the food area." The sheriff pushed back his wide-brimmed hat.

"That's right," Mel said. "I . . . uh . . . bumped into Mr.

Stokes earlier this evening, and he wanted some cupcakes, so my partner and I came looking for him. Unfortunately, we found him like this."

Sheriff Dolan nodded. "Slim already told me about the altercation."

"I was hoping the cupcakes would make things better," Mel said. The sheriff gave her a wry glance. "My wife, Ruth, always says there is no trouble that a good slice of pie can't ease."

"Ruth from the diner is your wife," Mel said.

The sheriff nodded.

"We had her coconut custard," Angie said. "She's got a gift."

"She is a remarkable lady," he agreed. Although his features remained staid, Mel could see the pride shine in his eyes. He took a small pad and pen out of the breast pocket of his tan uniform. "I have a few questions for you."

"All right," Mel and Angie answered together.

Tate stayed in between them as if to bolster them, and Mel was grateful for his solid warmth.

Sheriff Dolan asked them to repeat the events as they remembered them. Once they were finished, he made a few notes and then glanced up.

"Do you remember seeing anyone, anyone at all, in here when you came in?" he asked.

Mel and Angie glanced at each other while they tried to remember. Mel shook her head, and Angie did the same.

"It was eerily quiet," Angie said.

"It was," Mel agreed. "We almost didn't go any farther, but the man at Ty's trailer said that Ty and Shelby had left a half hour before and were headed this way."

Sheriff Dolan gave her a sharp look. "Could you repeat that?"

Mel did, and he looked thoughtful.

"We didn't see Shelby when we got here," Mel said. For some reason, she felt as if she were ratting out Shelby, but that was ridiculous. She was just telling him what had been said to her.

She glanced past the sheriff to see Slim watching their conversation. He looked worried, and Mel felt like a complete heel.

Sheriff Dolan closed his pad. "Thanks. If you think of anything else, let me know."

He fished two cards out of his pocket and gave one to Mel and one to Angie.

"I'm going to take these two back to the hotel," Tate said. "It's been a long day."

"Should I . . . ?" Mel gestured to the pile of cupcakes on the floor.

"We'll take care of it," Sheriff Dolan said. "After our crime scene techs are done."

"Oh, okay," Mel said. She felt bad leaving the mess, but it was out of her hands.

Mel wanted to talk to Slim before they left to apologize for mentioning Shelby's name to the sheriff, but she had no idea how she would go about doing that. The sheriff was talking to Slim and Tammy now, so Mel let Tate lead her away.

When they stepped out of the field house and into the cool evening air, she sucked in a deep breath and tried to relax.

"Mel, you're going to need to clean up," Angie said.

She gestured to Mel's jeans, and Mel glanced down. Her knees were saturated with a crimson stain, and she felt her head spin a little as she realized that she'd been kneeling in Ty's blood.

"Oh," she said.

"Are you all right?" Tate asked. He grabbed her elbow as if she might crumple like a paper bag under a heavy boot.

"No, not really," Mel said. "I'm feeling kind of nauseous."

"Come on," Angie said, propping Mel up on the other side. "Let's get moving. You'll feel better if you're in motion."

Mel certainly hoped Angie was right, because at the moment she really just wanted to put her head down, except that would put her face in proximity to her knees, which would definitely make her puke. So, motion it was.

The rodeo had finished for the night, and people were headed toward the exit. Laughter and loud conversations fluttered across the night air like the bats swooping above them catching bugs.

Mel realized that the calmness of the crowd meant that no one yet knew what had happened. That Ty Stokes, rodeo star, was dead.

She lowered her head and plowed forward. She felt as if the crowd was closing in on her, and she was having a hard time catching her breath.

Angie and Tate, as if sensing that she was struggling to maintain control, kept pace with her, and it wasn't until they'd reached the dirt road that led back to town that Mel slowed down.

"Was it just me or was it really crowded back there?" she asked.

"It wasn't you," Angie said. She was panting, too, and her long brown hair hung limply around her face. She reached up and twisted it into a knot at the back of her head.

"Come on." Tate led the way along the side of the road. "You'll feel better after a shower."

Mel felt as if the town of Juniper Pass was miles away instead of just up ahead. By the time they got to the Last Chance, she was ready to collapse.

She must have looked worse than she thought because when they entered the saloon, Marty, who was seated at the bar with Delia, hopped off of his seat and crossed the room in three strides.

"What happened to you?" he demanded. "Why are you covered in blood?"

"Not here, Marty," Tate said.

The eyes of the room turned toward them, and Tate was trying to get Mel out of there without having to explain about Ty in front of a crowd of people.

Marty looked ready to argue, but Angie gave him the "wait" hand gesture, which, coming from Angie, made it nonnegotiable.

Mel was just pushing through the small side door into the hotel lobby when the front door to the saloon slammed open, banging against the wall.

"Bull!" a man yelled, looking frantic. "A bull is loose on the town green!"

Sixteen

The customers in the bar ran to the doors. Mel and Angie exchanged a look. They had no doubt that it was "the bull."

"C'mon!" Henry the bartender shouted at them. "This is an emergency."

"What are we supposed to do?" Tate asked.

"Use that lasso you're so fond of," Angie said.

Mel frowned at her. The last thing they needed was for Tate to be dragged through town by a bull on a rampage.

"We need to get him back to the rodeo before he does himself or anyone else an injury," Henry said. "Delia, you stay here and mind the bar for me."

Delia bobbed her red head, and Mel could tell that had been her plan all along.

"I don't want you two going out there," Tate said.

Angie looked like she was going to kick him, but Mel was thinking he was talking good sense. She'd had more than enough drama for one day, and what the heck was she supposed to do with a loose bull anyway?

"There he is!" a shout sounded from outside.

Mel and the others crowded into the large picture window to see. It was dark outside, but the town's old-fashioned streetlamps illuminated the town green, and it wasn't hard to spot the boulder-shouldered, long-horned beast that was trotting around the green, lowering his head, and chomping at the petunias.

Several men, who looked as if they knew ranch work and how to deal with a burly behemoth on the move, were circling the green as if trying to get near him. A pickup truck with a horse trailer attached had been backed up to the green.

Mel assumed that the plan was to get the bull into the trailer. Given that this sort of event had not been covered at Le Cordon Bleu, she was more than happy to watch from the safety of the bar.

"Come on, Marty," Tate said.

Marty cast a quick glance at Delia, who was pressed to the window, then looked at Tate with a wide-eyed "you are crazy" stare.

"Your hat is too tight," he hissed at Tate.

"It's our duty as men," Tate said. "We have to help."

"Don't be ridiculous," Angie said. "You don't know a hoof from a horn from a hook. You'll get trampled to death out there."

"Oh, is that so?" Tate asked. Without another word, he pushed through the swinging doors out onto the sidewalk.

"Nice going," Marty snapped at Angie, and with a sigh, he followed Tate.

"Tate! Marty!" Mel hollered. "Come back!"

They ignored her.

"Oh, dear," Delia muttered from beside them.

Mel turned to glower at Angie.

"What?" Angie asked.

"Nothing had better happen to them," she said. "Instead of taking your foul mood out on Tate, maybe you should do some soul searching and knock it off!"

"Well, that's just—" Angie began but Delia cut her off with a gasp.

Mel and Angie turned to look at her and saw that her eyes were huge as she pointed out the window.

"Isn't that the young man who works for you? What's his name? Oscar?"

"Oz?" Mel peered back out the window. "What's he doing out there?"

"Looks like he's got a box of something," Delia said.

As he passed under a streetlamp, oblivious to the chaos around him, Mel could see that he did have a big Tupperware tub in his arms.

One of the men on the town green shouted and waved at Oz, but he had his iPod earbuds in and was bobbing his head to whatever punk band he was listening to, so he didn't hear the shouts, and before anyone could get to him, the bull spotted him and lowered his head.

"Sweet petunias," Delia muttered. "That bull is going to charge."

As one, Mel and Angie fell back from the window and burst through the doors.

"What do we do?" Angie cried.

"I don't know, but I am not returning Oz to his parents in a bucket."

Together Mel and Angie dashed across the deserted street, but before they could jump onto the curb, a strong hand grabbed each of their elbows and dragged them behind a parked car and held them.

"Don't move!" Jake Morgan hissed as they tried to jerk out of his grasp. "You'll get that boy killed if you spook the bull."

Mel and Angie watched helplessly as Oz continued down the sidewalk and the bull lumbered forward. Mel saw Tate hop over a park bench and angle himself so he could jump in front of the bull if need be.

"Oh, no, Tate, no," Angie whispered.

The bull stepped onto the sidewalk, and Oz stumbled to a halt. Mel couldn't see his eyes through the bangs that covered them, but she was betting they were wide-open now.

The bull snorted and pawed the ground. Oz slowly reached up and pulled out his earbuds.

Mel could hear Tate talking to Oz. She saw Oz shuffle toward the bench, but the bull shook its mighty crest, the top part of its shoulders, and Oz froze. Slowly, ever so slowly, she saw Oz move his hand toward the top of the Tupperware.

Carefully, he slipped his hand inside the tub. He held something in his fist, and as she watched, he lobbed it underhand right at the bull.

"Did he just . . . ?" Jake's voice trailed off, and his grip on their elbows loosened as he stared at the scene before him.

"Throw a cupcake at it," Angie said. "Yeah, he did."

They all held their breath as the bull snorted over the cupcake on the sidewalk. As they watched, the bull's large pink tongue came out, and he rolled the cupcake into his mouth like a cowboy packing chewing tobacco in his cheek.

While the bull worked on the cupcake, Tate called out to Oz to get behind the bench. Oz shook his head. Instead, he walked toward the bull.

"Oz, don't do it!" Tate ordered. "He's not a stray dog. He'll squash you like a bug!"

Oz took two more steps toward the bull. The bull eye-balled him, and Mel felt her breath stop somewhere in her windpipe. She was frozen with fear and could neither inhale nor exhale.

Then the bull gave a hoarse cry and stomped toward Oz, making him jump. Oz fished out another cupcake and tossed it at the bull. The bull snorted it up and looked up for more, but Oz was already running across the green.

"Run, Oz!" Mel yelled.

Several cowboys, including Tate and Jake, sprinted forward to help him, but the bull was gaining on him. Mel knew that if Oz tripped, he was a goner.

"Head toward the trailer!" Jake yelled.

Clutching the Tupperware to his chest, Oz veered across the grass, throwing cupcakes over his shoulders like they were hand grenades. The bull stayed in pursuit, but Oz had a good lead as the bull slowed down to snuffle up the cupcakes left in Oz's wake.

The bull was going full tilt after him right up until it spotted the trailer. Then the two thousand plus pounds of bull balked and threw itself into reverse.

Mel and Angie circled the back of the parked car and started to run. As they neared the trailer, Mel saw Tate grab a rope off of the gate and send it up in the air in a wide, looping circle that came down neatly over the bull's horns.

"Holy cow!" Angie cried. "Did you see that?"

Four other men, including Jake and Marty, jumped in, and together, with Tate controlling the horns with the lasso, the men chased the bull up into the trailer with a little help from Oz, who threw several more cupcakes into the back of the trailer.

Jake slammed the gate of the trailer shut and shot the bolt home. The men broke out into cheers. Oz and Tate were soundly smacked on the back, and they both looked sheepishly proud of themselves.

Angie ran across the grass and catapulted herself at Tate, who grabbed her close, much to the delight of the crowd that had gathered. Mel followed, feeling her knees knock against each other as she thought of what could have happened, especially to Oz, and the fact that she would have had to explain it to his parents.

She snatched Tate's hat off of his head, as it was the handiest weapon available, and began to swat him with it.

"Have you lost your mind?" she yelled.

"Hey!" Tate dropped Angie and spun on Mel. "Not the hat!"

Mel threw it at him and then turned on Oz. "And you! Do you have any idea what could have happened to you?"

Oz looked at the trailer where the bull was banging around in protest and then at Mel. He gulped.

"Yeah, I have a pretty good idea," he said. He visibly paled beneath his shaggy bangs, so Mel took pity on him and forced herself not to belabor the point, much as she would have liked to.

Instead she hugged him close and said, "Do not ever scare me like that again!"

"So, Oz, where did you get the cupcakes?" Angie asked.

She smoothed down the front of her shirt as if she were trying to appear casual. Mel glanced from her to Tate, who was watching Angie with an intensity Mel usually saw only on her true cupcake-connoisseur customers when they were trying to make a flavor decision.

"I made them," Oz said.

"Really?" Angie asked. "Where?"

"At the diner," Oz said. "Ms. Ruth let me use the kitchen."

"So you felt the need to bake more cupcakes because the ten thousand we brought weren't enough?" Mel asked.

Oz let out a sigh, and then he said, "This wasn't how I was going to tell you, but these are vegan."

Tate was the first to grasp the meaning, and he laughed and said, "So that explains why the bull liked them so much. They probably taste like grass."

"Soy, actually," Oz said.

Mel glanced into the Tupperware. "I've been thinking we need to offer a vegan alternative. Let's have it, then."

She held out her hand and waited for Oz to fish out a cupcake for her.

"They were prettier before I had to flee for my life," he said.

He handed Mel and Angie each a vanilla one and Tate a chocolate. The frosting was lopsided and mashed, but Mel could tell it had been lovely before the running of the bull.

Mel peeled off the paper wrapper and took a bite, making sure to get an equal amount of frosting and cake, since she considered the frosting-to-cupcake ratio critical, especially when trying a new cupcake.

She savored the first bite and then took a second. The cake was dense and moist with a definite hint of soy milk, but it didn't overpower. The frosting was as smooth as silk, and she marveled at its texture.

As if reading her thoughts, Oz said, "Organic margarine, organic powdered sugar, and vanilla bean paste."

Mel swiped some up on her index finger and tasted it without the accompaniment of the cake. It was delicious.

"I'm impressed," she said, and finished off the cupcake.

"I was thinking I'd like to offer organic cupcakes in the bakery," Oz said.

Mel could tell he was watching her through his bangs, as if afraid she was going to shoot him down.

"Well, I don't know," Mel said. "I really can't make an informed decision until I've tried your chocolate version."

Oz hurriedly reached into the box and grabbed a chocolate cupcake with chocolate frosting. His eagerness almost made Mel feel bad for teasing him, but then she bit into the chocolate and forgot that she'd been kidding.

Again, the cake was dense and moist, and the chocolate flavor was dominant. The frosting was luscious. She gave Oz a surprised glance, and he smiled.

"Unsweetened cocoa, agave nectar, and organic margarine," he said.

"It's a deal," Mel said. "You are hereby our organic cupcake chef."

Tate and Angie both nodded in agreement. "These are amazing."

"I need to try the vanilla," Tate said.

"I'm out," Oz said. "I used most of those on the bull."

Tate looked crestfallen.

"Oh, here," Angie said. She offered him the last half of her vanilla.

Instead of taking it from her hand, Tate leaned close and opened his mouth. Angie flushed bright pink and carefully fed him the cupcake from her fingers.

Mel watched as they gazed at each other with such naked longing that she had to turn away because she felt as if she were intruding.

She grabbed Oz by the elbow and spun him around, too. How offering a person a cupcake could be R-rated, she had no idea, but she really felt that Oz was too young to witness such an intimate moment.

"Let's get back to the hotel," she said. Marty was standing up by the horse trailer, talking to Jake, so she went that way to see if Jake had heard about Ty's death.

"Is this the bull?" Mel asked. "The one that should have been in the pen where . . ."

"Ty was found," Jake said. He blew out a breath. "Yeah, the sheriff wants us to bring him back down to the rodeo grounds so the vet can check him out."

"Check him out?" Oz asked. "Why?"

Mel glanced at Oz. If he'd been up at the diner making cupcakes, then he had missed hearing about Ty.

"Oz, Ty Stokes was found in one of the bull pens," Mel said. "He was gored to death."

Oz dropped his cupcakes.

Seventeen

"What?" he asked. "How did he ... Was it *that* bull?"

Oz's olive complexion faded as the blood drained from his face, and he wobbled in his size thirteens.

"Head between the knees, champ," Marty said, and he eased Oz down onto a nearby bench and had him hang his head down.

"We don't know," Mel said. "Ty was found in the bull pen, and the bull was gone."

"But why was he ... ?" Oz's head came up and his bangs parted. Mel could see he was thinking of something but had cut off his words before he spoke them aloud.

"What do you know, Oz?" she asked.

"Me? Nothing!" he said.

He was protesting a little too quickly for Mel's liking.

When she was about to press, Tate and Angie joined them, interrupting the moment.

"You okay, O-man?" Tate asked.

"Yeah, I'm cool," he said.

"He just heard about Ty," Marty explained.

"Speaking of which, I'd better get this bull back down to the rodeo," Jake said. "Thank you all for your help."

He tipped his hat and headed toward the truck. They stood and watched him haul the behemoth bovine away.

"What will happen if they do discover that it was the bull?" Oz asked.

The rest of them exchanged a look over his head: Marty to Mel and Mel to Tate and Tate to Angie and Angie to Mel.

Mel got it. It was her job to break the bad news.

"They'll probably have to put him down, Oz," she said.

"So, my cupcakes led him to his doom," Oz said. He shook his shaggy mane, and Mel felt helpless to console him. She didn't know how these things worked.

"Now, quit with the crazy talk," Marty said. "I got a nice close-up look at the bull, and those horns of his are clean. Don't you think if he gored somebody to death, it'd show?"

"Marty's right," Mel said quickly. "He certainly didn't look like he'd been in any . . . uh . . . incidents with his horns."

Oz glanced up at Mel. She knew it wasn't her best sell job in the world, but he seemed to accept it.

"I think we all need to get some shut-eye," Tate said. "It's been a hell of an evening, and who knows what's going to happen tomorrow."

"Do you think they'll shut the rodeo down because of Ty?" Angie asked.

Mel saw the line of customers outside of her cupcake truck disappear like a dust devil in a rainstorm. It was horribly selfish; a man had died, after all. She needed to get some perspective. But even as she chastised herself, she couldn't help but lament that they had been doing a bang-up business.

Tate shrugged. "It's up to the sheriff."

It was a somber group that made their way to the Last Chance to try to sleep. The bar was full of people who had been out chasing the bull. Mel glanced around the room. Some were laughing and clapping one another on the back, but others were looking anxious, and she knew without being told that word of Ty's demise was spreading through the room, moving amongst them like a cloaked specter of death wielding his scythe over all of their heads.

A chill shivered through her, and Tate gave her a concerned look.

"Are you okay?" he asked.

Mel nodded, but it was a lie. Suddenly, she was overcome with homesickness. She wanted to be curled up on her futon with Joe, watching old movies and chomping on popcorn while Captain Jack made them laugh by chasing his tail until he was overcome with dizziness and fell over.

Tate looked at her as if he understood. He gave her a one-armed hug and kissed the top of her head.

It helped.

\'\'\

Mel and Angie were up early the next morning. The sky was blue, the sun was warm, but the breeze was cool. They had a quick breakfast with the men at the Stardust Diner, and then they all trooped down to the rodeo to see what was happening.

It was early, but Mel saw both Slim and Lily near the grandstand. They were having a heated conversation with the sheriff.

"Tate!" Lily called, and waved him over.

Mel saw Angie glower, but she didn't say anything as Tate made his way over to the small group.

"Come on, sunshine," Marty said to Angie. "Let's go get ready for business."

"But what if . . ." Oz began, but Mel waved her hand.

"Assume it's business as usual unless you hear otherwise," she said. "I'll go find out for sure."

She made her way over to Tate and the Hazards. She wasn't sure how to break into the conversation, so she waited, hoping to hear one way or another if they were to open or not today.

"Oh, look, it's the fairy tale baker," a voice said behind Mel.

She spun around to find the Bubbas fast approaching.

"What's the matter? Are you hoping they'll shut the rodeo down so you can get out of our wager?" Billy asked.

"No!"

"She looks desperate," Bob said. "Maybe her cupcakes aren't such a happy-ever-after, after all."

"Go choke on a brisket," Mel said. She turned away from them and focused on what the sheriff was saying.

"Look, Slim, I know the rodeo is the lifeblood of Juniper Pass, but I've got a murder investigation on my hands now."

"Hadley, we don't know that it was murder," Slim argued.

"The bull came back clean," Sheriff Dolan countered. "Dr. Elway says it looks like Ty was gored by something else."

"He's a veterinarian," Slim said.

"The county crime lab agrees," Sheriff Dolan said.

"Are you shutting us down?" Slim asked. "I need an answer."

The sheriff pushed his hat back on his head and rubbed a hand over his eyes. He looked as if he hadn't slept at all last night.

"Not yet," the sheriff said. "But if anything else happens . . ."

"It won't," Slim said. "Ty's death was an accident. It had to be."

Mel glanced at the group surrounding Slim. No one, not even his daughter, looked as if they believed him.

"The rodeo will open same time as usual!" Slim called out, and the crowd dispersed.

Mel spun around and saw the Bubbas watching her with grins on their faces.

"What?" she snapped.

They both shrugged. Mel narrowed her eyes. She did not trust them.

She was halfway across the grounds when Angie came running up to her. Her long brown hair was wild about her head, and she was out of breath and looked panicked.

"Angie, what's wrong?"

Angie opened her mouth to speak but sucked in a gulp

of air instead. She held up one finger, took another breath, and said, "Cupcakes, all of them, ruined."

"What?"

"Someone unplugged our freezers. Thousands of cupcakes defrosted," Angie wheezed.

Mel broke into a run, and Angie, hugging the stitch in her side, followed.

Eighteen

When Mel reached the truck, she found Marty and Oz looking as perplexed and distressed as Angie.

"I'm sorry, Mel," Oz said.

Mel nodded and climbed up into the back of the truck. The freezers were hanging open, and it was easy to see that, yes, sometime in the night they had stopped working, and now all of her cupcakes—the red velvets, chocolate, vanilla, and lemon—were all defrosted.

Angie climbed up quietly behind her. She was still wheezing. Marty and Oz climbed in, too, and Mel looked at them and then back to the freezers.

"Do we know what happened?" she asked. She was pleased that her voice didn't reflect the full-blown panic that was coursing through her.

Marty gestured out the back of the truck. "We had the

146

freezers plugged in on backup power, and somehow the truck got unplugged."

Mel glanced out the service window to see the Bubbas, standing in their barbecue pit with barely disguised grins.

"I think 'somehow' is named Billy and Bob," she said.

"What?" Angie snapped. "You mean we were sabotaged by those backwoods barbecue buttheads?"

"I can't prove it," Mel said as she watched Billy and Bob give each other a high-five. "But, yeah, that's what I'm thinking."

"Argh," Angie growled, and spun on her heel toward the back of the truck.

"Oz, grab her!" Mel ordered.

Oz looped an arm out and caught Angie about the waist.

Mel knew that Angie fully intended to go over and put a hurt on Billy and Bob, but Mel had a better idea, and she was going to need all hands on deck to get it done.

"Angie, I know you want revenge," she said in a low voice only Angie could hear. "But the best revenge will be seeing the Bubbas pimping cupcakes in cute little pink aprons, yes?"

"How is that going to happen when we don't have enough product to get us to the end of the rodeo?" Angie argued.

"Oh, we'll have enough," Mel said. "How many cupcakes did we sell yesterday?"

"Almost two thousand," Marty said.

"Excellent," Mel said. "So, here's what we're going to do. Let's keep two thousand of the thawed cupcakes out for today and start frosting just like we would be anyway. Marty, Oz, can I count on you two to get it done?"

Both men nodded and set to work.

"And then that's it?" Angie asked. "The cupcakes won't be any good tomorrow. I mean, they'd be okay but not up to our standard."

"Yes, they will, because they won't be cupcakes; they'll be cake pops."

Angie shook her head. "Come again?"

Mel pulled Angie away from where Marty and Oz were working, so that they couldn't overhear her. She didn't want to have to explain about the bet to them and add pressure to an already ulcer-inducing situation.

"You heard me," Mel said in a low voice. "I'm not throwing out thousands of cupcakes, and I'm not losing the bet to those two idiots. Agreed?"

Angie met her gaze and nodded.

"Excellent," she said. "All right. Marty and Oz, you're going to be in charge. Angie, you and I will make a supply run. We're going to need candy coating, lollipop sticks, and small cellophane wrappers."

"Problem," Angie said. "We don't have a car."

"Well, we're just going to have to get one," Mel said.

Two ladies appeared at the truck window. Both wore Western shirts and jeans with cowboy boots, but neither of them looked as if they'd ever seen the back of a horse except from a distance.

"A half dozen French Toast cupcakes, please," the woman asked.

"Coming right up," Marty said. He had already set to work turning the defrosted vanilla cupcakes into breakfast food.

Mel stepped up beside him and started sprinkling the bacon on them.

"So did you hear about Ty Stokes?" one lady asked the other.

"Gored by that crazed bull," the friend replied. "I hope they put it down. It gives me the shivers to think of that beast roaming the streets looking for another victim."

Mel glanced over at Oz. His back had gone ramrod straight, and he looked like he was about to say something.

She hurriedly elbowed him out of the way and plastered a pleasant smile on her face.

"Here you go," she said, quickly boxing the six cupcakes and handing them out the window.

Then she spun around and arched her left eyebrow at Oz. "Do not get into it with the customers, or I'll put you down."

Oz bobbed his shaggy head, and Mel reached out to lift his bangs and make sure he understood her with some good old-fashioned eye contact.

"I mean it," she said.

"All right, I won't say anything," he said. "But the bull is innocent. He's just seriously misunderstood."

"So long as I'm not," Mel warned him.

Marty and Oz exchanged a look, and Mel got the feeling they were a little afraid of her. Normally, she was the easy one at the bakery, but maybe it wasn't so bad to be the heavy in a time of crisis.

"So where is Tate?" Angie asked. Her voice was scathing, as if she expected him to be rolling in the hay with Lily Hazard. Mel rolled her eyes. If they all survived this rodeo without being stomped by a bull or strangling one another, it would be a miracle.

"Tate was talking to the Hazards," Mel said. "I think he was trying to help them keep the rodeo open."

She hopped out of the truck with Angie on her heels. They were passing the barbecue pit when she heard Billy laugh. Instinctively, Mel grabbed Angie's elbow to keep her on course and prevent her from launching herself at the two hayseeds.

"We don't have time for a smackdown right now," Mel said.

"Fine. I'll give up on the battle so long as we win the war."

"The only way we're going to win the war is if you make nice with Lily Hazard," Mel said.

Angie stopped walking and glared at her.

"Oh, no," Mel said. "I do not have time for this. I've had it with you and Tate and Roach and the whole stupid thing. Now, you are going to help me find a car and you're going to help me make cake pops and put your personal life on hold. Period. Am I clear?"

Angie raised her eyebrows in surprise. "So, you're channeling my mother now?"

"Did it work?" Mel asked.

"Yeah," Angie said, and then nodded. "I'm good."

Mel released a pent-up breath.

"Excellent. Then let's go."

They ran into Tate when they were halfway to the main gate. He was wearing his hat and boots and had developed a rolling strut just as if he actually spent time in a saddle.

Mel gave Angie a quick glance out of the corner of her eye, but Angie's face was blank, giving no indication of her thoughts.

"Tate!" Mel shouted, then waved.

He glanced over and saw them and returned Mel's greeting.

"What's up?" he asked.

"We have a situation," Mel said. "Something happened with the truck's freezer, and all of our cupcakes are defrosted. I need to drive to the nearest big town to buy some supplies if I'm going to turn this fiasco around."

"Talk and walk." Tate gestured for them to follow as he started walking toward the stables.

Mel explained her plan, and Tate nodded. He looked pretty impressed with her idea, and Mel had to admit she was impressed with herself.

"Okay, we need a vehicle and a place for you to work because there is no way you're going to have enough room in the cupcake truck," he said. "Also, we're going to have to start keeping watch at night. Once you get these cake popsicles . . ."

"Cake pops, as in lollipop," Mel corrected him.

Tate nodded. "Cake pops, got it. Are you sure they'll be as popular as cupcakes?"

"Am I ever wrong about desserts?" Mel asked.

"No."

"Then trust me."

"Once you get them made, we're going to need to keep an eye on the truck and make sure we don't have another incident."

"Agreed," Mel said. "We'll have to take turns keeping watch. I don't want anyone touching my cake pops."

They entered the big barn and slammed into Jake Morgan. He looked surprised to see them there, and Mel imagined that they were quite a sight. Two women and one man all obviously very stressed. Mel forced her lips into a smile, trying not to look as freaked out as she felt.

"Hey, there," Jake said. He shuffled back around a bale

of hay to give them some space. "Can I help you with something?"

"I hope so," Tate said. He explained about the cupcake situation, and Jake nodded while he listened.

"I can loan you my truck," he said. "It's not pretty to look at, but it will get you where you need to go, and I'm pretty sure Tammy won't mind if you use the kitchen at the ranch house."

"Really?" Mel asked. She'd been afraid to hope for so much help, but now it looked as if she wasn't going to lose the bet and be forced into the Daisy Dukes, after all.

"I don't see why not," Jake said. "We're all on the rodeo grounds pretty much twenty-four/seven right now, so it's not like you'd be in anyone's way at the house."

He fished a hand into his pants pocket and pulled out a simple key ring with three keys on it.

"Tate, can you go help at the cupcake van?" Mel asked. "If we get hit as hard as yesterday, Marty and Oz are going to need backup."

"Sure," he said. "Thanks, Jake."

The two men nodded at each other, and Tate left. Angie watched him go, but her face remained impassive, for which Mel was grateful.

✁

Jake led them outside to the back of the stable. He stopped at an old-style Ford pickup that had more paint missing than it had on it.

"I need a craft store, like a Jo-Ann's or a Michael's," Mel said. "Any idea where the closest would be?"

"A what?" Jake asked.

"Craft store," Angie repeated.

Jake looked perplexed. "I pretty much only shop at the Feed and Tack store myself."

"Why, Jake, you've given up your sewing?" a snide voice asked. "Or is it that you're only interested in hemming yourself into my daddy's life—or would that be his fortune?"

Jake spun around, and Mel glanced over his shoulder to see Shelby coming around the back side of the truck. She was smoking a cigarette and didn't have her usual health-girl sparkle. There were bags under her eyes, and her hair was scraped away from her face and held back with a wide white hair band.

"Shelby, you shouldn't be smoking," Jake said. "You know how Slim feels about that around the barns."

Shelby made a disgusted face. "Could you be more of a kiss-ass?"

Mel glanced at Jake and saw his jaw clench and unclench, as if he were keeping his temper by sheer force of will.

"You know, I'll just head into town and see if someone can give me some directions," Mel said. She took the keys from Jake and slid into the driver's seat as Angie made her way around to the passenger's side.

"Good luck," Jake said. He tipped his hat and stalked away as if he couldn't put enough distance between himself and Shelby fast enough.

Mel turned the key in the ignition, and the engine purred. Whatever was under the hood was certainly in better condition than the outside, and Mel relaxed. She'd had visions of them stranded in the outlying area waiting for the cupcake van to come and save them.

Before she could move the steering column shifter into reverse, Shelby stepped forward and rested her elbow on Mel's open window.

"I like your cupcake boy," she said, and she blew a smoke ring up into the air. "He's cute."

Mel felt Angie grow tense beside her. She glanced up to see the smoke ring drift away, breaking apart on the breeze.

"He's underage," Mel said.

Shelby gave her a sultry look that said louder than words that there was no man she couldn't have if she decided she wanted him. Mel wanted to slap the conceit right out of her, but then something clicked in her head and she turned to face the sultry blond.

"I'm sorry, Shelby; maybe I'm mistaken, but I thought I'd heard that you were with Ty right before he died?" she asked. "Is that true?"

Nineteen

Shelby's expression faltered with a flicker of unease before she regained her composure.

"Yeah, so? What's your point?"

"Does Sheriff Dolan know you were with him?" Mel asked.

"Yes, I already explained it to him, and he's fine with it," Shelby said. "Ty and I are old friends, and we were just catching up. I didn't kill him."

"Hmm," Mel said. "An animal-rights advocate and a rodeo star is an interesting combo. Seems to me an animal-rights person might be just the sort to murder a rodeo star."

"Oh, please," Shelby said. "I couldn't care less about these dumb animals. It's just the Hollywood thing to do, to help my career, you know?"

"I'd rethink, if I were you," Angie said, leaning around

Mel to glare at Shelby. "Since it doesn't seem to be doing much for your career, and it does seem to be affecting a friend of ours."

"Are you threatening me?" Shelby asked. She crushed the tip of her cigarette between her fingers before flinging it away.

"Oh, that's such an unpleasant word," Angie said. "Let's go with warning. Stay away from Oz."

Shelby tipped her head back and laughed without humor. "Even if I did, how can you make him stay away from me?"

She turned and sauntered away from the pickup with her hips swinging in a come-hither way that was completely wasted on Mel and Angie.

"So, backing over her would be a bad thing, right?" Angie asked.

"Sadly, yes."

Mel reversed the pickup out of its space and then put it in drive to head to the dirt road that would take them to town.

Not knowing anyone in town, she figured her best bet would be Ruth at the diner. They had the foodie thing in common, and Ruth seemed like the sort who would know where to hunt down unusual ingredients at a bargain.

They parked beside the Stardust, which looked to be in the midst of its morning lull.

The bells on the door jangled when they walked in. There was one customer at the counter and a family at a booth, but that was it. Ruth was refilling the ceramic mug for the man at the counter, but she smiled at Mel and Angie in recognition.

"Hey, there," she said. "Don't tell me you've come for

the strawberry rhubarb. I've been cleaned out, but I have a nice peach pie if you're interested."

"I'm always interested in pie," Mel said. She took an empty seat at the counter.

"Make it two," Angie said. "With coffee."

"I didn't see you when we came in for breakfast this morning," Mel said.

"No, Hadley was up most of the night because of, well, you know," Ruth said. She *tsk*ed and shook her head while she got two fresh cups and poured them each a coffee. "I didn't get much sleep, either, and this morning, I slept right through my alarm. First time I've missed a morning shift in forever."

"Is there any word on . . . you know?" Mel asked. "Do they know what happened yet?"

Ruth shook her head. "Nasty business."

"But they know it wasn't the bull," Angie said.

"Yeah, but honestly, I don't find the alternative that comforting," Ruth said.

"Murder," Mel said. "No, I don't suppose that is a pleasant option."

"Ty Stokes was a miserable, greedy, mean little man," the man sitting down the counter said. "You ask me, he got what was coming to him."

Angie lifted her eyebrows as she met Mel's interested gaze.

"Hush, Whitley," Ruth said. "The man is dead. There's no need to talk badly about him."

"Oh, I'm not saying anything that folks don't already know." The man called Whitley took a big gulp of his coffee and didn't look at all repentant.

Jenn McKinlay

He was a large man who used the counter to prop up his middle while he balanced himself with an elbow on each side. He had a plate in front of him that looked to have been licked clean.

"I mean, do you really think it's a coincidence that Slim was shot at the opening parade?" Whitley asked.

"They say it was just random gunfire," Ruth said. She had turned her back on them and was taking a pie out of the display case.

"Huh," Whitley grunted. "There was nothing random about Slim getting winged like a duck in flight."

"You can't prove that," Ruth said. "Besides, who would want to harm Slim? He's the life of Juniper Pass."

"Since you're already dishing, Ruth, add a slice of pie to my tab," Whitley said.

She gave him a look that said he needed pie like a sinking boat needed a cinder block but politely said nothing.

Mel could see the yellow and red of the peaches glistening between the flaky crusts as Ruth cut two generous wedges and placed them on the thick white dishes with the cobalt blue edges. Without asking them, Ruth warmed the pie in the microwave and then put a generous scoop of vanilla ice cream on each before placing them on the counter in front of them.

"I think I'm drooling," Angie whispered, and Mel nodded in understanding.

"I hear that," she said, and surreptitiously checked her chin.

Whitley, however, was not one to be distracted by pie. He waved his fork at Ruth as he continued his discourse.

"I bet Slim and Ty had another falling-out," he said.

158

"And I'm betting one of Ty's boys shot Slim, and as retribution Ty was found gutted in the bull pen."

"Surely you don't think it was Slim," Ruth said. "The man is in a sling."

"But his daughter isn't," Whitley said. Then he shoveled in some pie as if that ended the conversation.

Angie looked surprised and asked, "Is he referring to Lily?"

Ruth patted back her gray hair with one hand and frowned. "That's just silly. Lily Hazard is one of the finest young women in Juniper Pass. She's on the hospital board, the museum board. Why, she even works with at-risk youth in the church."

"Huh." Angie grunted and shoved a piece of pie in her mouth, probably to keep from saying something not nice.

Mel had forked up a bite of her own and was enjoying the taste-bud sensation of warm, tart peaches with cold, sweet ice cream in a buttery, flaky crust. Nirvana.

"Now, that sister of hers, Shelby, why, I wouldn't put anything past her," Ruth said.

"Well, who did you think I was talking about?" Whitley asked. "It's the younger one that's the wild card."

"True enough," Ruth agreed. "She caused Slim more heartache than any father should have to bear."

Mel felt her curiosity rear its nosy old head. "How so?"

"After their mother died, she ran away," Ruth said. "Slim was beside himself, but he finally tracked her down in Las Vegas. She was working in one of the casinos."

"Then what happened?" Angie asked.

"He brought her back to the ranch, and she took up with any no-account who came along," Ruth said. "She was determined to get to California and be a big star."

"Might help if she had a lick of talent," Whitley said.

"No argument there," Ruth agreed. "Anyway, then she took up with Ty, and that was the final straw for Slim. He sent her away."

"Why?" Mel asked. "I thought Ty was his protégé. I'd think he'd be happy if she and Ty were together."

"Things had soured between Ty and Slim," Ruth said. She glanced out the window as if remembering. "Ty was angry with Slim."

"Tell them why," Whitley said.

"That's gossip that I want no part of," Ruth said, and she shook her head.

"Oh, phooey, it just proves that Slim is no saint, and no one likes to admit that," Whitley said.

Ruth glared at him.

"What? I'm just telling the truth," he said. He put his fork down with a clatter. "I like Slim as much as the next guy, but there's no denying that he was a hothead in his youth. And it was that temper of his that got Ty's father, Caleb Stokes, killed."

Mel gaped. She turned and saw Angie doing the same.

Angie recovered her powers of speech faster and asked, "How?"

"They were both bull riders on the circuit," Whitley said. "One night they got into a pissing match—needless to say they'd been drinking—and they broke into the bull pen at the Cheyenne Frontier Days Rodeo."

Mel cringed. She could tell this wasn't going to end well.

"Caleb went first, and from the witnesses who saw what happened, it was determined that he managed to ride 'A

Hard Day's Night' quite well considering his condition. But when he got off the bull, it swung around and got him in the ribs, hard. He tried to scramble out of the pen, and Slim did jump into the ring and try to draw the bull away, but Caleb fell and the fall caused his broken ribs to sever his pulmonary artery. There was nothing they could do to save him."

"Well, I don't see how that's Slim's fault," Angie said. "It sounds like a tragic accident."

"To a young boy who lost his father, it's more than that. How can he help but think if Caleb and Slim hadn't been drinking, or if Slim hadn't lost his temper and challenged Caleb, or even if Slim had gone first, there probably would have been a different outcome and he would have grown up with a father."

Mel let out a heavy sigh. They were all quiet for a bit.

"I thought Slim was Ty's mentor," Mel said.

"He was," Ruth said. "Slim wanted to help raise Ty to make up for what happened, so he helped Ty's mom as best he could."

"Which was pretty good," Whitley cut in. "That boy never wanted for anything."

"But then, the truth will out as it always does," Ruth said. "Someone told Ty about Slim's role in his father's death. Ty was devastated."

"As compensation for his father's death, Ty wanted part ownership of the rodeo. Slim said no. Shelby got in the middle of it, mucking it up and making it worse," Whitley said. "They've been at odds ever since."

"And Shelby has done her level best to make sure the bad blood remains," Ruth said.

Mel glanced down at her plate and saw that it was

scraped clean. She glanced back up and saw Ruth gazing out the large picture window at the town green. She looked wistful for days gone by.

"You don't think Shelby could actually have killed Ty, do you?" she asked.

"No!" Angie said.

Ruth, Whitley, and the family in the booth all turned to stare at her.

Angie cleared her throat. "What I mean is, that's really none of our business, right?"

Mel knew where she was going with this. Angie thought Mel was a big buttinsky and that she needed to back away from asking any questions about what happened to Ty, but Mel liked the Hazards, and she couldn't help but worry about what Ty's death would mean for them and the rodeo.

"The Hazards are our friends," Mel said. "Slim gave us this opportunity to work the rodeo, and you have to admit business has been good."

"I did hear about your Red Velvets," Ruth said. "And your young man, Oz—he's quite a character."

"He's also under Shelby's spell," Mel said.

"I figured when he showed up here asking to use my kitchen to make vegan cupcakes and all," Ruth said. "Still, they were very tasty, and he seems like a good kid."

"I heard the bull liked them just fine," Whitley said with a wheezy laugh that made his belly shake.

He pushed off of his stool and struggled with his belt. He looked as if he was trying to figure out whether it would be more comfortable riding over or under that last piece of pie. He settled on under and ambled over to the cash register.

Whitley paid up and headed out the door with a wave.

Mel and Angie stood up and handed their check to Ruth, too.

"Ruth, can you tell us where the nearest craft store is?"

"What sort of craft are you looking for?" she asked.

"We need lollipop sticks and candy coating," Mel said.

Ruth looked intrigued but didn't ask. "Well, there are a couple of stores over in Show Low, but depending upon how much you need, you may have to trek all the way to Flagstaff."

"We'd better get going, then," Angie said.

Mel paid the tab with a healthy tip. "Thanks, Ruth."

They left the diner behind, and Mel could feel Angie staring at her.

"What?" she asked as she climbed into the truck.

"Do not start asking questions about Ty's death," Angie said. "We need to focus on making enough money to pay Tate back for the van. That is our sole purpose."

"I know," Mel said. "That's why we're driving all the way to Flag if need be for supplies."

Mel turned onto the main road that led to the route that would take them to a bigger town.

"So long as we're clear," Angie said as she fiddled with the radio. "I'd hate to have to call Joe and tell him what you're up to."

Twenty

Mel stood on the brakes, and the truck did a wobble and squeal. They were in the middle of the road, but she didn't care, not even when a car coming up behind them honked and then swung around them, with the driver sending them a stiff-fingered salute.

Angie had been held in place by her seat belt, and as she leaned back in her seat, she looked at Mel as if she'd lost her nut.

"Are you crazy?"

"Me? You're asking me?" Mel countered.

"Do you see anyone else in the car?" Angie asked.

"Listen, Angie, you've been my best friend for more than twenty years, and I love you, but—" Mel paused. She realized she needed to go for tactful here and not let her temper get the best of her.

"But?" Angie prodded.

"You have no reason to be calling Joe about anything," Mel said. "And I don't like that you dropped that little bomb on me when I could easily say the same about Roach."

Angie sucked in an outraged breath. "I am not the one asking questions about a dead guy."

"No, you're the one glaring daggers at Tate and his new friend," Mel said. "Angie, you can't have it both ways. You can't date a rock star and then be all hurt if Tate is spending time with someone else. He does not deserve the endless case of stink eye you've been blasting him with."

"Nice change of subject," Angie said. But her scathing tone made it clear that she found nothing nice about it.

She turned to face the window, and Mel was afraid she'd been too harsh, but it was time. Angie had to woman up and make a decision. And besides, she had no right saying that she was going to call Joe and report on Mel. That was most definitely not in the best girlfriend's handbook.

Mel eased her foot off of the brakes and stepped gently on the gas. She could tell by the stiff set to Angie's shoulders—well, that and the fact that she wouldn't look at her—that Angie was mad at her. Fine. Whatever. It was going to be a long drive to Flagstaff.

‛∕‚∖‚∕‛

They got back to Juniper Pass by early afternoon, and Mel took the truck right down to the rodeo. The man at the gate waved them on in, and Mel parked behind the cupcake van.

She was relieved to be back. Although she and Angie

had spoken while they were purchasing their supplies, they had said little else during the trip, and Mel was feeling guilty. Perhaps she shouldn't have been so tough.

When they pulled up to the cupcake truck, all thought of Angie and their tiff fled as Mel saw Tate and Sheriff Dolan going nose to nose while Deputy Justice stood next to Oz, looking as if he would Tase the boy if he made one false move.

Mel banged out of the truck and raced over to where they were standing.

"What's going on?" she demanded.

"The sheriff wants to take Oz in for questioning," Tate said.

"What for?" Angie demanded. She moved to stand between Oz and the sheriff as if she were a human shield.

"It's just routine questioning," Sheriff Dolan said. "Nothing to get excited about."

"I'm sorry, Sheriff," Mel said. "But he is a minor in my employ and under my supervision. You're going to have to give me more than that if you want me not to call my attorney—well, my assistant-district-attorney boyfriend—in on this."

Sheriff Dolan looked at her and raised his eyebrows in surprise.

"Joe DeLaura," Mel said. "If you want to verify, you can call him. We own a cat together."

Why ownership of Captain Jack made it seem more legally binding, she had no idea, but given the panic coursing through her at the thought of Oz being arrested, she felt the need to stack the deck, as it were.

"Joe's also my brother," Angie added.

The sheriff pushed back his hat and scratched his head. "All right, here's the thing. I have a witness that says she saw Oz at the bull pens just before Ty was killed."

Collectively, they started to argue.

"But that's not—"

"Impossible—"

"He was baking cupcakes at the diner—"

The sheriff held up his hands and looked at Oz. "Do you want to tell them or should I?"

Oz hung his head and scuffed the toe of his sneaker in the dirt. Mel felt her heart sink like a stone in a pond.

"Oz," she said. "Tell me this isn't true."

"I was down at the field house," he said. "But I didn't do it. I didn't hurt Stokes. I was just looking for Shelby to tell her about the vegan cupcakes."

"Did you tell her?" Angie asked. "Did she see you?"

Oz shook his head. "I saw her and Ty together, so I split."

"Together how?" Sheriff Dolan asked.

Oz blew out a breath, and his shaggy bangs lifted off of his forehead. The look on his face said it all.

"Oh," Sheriff Dolan said.

"Hey, we've got a line of people over there," Marty said as he came around the side of the cupcake van. He was holding two large frosty lemonades, and he stumbled to a halt as he took in the sight before him.

"So, are we having a meeting?" he asked. He handed one of the lemonades to Oz and glanced around the group.

"Sheriff Dolan seems to think Oz had something to do with Ty Stokes's murder," Angie said. Her voice was a low growl.

"Now, we're just trying to establish his whereabouts, since a witness put him at the bull pens a few minutes before the murder."

"Yeah, that's right," Marty said.

Tate, Angie, and Mel all snapped their heads in his direction. Clearly, Marty had taken a sudden spin into senile old man. What the heck was he thinking?

"Oh, really?" Sheriff Dolan asked.

"Yep, and I should know, because he was with me," Marty said.

Everyone was silent for a beat. Mel glanced at Oz. He didn't so much as flicker an eyelash, not that she could have seen it if he did.

"Is that so?" Sheriff Dolan asked.

"Yep," Marty said. "I ran into him after he'd made those vegan cupcakes, and we walked around the rodeo together looking for Miss Hazard so he could tell her about them. When we saw that she was otherwise occupied"—Marty paused to cough—"then we headed up into town. I went to the Last Chance to see Ms. Delia while he went to get his cupcakes from the diner."

"So you weren't together the entire time?" the sheriff asked.

Marty narrowed his eyes at the sheriff as if he knew exactly what he was getting at, and he didn't like it.

"Ten minutes is all it took for him to go get his cupcakes and come back to the saloon, you know, after he stopped to help capture that runaway bull," Marty said.

Everyone glanced between Marty and the sheriff, and Mel felt as if she were suddenly in a standoff in the Old West.

"Are you willing to swear to it?" the sheriff asked. Marty opened his mouth to speak, but the sheriff stopped him with a hand. "Swear to it, knowing that if I find out you're lying to protect him, I'll haul your scrawny butt into jail for obstruction of justice, and there won't be any visits from Ms. Delia to make your stay more pleasant."

"I swear." Marty met his gaze without flinching, and that seemed enough for the sheriff.

"I expect all of you will be staying for the entire rodeo," he said. "Just in case I have more questions."

"We will," Mel answered for the group.

"Hey, are you all closed or can a gal get a cupcake around here?" a woman asked as she came around the side of the van.

"Are you up to working this afternoon, Oz?" Mel asked.

He nodded. "I think it would be for the best."

"Tate, will you stay and keep an eye on things?" Mel asked.

"Will do," he said.

"Good. For now, could you help us load up all of the extra defrosted cupcakes?" Mel asked. "We need to get moving if we're going to be ready by tomorrow."

They spent the next half hour loading up the defrosted cupcakes into Tupperware tubs. Then Mel and Angie drove over to the Hazards' house. Mel felt a little awkward arriving at the ranch house and hoping to commandeer their kitchen, but she was out of options.

She climbed out of the truck and crossed the wooden porch. She knocked three times on the thick wooden door and waited.

Tammy Hazard answered after a moment and gave them her former-beauty-queen smile.

"Well, hi, Mel. Jake told me you were coming over to use the kitchen. Let me show you where it is."

Mel felt all of her tension release. Thank goodness Jake had given Tammy a heads-up. It made it so much easier for Mel to barge into her home.

"I am so sorry about this," Mel said. "You're really helping us out. I can't thank you enough."

She turned and gestured for Angie to come and join her. Angie was furiously texting on her phone again, and she nodded to let Mel know she'd be right there.

The ranch house was exactly what Mel thought a ranch house should look like. She followed Tammy from the foyer to the main room. It was all lightwood with a beamed ceiling and white stucco walls. A shelf of trophies and blue ribbons and photographs graced one wall beside a huge stone fireplace. Big, squashy-looking leather furniture filled the room, and Mel felt the longing for a nap pull at her from down deep.

She followed Tammy into a brightly lit room beyond. It was a gorgeous kitchen, built for cooking with a professional range, granite countertops, two dishwashers, an enormous refrigerator-freezer combo, and two large windows that overlooked the pasture beyond.

"This will do," Mel said. She gave a low whistle of appreciation so that Tammy would know she was teasing.

Tammy laughed. It was a musical sound and made Mel feel at ease. She wasn't surprised Slim had been so taken with the blonde. She seemed genuinely kind and good-natured.

"I'll just start hauling in my stuff," Mel said.

"I can help," Tammy offered.

Mel was about to refuse. It was bad enough she was taking the woman's kitchen, but Tammy shook her head.

"I wouldn't have offered if I didn't want to help," she said. "I am so sorry you've had troubles at the rodeo. Do you have any idea how your freezers lost power?"

"I have ideas," Mel said. "But nothing I can prove."

They met Angie in the door, and in no time the three of them had all of the tubs in the kitchen.

"All right, master chef, now what?" Angie asked.

"Now for the fun part," Mel said. She handed Angie a pair of plastic gloves. She looked at Tammy and she nodded, so Mel handed her a pair of gloves, too.

Once the three of them were properly gloved, Mel took eighteen cupcakes, peeled off the wrappers, and dumped them in a bowl.

Angie gave her a concerned look, and Mel smiled. Then she put both hands into the cupcakes and started mashing.

"Now we get messy," Mel declared.

Twenty-one

Tammy and Angie each took eighteen cupcakes, dumped them into their own bowls, and followed Mel's example. Once all of their cupcakes were sufficiently crumbled, Mel opened up a tub of her buttercream frosting and plopped a healthy amount into each bowl.

"Keep mixing," Mel said.

Tammy squished the frosting and cake between her gloved fingers and said, "This is therapeutic. Instead of choking someone, I can mash cupcakes and frosting."

"Is there someone who needs choking?" Angie asked.

"Shelby," Tammy spat. Then she gasped as if she hadn't meant to say that.

"It's all right," Mel said. "She's not high on our list right now, either."

"She's just the most selfish, irresponsible person I've

ever—" Tammy cut herself off. "Still, she's my stepdaughter, and I should try to be more understanding."

"You don't pick your family," Angie said. Her words were full of sarcasm, and Tammy looked at her. "I'm the youngest of eight with seven older brothers."

"Oh, my," Tammy said.

"And the reality is even worse than it sounds," Mel said. "I should know. I'm dating one of them."

Tammy glanced between them and continued smashing. "How mushy do I want to make this?"

"It should be the consistency of a truffle," Mel said. "You are just about there."

Mel finished mixing hers and then began to roll the cake-frosting mixture into a ball the size of a large walnut. Then she placed it carefully on a cookie sheet, quickly followed by twenty-nine more. When the cookie sheet was full, she put it in the fridge to chill.

While the first batch was chilling, they mixed up more cake and frosting. While Angie and Tammy took over the cake balls, Mel started melting big pots of candy coating.

She figured the red velvet and lemon cake balls would go into the vanilla candy coating. She planned to sprinkle red sugar on the red velvets and yellow sugar on the lemon to differentiate. The vanilla cake and chocolate cake she would put in the chocolate candy coating. The vanilla she would sprinkle with white sprinkles and the chocolate with chocolate sprinkles to help keep them straight.

She set out the foam flower-arranging blocks that she'd picked up, because once the cake balls had been dipped, they'd need a place to dry.

When the candy coating was finally melted, Angie and

Tammy sat down with large glasses of iced tea while they watched Mel work out the logistics of putting the cake balls on the sticks.

She started with the red velvets. She dipped the end of the lollipop stick into the candy coating and then slid the cake ball onto the stick about a half inch down. Then she set it aside to let the candy coating between the stick and the cake ball harden. She did eleven more and then took up the first one and dipped the entire cake ball into the candy coating. She tapped it twice on the side of the melted candy pot. The cake ball held and she let out a huge sigh of relief. She then put the cake pop back into the foam block to let it dry completely.

She glanced up at Tammy and Angie, who were watching with bemused expressions, and grinned. "I think we have cake pops."

The rest of the afternoon was spent in a blur of candy coating and sprinkles. Once the cake pops were completely dry, Mel and Angie carefully put small cellophane bags over them and tied them with silver twist ties. Very festive.

When Lily and Slim came through the front door, it was to find Tammy, Mel, and Angie all supine on the leather furniture with their feet up and toasting one another with white wine spritzers.

"Happy hour hit early today?" Lily asked.

The wine must have mellowed Angie toward her rival, because she raised her glass and said, "The cake pop factory is proud to announce several hundred cake pops ready to go."

Tammy hopped out of her seat and grabbed Slim's hand. "Honey, you have to try these. They are amazing."

"Well, I don't know," Slim said. He looked haggard, and Mel wondered if it was his arm or Ty's death, or a combination of both, that had him looking as beaten up as a boxer in round twelve.

Tammy patted his hand and said, "Take a load off. This will cheer you up a little bit, I promise."

She vanished into the kitchen and then returned with a red velvet for Lily, who had taken the seat next to Angie, and a chocolate for Slim.

They each unwrapped the treat and looked at it as if they hadn't seen anything quite like it before.

"So, you made lollipops?" Lily asked.

"Cake pops," Tammy said. She waved her hands at them. "Go ahead, try them."

Slim and Lily took tentative bites. Mel knew the minute their taste buds had signaled to their brains that their mouths were full of yummy goodness as identical smiles of joy spread across their faces.

"These are fantastic," Lily said.

Angie lifted her glass and said, "Mel's idea. Genius, as always."

"Well, I didn't invent them," Mel said. "They're the latest dessert rage right now, and I had thought about making them in the shop but haven't had time. I may have to rethink that and make the time. For now, these are just a way for us to salvage what was defrosted last night."

"I heard about that from Tate," Lily said. "What happened?"

"Somehow, we got unplugged," Mel said.

"You mean thanks to someone," Angie corrected with a glower.

"We can't prove it," Mel said. "Besides, if these are as popular as I think they're going to be, then the barbecue brothers are going down."

"If Billy and Bob are responsible for your cupcakes getting sabotaged, I can have a chat with them," Slim said.

"You have enough on your plate," Mel said. "Besides, you gave us your kitchen and an assistant for the day. We can't ask for more, and truly, we're going to be just fine."

Angie held up her fist and she and Mel banged knuckles.

"Come on," Angie said. "We need to pack up the pickup and get back to the rodeo."

"Let's hope the boys haven't run out of cupcakes," Mel said.

"I'll give them a call and get a status report," Angie offered. She took her phone out of her pocket and headed to the kitchen.

"Well, I'm going to snatch me another of those pops before you pack them all up," Slim said, and he rolled out of his seat.

"Help yourself," Mel said.

"Oh, don't say that," Tammy said. She gave Mel a comically alarmed look. "He'll take you at your word and eat them all."

She hurried after Slim, and Mel smiled at Lily. "They're cute together."

"Yeah, I was a little worried that Tammy was going to get Dad to pull up stakes and move to Dallas—she's a

Texan—but so far, he's held his ground and she's stayed with him."

Mel stood and stretched and wandered over to the wall full of ribbons and awards. She saw several pictures of Lily and Shelby and a younger-looking Slim. There were also pictures of another woman that Mel assumed was Lily and Shelby's mother, since she had the same eyes and smile.

Another picture, which looked to have been taken when Slim was just a teenager, showed a whole family sitting on the same split-rail fence that surrounded the pasture off of the kitchen.

Mel picked it up to study it more closely. She liked the faces in it. They were long, careworn faces of people who lived on the land they loved. Smiles were tucked into their eyes, and they all had the same wavy brown hair and dimples in their right cheeks.

"Those are the Hazards back in the fifties," Lily said. "The heyday of ranch life."

Mel liked that they were all wearing Western shirts, jeans, and boots. There was definitely a fifties feeling in the shoulder-length curls of the women and the stitched brims of their hats.

"That's Daddy," Lily said, and she pointed to a young boy sitting on the top rail.

"He looks like Opie." Mel laughed. "But don't tell him I said that."

Lily laughed. "No, it's fine. I said the same thing when I first realized it was my dad."

"Who's the girl next to him?" Mel asked.

"My aunt Hannah," Lily said. "She was a famous barrel

rider in her teens." She pointed to a picture on the wall, and Mel could see the resemblance between the pretty teen and the young girl.

"Does she live in Juniper Pass, too?" she asked.

"No." Lily shook her head. "She was killed in a car accident in California when she was twenty. I never got to meet her. It broke my dad's heart."

"Oh, I'm sorry," Mel said. She carefully put the picture down.

"Time marches on," Lily said. She traced the picture of a pretty woman holding two little girls. Mel knew without asking that it was her mother. "But some people, you never forget."

Mel thought of her dad. He'd been gone more than ten years to the all-you-can-eat buffet in the sky, but still when she thought of him she could hear his laugh as clearly as if he were in the room with her. Charlie Cooper had one of those laughs that rumbled up from deep inside of him and roared out to bear-hug everyone who heard it.

She missed a lot of things about her dad, but most especially his laugh, or rather, the way his laugh made her feel when she heard it.

"I know how you feel," she said. "Some people stay in your heart forever."

Lily met her gaze, and she seemed to know without Mel saying it that Mel understood the sharp pain that came with the loss of a beloved parent.

Another picture caught Mel's eye. It was Slim when he was middle-aged with a young man. From the electric smile and the dark hair, she knew it was Ty.

"Dad keeps that picture to remind him of the Ty he used

178

to know and love," Lily said. "Dad took Ty in when his grandparents passed away, as both his parents had already died. He mentored him in bull riding. They used to be so close that sometimes I'd get jealous. I felt like Ty was the older brother I never wanted, and I used to wish he'd just go away. I never wanted this, however, not the rift with him and Dad and definitely not his death. Dad is really struggling with losing Ty, especially since they were at odds. I'm worried about him."

They were both silent, giving a moment of respect to the slain bull rider.

"Well, I'd better go help Angie," Mel said.

She turned and headed to the kitchen. She was tempted to ask Lily about her relationship with Tate, since they were sharing a moment and all, but she refrained, figuring it was none of her business, even though she was dying of curiosity.

She entered the room to find Angie snapping the phone shut. "We'd better move it. The boys are almost out of cupcakes, and there's a dance in the arena tonight, so they're expecting a big crowd."

"Well, I guess this will be a good test for our cake pops," Mel said.

"You're going to be working in the van tonight?" Lily asked as she entered the kitchen.

"Yes," Mel said. "The boys undoubtedly could use a break."

"Well, that's too bad," Lily said as she passed through the kitchen. "I promised Tate I'd teach him how to two-step tonight, and I'd love it if you could join us."

Mel glanced at Angie, whose lips were pressed so tightly together, they formed a straight white line.

"Yeah, that's too bad," Mel said, stepping between Lily and Angie and ushering Lily through the opposite kitchen door. "We don't want to keep you from getting ready for the dance. Make sure you drop by the cupcake van later."

She whirled around and caught Angie's arm right as she extended it back to lob a cake pop at Lily.

Twenty-two

"Angie, no!" she said as she wrestled her arm down.

"What?" Angie dropped the cake pop into its bucket. "I was just sorting them."

"Uh-huh." Mel was not fooled for one second.

Angie gave her a mutinous look but hefted up the large Tupperware bucket and headed to the truck. Mel glanced around the kitchen. They had left it as spic-and-span as it was when they arrived, which had been no small task, since that candy coating had gotten all over the counter.

She lifted her own box and followed Angie, and after three more trips, they were ready to go.

When they pulled up beside the cupcake truck, it was to find three very haggard men hanging out the window.

"How was business?" Mel asked.

"We are about cleaned out," Marty told her. "You got here just in time."

"Good thing," Angie muttered. "I heard someone has a date."

She shoved past Tate, who gave her a funny look and then glanced at Mel with his eyebrows raised. She shrugged, refusing to get into it.

"How did you hear about my date?" Marty asked. "Oh, man, is that the time? I have to go. Delia is going to be waiting, and I can't pick her up smelling like . . ."

"A cupcake?" Oz supplied with a laugh. "If I were you, I'd go with it. Chicks dig cupcakes."

Marty cuffed him gently on the head. "Ladies don't like to be called *chicks*; mind your manners."

Oz shrugged, and Marty leaned close and said, "I'm serious. They don't like to be called *broads*, *dames*, or *honeys*, either."

"I would never call a woman a broad," Oz protested.

"Good thing," Marty said. "The last time I did, I got a swift knee in the privates."

All three of the men winced.

"And you deserved it, no doubt," Angie said. "Honestly, calling a woman a broad."

"Hey, it was 1958," Marty said. "I've smartened up lots since then."

"Go!" Mel ordered. "Delia is too nice to be kept waiting on you."

Oz and Tate helped them unload the cake pops. Oz looked dubious until Mel coerced him into trying one.

"Amazing," he said. "It takes all the work out of figuring out the cake-to-frosting ratio."

Mel beamed at him. He was such a quick learner.

While Angie was setting up a display of cake pops, Mel took Tate aside and said, "So, you told me not to worry about you and Lily, and then I hear you have a date with her."

"It's not a date-date," Tate said. "She's just going to teach me some two-stepping. Why? Is Angie jealous?"

"Ask her," Mel snapped, refusing to get into it. "Now, listen, since you're going to be with Lily, it might give you a chance to chat her up about Shelby."

"Why would I want to do that?" he asked.

"Because Shelby threw our boy Oz under the bus to the sheriff, and I for one want to know why."

"We don't know that it was her who told the sheriff she saw Oz in the stable."

"Yes, we do," Mel said. "Just like we know Marty wasn't with Oz but lied to give him an alibi."

"You think so, too?" he asked.

Mel looked grim. "It was noble of Marty, but if he gets found out, it will only make Oz look even more guilty."

"Agreed," Tate said. "Okay, so what should I be asking?"

"Anything about Shelby," Mel said. "Let's try to get as much info on her as we can. I don't trust her, and I can absolutely see her killing Ty if he wasn't giving her something she wanted."

"That's a strong accusation," Tate said.

"She made a major mistake when she went after Oz," Mel said.

"He's lucky to have you," Tate said. He rested his hand on Mel's shoulder. "We all are."

"Aw, shucks," she said. She hugged him tight. "Go have fun but not too much."

He ambled off in the direction of the road that would take him to the arena. Mel wondered what a non-date date consisted of besides two-stepping; then she shook her head, refusing to think about it.

The phone in her pocket chimed with her *Gone with the Wind* ringtone, and she dug it out and checked the tiny screen. It was her mother.

"Hi, Mom," she answered.

"Now, I don't want to worry you," Joyce said without a greeting, which made Mel's short blond hair stand straight up in a full-on panic. "But Captain Jack is missing."

"What?" Mel cried. "What do you mean, missing? Did he get outside?"

"I don't think so," Joyce said. "But he didn't come when I called him, and I can't find him in any of his favorite spots. He didn't even come when I opened up a can of tuna for him."

"That's not good," Mel said. "Have you looked everywhere?"

"Hang on, Mel; dear Joe is here," Joyce said.

"Wait. Joe is there? What is Joe doing there?"

"Well, I called him, naturally," Joyce said. "You know how much Captain Jack loves him."

The phone went quiet, and Mel knew her mother had put it down to go and answer the door.

She paced around the outside of the cupcake van. Her chest felt tight. If anything had happened to Captain Jack . . . No, she couldn't even go there.

"OMG! These are yummy!" a young female voice said from the front of the truck. She was holding two cake pops, a vanilla and a chocolate with a bite taken out of both of them.

"I have to get two more," she exclaimed, and got back in line.

At any other time Mel would have done a cartwheel of joy, but not right now. Not when her baby was missing.

"Mel?" Joe said into the phone.

"Joe, what's going on? How long has he been missing? Do you think he got out?"

"Mel, breathe," Joe said. "It's going to be all right. I'm going to search the house top to bottom until we find him. You know how he is."

Mel's throat was tight. She felt so powerless being so far away. "Yeah, remember when he got stuck in your shirt-sleeve?"

Joe laughed. It was a warm and reassuring sound that made her miss him desperately.

"The fur ball was squeezed in so tight he looked like blue sausage with whiskers."

Mel had a picture of the Captain Jack sausage on her phone. He'd wedged himself in so tightly, they'd had to cut him out of the shirt to free him.

"You think he got into Joyce's closet?" she asked.

"Maybe," he said. "But don't worry; I'll find him. I'm not his kitty daddy for nothing."

"Thanks, Joe," she said.

"Hey."

"Yeah?"

"I miss you," he said.

His voice made her insides buzz, and Mel felt as reassured as if he'd hugged her.

"I miss you, too," she said.

"How are things at the rodeo?" he asked.

Mel had called him daily and kept him up-to-speed on Slim's shooting and Ty's death. Joe had not been happy about any of it, but he knew that she had to stay, not only for business reasons but because it would look mighty suspicious if they packed up their cupcakes and left.

"It's been interesting," Mel said. "I'm on my cell, so I don't know how much I should say."

"Good idea," Joe said. As an assistant district attorney, he had a healthy paranoia about security. "Listen, I'll go look for Captain Jack, and I'll call you as soon as I find him. And then we can have a longer chat later when you're in your room on a secure line."

"Thanks, Joe," she said.

"See ya, Cupcake," he said.

"Bye," Mel said. She ended the call and slid her phone into her pocket. Captain Jack loved Joe almost as much as he loved her. If anyone could find him, it would be Joe.

She climbed up into the back of the cupcake truck to help sell the cake pops. She glanced out the window and saw that the word had gotten out amongst the rodeo people. A line twenty-five deep wound itself out to the road and back toward the barbecue pit.

Angie gave her a gentle nudge and pointed to where Billy and Bob were standing behind the smoker, as if Mel and Angie wouldn't be able to see them, and they were frowning.

"I hope they are shaking in their snappy red bandannas," Angie said. "We are killing here."

Mel glanced at the window to see Sheriff Dolan standing there.

"Not exactly the best choice of words," she said to Angie as the sheriff gave them an interested look.

"Do tell," he said.

"We have a bet with the Bubbas over there," Mel explained.

"Yeah, whoever sells the most wins, and the loser has to spend the last day of the rodeo working in the other's booth," Angie finished.

"Well, I hope those boys like pink," Sheriff Dolan said.

Ruth appeared next to him, and she said, "These look fantastic. We'll take one of each."

The sheriff gave his wife an indulgent look as Oz handed them each two cake pops.

"Now, let's go do some dancing," Ruth said as she looped her hand through her husband's arm and led him away to the arena.

"They make a cute couple," Angie said.

"Her half is cute," Oz said. "His half is scary."

The line drew their attention back to the work at hand. Mel checked her phone repeatedly, hoping to get a call from Joe. An hour passed, and there was still no word as they began to close down the cupcake truck for the night.

They decided to monitor the truck in pairs. Since Mel and Angie were dateless, they would camp out in the truck first while Tate and Marty enjoyed their dates. Mel didn't want Oz out of sight, given that the sheriff had not cleared him as a person of interest, so he was stuck in the truck with Mel and Angie.

This plan didn't work out so well, as Oz, who'd been working in the truck all day, began to pace back and forth up and down the narrow aisle in the back like the bull he'd helped to pen.

"Oz, sit down," Angie said.

"Ugh, I've been in this truck all day," he said. "As much as I love it, my brain is going to explode if I don't get out of here."

"Why don't you two go for a walk?" Mel asked. "Stretch your legs."

Angie tossed down the cooking magazine she'd been thumbing through by the overhead light in the van's ceiling. "Oh, all right. But only because if I don't move, I'm going to fall asleep."

She and Oz climbed out of the truck, and Mel pillowed a bunch of jackets on the door rest and positioned her body across the seat. The windows were down, letting the cool night breeze drift through the van.

She watched as Angie and Oz walked along the road toward the stables. She had assumed they would be heading to the dance, but maybe Angie wasn't too keen to see Tate learning the two-step with someone else.

The chime on her phone started, and she saw it was Joe. She sent up a silent prayer that it was good news before she answered.

"Well, I found him," Joe said.

"Is he all right? Where was he?" Mel asked.

Joe made a strangled noise as if he was trying not to laugh.

"Joe!" Mel chided him.

"Melanie, it's your mother," Joyce said. She had obviously commandeered the phone from Joe, who was laughing in the background. "Captain Jack is fine."

"Thank goodness," she said. "But where was he?"

"In the closet of your old room," Joyce said. "I think he must have figured out that it was your old room from the smell."

"But how did he get in there?" Mel asked.

"Probably he snuck in when I went in to do my weekly cleaning," Joyce said. "Anyway, he wedged himself into one of your old boots and he was stuck."

"Which boots?" Mel asked.

"Those black ones," Joyce said.

"The patent leather ones with the nice heel?" Mel asked.

"Yes, those are the ones."

Mel let out a small sigh before she asked, "Did you have to cut them?"

"No, Captain Jack was wedged in with just his behind sticking out, but dear Joe managed to shake him loose."

"Oh, good grief," Mel said. "Is he all right now?"

"He's fine," Joyce said. "But I think dear Joe is going to herniate something from laughing. He keeps talking in a Spanish accent and saying, 'How strange it was to be a cat in boots, but woh, I look good.' You don't know what he's talking about, do you?"

Mel smiled. "Yeah, he's quoting *Puss in Boots*— remember we took the nephews to see that movie?"

"Oh, how cute," Joyce said.

Mel rolled her eyes. When it came to Joe, her mother always thought he was perfect.

"Tell him I'll call him later," Mel said. "Love you, Mom. Give Captain Jack lots of pets and some scolding from me."

"Yes, dear," Joyce said.

Mel slid her phone back into her pocket. The sound of the dance was far enough away that she could hear the music only faintly, as if the notes were sprinkled on the breeze.

She yawned again. The long day spent driving, making cake pops, and working the evening shift in the truck had taken its toll, and her eyelids felt as if they were made of cement. She tried to keep them open. She forced herself to take deep breaths of the cool night air. She was sure she was awake, but then she'd start and discover she'd dozed. She thought about getting up and walking around the van to try to stay awake, but sleep hit her like a roundhouse punch to the temple, and she was out.

When she awoke, Mel had no idea if she'd slept for a solid fifteen-minute power nap or if she'd conked out for an hour or more. All she knew was that the sound of whispered voices woke her up, and not because they were whispering sweet nothings, but rather because they had the frantic sound of people having a low-grade case of hysterics.

Twenty-three

Mel lurched upright. She could hear the voices just outside the van. Was it the Bubbas coming to unplug them again? She scrambled around looking for a weapon, but all she had at hand was a wadded-up jacket, the magazine Angie had been reading, and the emergency flashlight Oz kept under the dashboard.

She grabbed the flashlight. She wasn't sure whether she would clunk them on the head with it or freak them out by shining the light in their eyes, but she'd worry about it when she was closer.

She crawled through the two front seats and eased herself into the back. The voices were coming from below the service window in the van. She could see two shadowy figures just beyond the window. They were having a heated discussion, and she wondered if it was the Bubbas debating lighting the van on fire.

She eased the window open and, in one motion, popped her head through the opening, snapped on her flashlight, and yelled, "Aha!"

The two shadows shrieked and then slammed into each other in their attempt to get away.

It was then that Mel recognized the short, curvy woman with dark hair and the tall young man with shaggy hair and many piercings.

"Angie! Oz! It's me," Mel said.

Angie had her hand over her chest, probably to check that her heart had resumed beating, and Oz slumped against the side of the truck, looking like he was afraid he might faint.

"What are you two doing, skulking around out here?" Mel asked. "You scared me half to death."

"'I don't usually skulk, but I suppose I could skulk if skulking were required,'" Angie quoted.

"*Four Weddings and a Funeral.*" Mel and Oz identified the movie quote at the same time and pounded knuckles.

"We have to tell her," Angie said to Oz.

"No, no, let's just pretend we didn't see it," he said. "You know, mind our own business; butt out."

Mel got a sinking feeling in her stomach.

"Tell me what?" she asked.

"We think we found what killed Ty," Angie said. She whispered it as if whispering would make it less real.

"Really?" a voice asked from behind the truck. They all

stood frozen as Sheriff Dolan and his wife Ruth appeared in the shadows.

"Uh-oh," Oz said.

"And to think we came just hoping for another cake-on-a-stick thingy," Sheriff Dolan said.

"Cake pop," Ruth corrected him.

"Okay, we can explain," Angie said. "I'm sure that sounded worse than it is."

Sheriff Dolan pushed back his hat and scratched his head, a gesture Mel was beginning to recognize as one he made when he was not happy.

"Now, Hadley," Ruth said. "Hear them out."

He gave her a look that mingled consternation and affection. Mel had seen the same look from Joe upon occasion. Somehow, this comforted her.

"Okay, it's like this," Angie said. "We were taking a walk because Oz has been cooped up in this truck all day and he was getting a little stir-crazy."

Sheriff Dolan looked at Oz, who nodded vigorously.

"So, we went for a walk . . ." Angie began. She took a big breath as if bracing herself for the next part of the story. "We decided that we wanted to go and check on the bull and make sure he was okay."

The sheriff looked between them as if they were certifiably cuckoo. "You say that like he's some stray dog you found wandering loose. You are aware that he's about one thousand, nine hundred pounds heavier than a dog? And he has horns, big ones."

"We weren't going to pet him or anything," Angie said. Then she gave Oz a funny look and asked, "Right?"

"Right," he said. "I just felt bad 'cause it was my cup-cakes that got him captured."

"Son, you probably saved someone's life," the sheriff said.

"Which would be a really good thing for you to keep in mind," Angie said. "So, where was I?"

"The bull," Sheriff Dolan prompted.

Mel handed two cake pops out the window to the sheriff and Ruth. She was not above bribery with baked goods if the situation warranted it. And, judging by the way Angie was shuffling her feet from side to side, she was guessing it was warranted.

"We figured he was back down in the bull pen," she said. "When we got there the place was deserted, probably because of the dance, so there wasn't anyone to ask where they'd put the bull, so we decided to work our way through the pens."

The sheriff bit into his cake pop while he listened. Mel didn't see any softening of his features. Damn. She didn't want to be wasting cake pops.

"Well, I took one side, and Oz took the other," Angie said. "I was halfway through the pens when I tripped on a handle poking out between two hay bales. When I pulled it out . . ." She paused, and a shudder ran through her. She took a deep breath and continued, "When I pulled it out to keep anyone else from tripping on it, I noticed that the tips were covered in blood."

The sheriff's jaw dropped, and Ruth gasped.

"Show me," he ordered.

Mel hurriedly put up the windows and locked the back of the van. She didn't want to leave it unguarded, but she didn't want to send Oz, too young, and Angie, a hothead, off with the sheriff on their own.

She decided to text Tate, telling him to get back to the van. Odds were that, with the sheriff on the premises, no one would mess with the van anyway—at least, she hoped so.

Angie and Oz led the way with Sheriff Dolan while Mel and Ruth brought up the rear. Ruth was still nibbling on her cake pop, but her eyes looked worried.

When they entered the field house that contained all of the bull pens, it was to find several of the bull owners present. They were standing at one end of the barn talking, but they stopped as soon as they took in the sight of the sheriff.

"I tripped here," Angie said, and gestured to several large bales of hay. "And I pulled the handle out of here."

She knelt down beside the hay bales. The bull owners walked over to where they all stood.

"What's going on, Hadley?" one of them asked.

"I don't know just yet," the sheriff answered evenly.

Mel glanced at the three men, who all wore the requisite plaid shirts, jeans, and work boots. Their faces had a similar weather-beaten look to them, and their hands were big and square. These were not the type of men who lived in cubicles, but rather spent life outside, taking on the fickle temperaments of their animals and Mother Nature.

"When I pulled it out, I didn't realize at first that it was bloody," Angie said. "I just thought someone had been really careless."

"More like sneaky," Ruth said.

"Then what happened?" Sheriff Dolan asked.

"Well, then, when I realized what it was—you know,

that it had probably been used to stab Ty Stokes—I called Oz over. We weren't sure what to do with it."

One of the ranchers let out a low whistle.

"It didn't occur to you to call me right away?" the sheriff asked.

"It did," Angie said. She gave him a mutinous look. "But you'd already made a big stink about Oz being a suspect, so we weren't sure if we should be the ones to tell you about it."

"Where is it now?" the sheriff asked. His voice was very soft, and Mel got a sick feeling in her stomach that they had better be able to produce the pitchfork, or things were going to go very badly for Angie and Oz.

"I put it up there until we could agree about what to do," Angie said. She pointed up at a loft, and they all looked up.

"Lead the way," the sheriff said.

Angie climbed the wooden ladder that led up to the loft.

"I told her we should call it in," Oz said. "But she wanted to leave an anonymous tip."

The sheriff scurried up the ladder after Angie. Everyone on the ground was looking up at the loft as if they expected to see fireworks explode out of it. "No, don't touch it," they heard the sheriff say. "We don't want to compromise any evidence that might be left on it."

He and Angie climbed back down the ladder, and Angie nodded at Mel and Oz to let them know that the pitchfork was still up there.

The sheriff pulled his phone out of his pocket. He pressed two buttons. "This is Sheriff Dolan. I need a crime scene investigator at the Juniper Pass Rodeo ASAP."

He turned his back to them and continued his conversation.

The rest of them lingered, uncertain of what to do. As if the quiet were too much for her, Angie turned to Ruth and asked, "How much trouble am I in?"

Ruth opened her mouth to answer, but the sheriff returned to their group and said, "Ms. DeLaura, I'm going to need you to stop by the station to be fingerprinted."

Twenty-four

"What? No!" Oz and Mel protested at the same time.

Sheriff Dolan held up his hands. "Relax. She's not a suspect, but we need to have a copy of her fingerprints so we can rule them out when we check the pitchfork."

Mel and Oz both nodded and stood down. Angie looked at Mel and said, "It's fine—anything to help them catch whoever did it."

"We should call Tate and Marty," Mel said. "They'll want to know what's going on."

"No, don't ruin their dates," Angie said.

Her tone was a little sharp, but Mel let it go. She didn't envy Angie having to explain to the brothers why she had been fingerprinted in Juniper Pass. They never took that sort of news well.

"You two need to get back to the truck," Angie said.

"I texted Tate to tell him to get back there," Mel said. She checked her phone. "I haven't heard back from him yet."

"I imagine he's busy," Angie said. "You'd better go. We can't risk having anyone vandalize our product again."

"Vandalize?" Sheriff Dolan asked. "Explain."

"It's just speculation on Angie's part," Mel said with a warning glance at her friend. "The reason we had to make cake pops was because somehow our van got unplugged, and all of our cupcakes were defrosted. We didn't think we could keep them fresh until the end of the rodeo unless we re-created them into something else."

"Well, those pops are mighty tasty," the sheriff said.

"Indeed," Ruth said. "Before you leave Juniper Pass, you have to teach me."

"Pie secrets for cake pop secrets?" Mel bargained.

They shook on it.

"Now, go before someone breaks in and steals all of our yummies," Angie said.

"Call me if you need me," Mel said. She gave Angie a quick hug.

"Don't worry," Ruth said. "I'll stay with her through the whole thing."

"Sorry about this, darlin'," Sheriff Dolan said to her as he opened his phone to make another call.

"It's our date night," Ruth explained with a shrug. "Such is the life of being married to a lawman."

Mel thought of all the times court cases had taken up all of Joe's time, to the point where she'd pretty much only see him when he was unconscious.

"I know the feeling," she said. "Thanks for babysitting our girl."

"I heard that," Angie said.

"You were supposed to," Mel said, and then winked at her. Angie gave her a grumpy but not-really-annoyed *humph* and went with Ruth to sit on a bench by the wall.

Mel and Oz walked back to the truck. Oz was quiet, and Mel suspected he was mentally beating himself up.

"It's not your fault that you wanted to go and see the bull," Mel said.

His head snapped in her direction as if surprised.

"How did you know?"

"Because you're a nice person, so it would make sense that you would think that it's your fault that Angie has to go to the police station," Mel said. "On the upside, you've absolved yourself of anything to do with the murder, because now that they have what appears to be the murder weapon, they'll hopefully get a clue as to who did this."

"I suppose," Oz said, but he didn't sound convinced.

They got back to the cupcake truck, which looked to be untouched. Mel checked that the doors were still locked, and when she climbed into the back, the first thing she did was make sure that their cake pops were secure.

"Looks like we're good," she said.

She and Oz sat in the front of the truck. She wondered if it was really necessary to stake out the van, but then, could she risk having the last of her product destroyed if someone broke into the truck?

No. So, that answered that. They sat quietly for a few moments, and she noticed that Oz's head was drooping. Poor kid. He must be exhausted.

She wondered if he was beginning to see Shelby for what she was. He certainly hadn't seemed to be as enamored of her as he had been before she fingered him to the police. Mel still didn't like her. And now that she knew that Ty and Shelby had a history, she wondered if a lovers' spat had caused Ty's death.

She knew it was none of her business. She knew that Joe would tell her quite plainly to butt out, but still, now her best friend was going to the police station to have her fingerprints taken. Her employee had been sighted near the scene of the murder. Even if she was actively trying to ignore the whole situation, it was a bit more in her face than could be avoided.

Marty and Tate showed up about an hour later. Marty was whistling a tune that sounded like one from Old Blue Eyes about Jupiter and Mars. Mel eased her door open and climbed down. Oz was full-on snoring in his seat, and when Mel shut her door, he didn't even flinch.

"Martin Zelaznik, reporting for duty," Marty said with a salute that wobbled. He looked a little too happy, and Mel frowned.

"Had a good time, did we?"

"I only had the fruit punch," Marty slurred.

"Which was spiked," Tate added with a grin.

"Oh, you are kidding me," Mel said. "Is he . . . ?"

"Wasted," Tate confirmed.

"Oh, for the love of Pete," Mel said.

"No, no, the name is Marty," Marty said. Then he walked around her and opened the door to the truck and took her vacated seat. "You two go on; me and the kid have it all under control."

Mel looked at Tate. "Does that seem wise?"

"I don't think he can manage the walk back to town,"

Tate said. "He'll end up sleeping it off on the side of the road somewhere."

Mel had to admit that seemed likely, and Oz still hadn't moved. She went over to the open window, and looked at Marty as he burrowed himself into the seat like a dog circling for just the right spot.

"Do not get into any mischief," she said. Marty gave her a bleary-eyed look. "I mean it."

"No mischief," he said. "Got it."

Then he passed out with his chin on the windowsill.

"Well, at least he really can't get into trouble in a state like that," Tate said.

Mel gave him a dark look. She made sure the van was locked and secure, but she couldn't really imagine anyone disturbing it with two men, even sleeping men, in attendance.

Now that they were out of cupcakes, the beauty of the cake pop had hit Mel. Cake pops needed to be stored in a cool, dry place, because freezing them would cause them to go soft with condensation when they were thawed. Once the freezers were cleared out, they hadn't turned them back on; instead they'd used them as the perfect cool, dry place for the cake pops. So unless someone actually broke into the van and destroyed the pops, their product was safe. Unplugging the power for the freezers on the outside of the truck would no longer do any harm.

"Fine," she said.

She pushed Marty's head over and grabbed her purse from the floor. He mumbled and smacked his lips together and slid back against the seat, sound asleep.

Tate fell into step beside her. She felt his gaze on the side of her face, and she sensed he wanted to ask her something but wasn't sure how it would be received. Smart man.

"Angie's at the jail," she said.

"What?" Tate skidded to a halt in his shiny new boots and gaped at her. She knew full well that he wanted to know where Angie was. She decided to take pity on him but only a little.

"You heard me," she said.

Okay, she could have eased his mind with more information, but no. Let the two-timing, two-stepping potato head figure it out for himself.

She strode ahead, and Tate hobbled along behind her, trying to catch up. Apparently, after a night of dancing, the new cowboy boots pinched. She found it hard to dig up any pity for him.

"Mel," he called from several paces behind her.

She ignored him. She heard him heave a sigh as he tried to keep up and failed miserably.

"Are you forgetting that you asked me to find out what I could about Shelby?" he hollered when they were halfway to town.

Mel paused. Drat. She had asked him to cozy up to Lily and find out more about Shelby, but that had been before Angie found the murder weapon and had to give her fingerprints.

"Fair enough," she said. She waited for him to catch up. "What did you find out about Shelby?"

"Oh, no, you tell me what is going on with Angie first," he said.

They were on the edge of the main road, just a few doors down from the Last Chance.

"Come on, you're going to need a drink when I tell you about this new development."

The band was playing, Henry was tending bar, and the Last Chance was comfortably full without being overly crowded. Mel glanced at her watch and figured most people had shuffled off to bed after the dance. Only the hard-core had come out to continue the party at the Last Chance.

They ordered two beers and found a vacant corner table. Mel took a sip off her ice-cold mug and felt her entire body relax. Tate was staring at her as if he could will the words out of her.

"Angie found what appears to be the murder weapon, and they need her fingerprints to rule them out when they test the pitchfork themselves."

"Pitchfork?" Tate gaped at her. "How did she just happen to find a pitchfork?"

"She and Oz were going to see the bull," Mel explained.

"Why?" he asked.

"Because Oz had been cooped up in the van all day, and he wanted to go and check on the bull, so Angie went with him."

"And she managed to stumble on a pitchfork?"

"A bloody pitchfork," Mel said.

They both paused to sip their beers.

The doors to the Last Chance swung open, and in strode Angie. Her long hair was mussed, and she looked pasty, pale, and tired.

"Angie!" Tate sprang up from his seat and crossed the room in several strides. "Are you all right?"

She spun around and stared at him as if she had so many

things that she wanted to say, she couldn't seem to pick which she wanted to say first.

"What? Is your date over?" she spat.

Tate leaned back from the venom in her tone.

"Hey, I was worried about you," he protested.

"Really?" Angie blew her bangs off her forehead and planted her hands on her hips.

Mel knew this stance. This was volcano Angie right before she erupted. Tate knew this stance, too, and if he had a brain in his head, he would be backing up now.

"Yeah, really!" he argued.

Nope, no brains.

"I'm surprised you managed to tear yourself away from your date to even notice that I was having a less-than-two-stepping evening myself," she said.

"For the hundredth time, it was not a date."

"Ha!"

"It wasn't," he protested. "Besides, why do you even care? You have a boyfriend—a rock-star boyfriend."

"Don't you bring Roach into this," she said.

"How can I not?" he asked.

Mel noticed that all of the clientele in the bar was watching the drama unfold before them. She wondered if she should give her friends a heads-up, but figured they were having too heated a confrontation to notice; besides, maybe this would finally clear the air between them.

"You have to make a decision, Angie. Are you moving to Los Angeles with Roach or not?"

"I don't know," she said. "I haven't decided yet."

She crossed her arms over her chest and looked away. It

made her seem vulnerable, and Tate must have seen that, too, because he went in for the kill.

"Well, don't you think it's about time you decided?" he asked. "It's pretty simple, really—either you love him or you don't. So, what is it, Angie? Do you love him or not?"

"It's not that simple," she argued.

"Yes, it is," he said. He took a step toward her. "Decide, Angie."

"Listen, when I'm with Roach, I feel like I am somebody," she said. "Not a schoolteacher, not a baker, not a little sister or best friend, but I feel like I'm somebody special and important."

Her cheeks were flushed, and she was looking down at the floor as if it cost her to admit this. Tate reached out and cupped her chin, lifting her face until she met his gaze.

Mel was clutching her mug so tightly, she was afraid her fingers had frozen to the glass.

With his other hand, Tate brushed the bangs out of Angie's eyes.

"You've always been somebody to me," he said. Then he stepped back and walked around Angie, heading out the front door of the saloon, like a cowboy hitting the trail.

Twenty-five

Angie stood, staring after him, looking stricken. She turned and glanced at Mel.

"Ange," she said, rising up out of her seat.

Angie shook her off with a shake of her head. Then she bolted through the small door that led to the rooms above.

Mel let out a breath and sank back into her seat. Both Tate and Angie were her best friends, so whom did she go after? Or for once in her life should she just mind her own business and stay put?

" 'We're the last of the holdouts,' " a voice quoted from behind Mel's chair.

She spun around to find Jake Morgan standing there.

"*The Outlaw Josey Wales*," she said, identifying the movie.

He lowered his head in acknowledgment. "I noticed you all like to quiz each other. I figured you'd know a classic."

"Clint Eastwood and me are like that," Mel said, and she held up crossed fingers. Jake smiled.

"Can I buy you a beer?" she offered.

"No, thanks," he said. He held up a mug with dark liquid. "I'm sticking to root beer, as I'm on duty."

"On duty?"

"I've been shuttling the drunks up from the dance for the past hour in my truck. Apparently, the punch got spiked again. It happens every year, so I try to get as many folks home as I can."

"That's nice of you," Mel said, and he shrugged, as if he didn't think it was particularly nice of him; it was just what he believed one neighbor should do for another.

"I couldn't help but notice the . . . uh . . ." His voice trailed off as if he didn't know how to describe the scene between Angie and Tate.

"It's all right," Mel said. She gestured for him to take Tate's abandoned seat. "I don't know what to make of them myself. And you're right: I do feel like a bit of a holdout. I mean, they're both my friends; I don't want to look like I'm choosing sides."

She took a long sip of beer.

"I think staying out of it is probably the wise choice," Jake said.

"So, you like old movies?" Mel asked. She desperately wanted to talk about something besides Angie and Tate.

"Westerns, mostly," he said. A slow grin crept over his face, making him handsome in a rough-and-tumble sort of way. "Big shock, huh?"

Mel laughed. She liked Jake. He was a no-nonsense kind

of person, and, given the state of the ridiculous surrounding her right now, she really appreciated his down-to-earth way.

"So, how did it go with the . . . um . . . What was it you were making?" Jake asked.

"Cake pops," Mel said. "It went well. They're selling like gangbusters, so whoever tried to sabotage us failed."

"Do you think someone is trying to drive you away from the rodeo?" he asked. "Pun intended."

Mel smiled. "Oh, I know a few people who'd like to see us gone."

He looked surprised and concerned. Mel told him about Billy and Bob, and his face relaxed a bit.

"It sounds like a friendly wager," he said. "I'd be more worried about someone chasing you out because, well, you and your crew seem to be in the wrong place at the wrong time a lot."

Mel blinked at him. Coming from Jake, this felt like some fairly harsh criticism.

"I'd say it's more a case that trouble seems to find us," she said. "Angie certainly didn't mean to find the murder weapon."

"What?" Jake shook his head as if he'd heard her wrong, and he slowly lowered his mug of root beer to the table.

"Oh, you hadn't heard about that yet?" she asked. "Well, I suppose it's premature to call it the murder weapon, but a bloody pitchfork in a barn where a man has recently been gored sort of makes it seem likely, doesn't it?"

"Did she report it to the sheriff?"

"Yes, she had no choice, since he arrived right when she and Oz were arguing about telling him or not," Mel said. "It sort of took the decision out of her hands."

"See? This is what I'm talking about," Jake said. He shook his head in bewilderment. "What is it about you people?"

"Hey!" Mel protested. "It's not our fault that Ty Stokes was an egomaniacal jerk with a lot of enemies. Besides, Angie was just walking with Oz to see the bull when she tripped over the handle, so it was hardly her fault."

"Have you ever noticed that some people attract bad luck?" he asked.

Mel shrugged. She wasn't so sure she liked where this conversation was headed, especially given that it was hard to ignore that over the past year, she was quite sure she had stumbled over more dead bodies than the national average for cupcake bakers.

"It's like a hard-luck Charlie, you know, the sort who can never seem to get a break in life," Jake said. "Only instead of hard luck, it's just plain bad luck."

"I don't know," Mel said, fretting her lower lip. She was afraid to do too much self-examination in this particular area, as it might make her paranoid.

"Jake, do you think Slim's shooting and Ty's stabbing are connected?" she asked.

She wasn't sure why she asked, but the question had been bothering her for days, and since Jake was more familiar with all of the players in this particular drama, maybe he knew something she didn't.

"I can't imagine that they are," he said. "But again, perhaps this is not something you should be thinking about overmuch, as it might land you into more trouble than you're already in."

"We're not in trouble," Mel protested.

Jake gave her a disbelieving look and said, "You've got one employee who was seen at the scene of Ty's murder, and now your other employee found the murder weapon. You don't consider that trouble?"

Mel took a deep breath. When he put it like that, it didn't look so good for the Fairy Tale Cupcake crew, and she couldn't even blame it on the Bubbas.

Jake stood and drained his glass. "I'm just saying maybe you all need to be a little more careful."

He tipped his hat to her before he headed back to the bar to give Henry his empty mug.

Mel watched him leave through the swinging doors, feeling seriously unhappy. Maybe Jake was right. Maybe they were a bunch of Lousy Luck Louies, or maybe some spoiled rancher's daughter was causing them unnecessary grief. Tate had never gotten the chance to tell Mel what he had found out about Shelby, but that was okay; she had other avenues for getting information.

She took out her phone and called her uncle Stan. It was late, but as a detective for the Scottsdale police department, he kept some pretty late hours.

"Mel, how's the north country?" he asked, letting her know he'd checked the number displayed on his phone before he answered.

"That depends—are we talking about the weather?" she asked.

"Mel, it's a hundred and eight, and the sun is down," he said. "Of course I'm talking about the weather."

"Cool pine-scented breezes," she said. "Warm sun shining but not enough to cause even a bead of sweat."

Uncle Stan gave a longing sigh and then asked, "Okay,

so why are you really calling me? I know it's not just to taunt me about the weather."

"Uncle Stan, have you ever heard of the Hazards from Juniper Pass?" she asked.

"Well, sure, anyone who gives two hoots about Arizona history knows about the Hazards. I think state historian Marshall Trimble mentions them in a few of his books. Why?"

Mel noticed Stan's tone went from conversational—he was an Arizona history nut himself—to suspicious.

"Did you hear about the shooting?" she asked.

"I heard a moron shot off a gun at the parade and Slim Hazard got winged, but he was okay."

"And did you hear about the murder?" she asked.

"Murder?" Stan's voice got loud and seemed to roar into the phone, as if he had been reclined but now was leaning forward as she had just gotten his full attention. "Who got murdered?"

"The rodeo star Ty Stokes," she said.

"The news said he got gored by a bull."

"More accurately a pitchfork."

"And you know this because?"

"Angie found the murder weapon."

There was a beat of silence on the phone, and the band in the bar, who'd been taking a break, got back on the stage. In the time it took Uncle Stan to process what Mel had said, the band began to play.

"What is that noise?" he asked.

"The country band just started to play again," she said. She finished off her beer.

"Where are you?" he asked.

"The Last Chance Saloon," she said.

"Is Angie with you?" he asked. "I want to talk to her."

"No, she went to bed," she said.

"Tate?" he asked.

"Out for a walk."

"Melanie Cooper, are you sitting in a bar all alone?"

"Uncle Stan, I am more than of age, painfully more than of age," she said.

"I'm telling Joe," he said.

"Oh, good grief, how old are you?" she asked. "Listen, I'm calling because I'm curious about the Hazards. Is there any way you could find out more about them than what might be read in a history book?"

"Like what?" he asked.

"Well, I'm curious about Shelby Hazard, Slim's daughter, in particular," she said. "I'm pretty sure she was with Ty right before he was killed, and I heard that they were once a couple."

"And you'd be sticking your nose into this because . . . ?"

"She told the local sheriff that Oz was in the barn right before Stokes was killed, and because Angie found the murder weapon and had to be fingerprinted. I'm feeling a tad paranoid," Mel said. "I don't like Shelby and I don't trust her, and I don't like that she seems to be getting my people in trouble."

Uncle Stan was quiet for a minute. "I'll see what I can find out for you on one condition."

Twenty-six

Mel hesitated. She'd been on the receiving end of Uncle Stan's conditions before.

"Is this like the affidavit you had me sign when I was fifteen saying that if I didn't get a tattoo until after I was twenty-five, you'd give me five hundred dollars?"

"Yes, but this time I'm willing to take a verbal promise, since you followed through on the tattoo thing," he said.

Mel had to plug her other ear so she could hear Uncle Stan over the bar noise.

"Fine," she said. "What's the condition?"

"You've got to stay out of this, Mel," he said.

Mel was quiet for a minute. In fact, she was quiet long enough that Uncle Stan had to ask if she was still there.

"Yes, I'm here," she said. "But I fail to see why you'd

get me information about the Hazards and then want me to stay out of it. I can't help but be in it."

"Let me clarify," Uncle Stan said. "I want you to keep Angie and Oz out of trouble, and if finding out about the Hazards helps you to do that, then fine. However, I don't want you getting mixed up in this thing. If I do find out anything of particular interest, I will be calling the sheriff up there to share."

"Okay," Mel said. "I think I can safely commit to these conditions."

"Excellent," Uncle Stan said. "I'll call you as soon as I know something."

Mel ended the call and slid her phone into her pocket. Why was it when she made a deal with Uncle Stan, she always felt as though she'd been outmaneuvered?

She walked her empty mug over to the bar and left it with a wave to Henry. Then she headed through the door into the hotel. She climbed the stairs and eased into the room she shared with Angie as quietly as she could.

She assumed the body-shaped lump in the other bed was Angie. She watched her for a moment and debated asking whether she was awake, but figured if she was and she wanted to talk, she'd hear Mel and start the conversation. The lump didn't move, so Mel figured Angie was asleep or faking it, which she could respect.

She wondered whether Marty and Oz were okay, but then, she had a feeling that Tate had probably headed back in that direction. She thought back to the scene in the bar between her friends. When had all of this gotten so complicated?

She shook her head and started to get ready for bed. Despite her nap in the truck cab, she was exhausted. When her head hit the pillow, she had thought she'd be up thinking, but no. It was as if she were a puppet and someone had cut her strings. In the time it took her to exhale, her body went limp and everything went dark.

⸙

Mel blinked against the sun that was streaming through the window. She didn't want to get up. She didn't want to face another day of chaos and emotional upheaval. Then she thought about her cake pops and what might have happened during the night.

She lurched out of bed and put her feet on the floor, realizing that the bed next to her was empty and neatly made with hospital corners and fluffed pillows. Angie was already gone, and Mel hadn't even heard her get up.

She hustled over to the bathroom and found it empty. She raced through her morning routine, which, with her short blond hair, was not so much a routine as it was a wash-and-go.

She locked the door behind her and pounded down the stairs, eager to get to the rodeo and find out if anything had happened with the van last night. She'd had a fitful sleep worrying about her product and her employees, and not necessarily in that order.

As she approached the van, she was surprised to find Tate and Angie working together. They didn't seem on exactly chummy terms, but they weren't nose to nose arguing, either. There was no sign of Marty or Oz.

She tried to gauge her friends' expressions as she approached. Angie had her lips pursed and was looking miffy, while Tate's shoulders were clenched almost as tightly as his teeth. They were working together but looked as though they were actively trying not to touch each other. Yeah, not easy to do in a van the size of a closet.

She skirted the line that had already formed and climbed into the back.

"Need any help?" she asked.

"Sure, take my spot," Tate said. He didn't even look at her. He pulled his apron over his head, dumped it onto a shelf, and climbed out the back.

"Something I said?" Mel asked.

"No, I'm sure it's probably something I said," Angie answered. She leaned out the window and took the next order.

Mel slipped on her apron and joined her in the window.

As the next customer stepped up, Mel felt a grin spread over her face. She couldn't help it. Wearing a pink cowboy hat, clown makeup, a striped shirt, and suspenders was a rodeo clown.

"Good morning," she said. "What can I get you?"

The clown blinked at her and then pantomimed eating corn on the cob.

"Sorry, no corn here," she said. "Cake pop?"

The clown gave her a mockingly suspicious look, and Mel heard a few people in the line chuckle. Then he mimed cutting a steak and taking a bite off of a fork.

Mel chuckled and shook her head. Then she held up one of each of the four cake pops and said, "Vanilla, chocolate, red velvet, or lemon."

The clown jumped in the air in glee or surprise—Mel

wasn't sure—but it scored some laughs, and Mel noticed that his performance was drawing even more customers to the truck.

The clown took the two cake pops and then began to walk away.

"Oh, no, you don't," Angie said. "Those will cost you."

The clown hid behind the lady behind him in line and looked at Angie over her shoulder. The lady laughed, and so did Mel. Angie did not look amused.

"Pony it up, big boy," she said. She gave him her best DeLaura scowl.

The clown took one exaggerated step back to the truck and offered Angie his hip pocket.

"Oh, for Pete's sake," Angie said. "I am not going to fish through your pockets for you. Let me hold the cake pops."

The clown wagged his hip at her, the crowd laughed, and Angie glowered at him again. Knowing she'd lost the public opinion poll, she dutifully hung out of the window to reach into his pocket.

"You'd better not be getting any jollies out of this," she said as she pulled a rubber chicken out of his pocket.

Mel had to press her lips together to keep from cracking up, but she could see even Angie was tucking in a smile.

The clown jumped back, as if startled to find a rubber chicken in his pocket. Then he turned and offered his other hip to Angie. She gave him a feigned look of exasperation but bravely reached in and pulled out two perfect pink roses.

Angie laughed and went to hand them back to him, but he shook his head and stepped back, pointing the cake pops at the two of them to indicate there was a rose for each of them.

"Oh, thank you," Mel said as Angie handed her the other one.

"Consider your tab paid," Angie said.

He jumped up and clicked his overly large heels together. Angie reached out the window and tucked the rubber chicken under his arm. The crowd laughed and clapped as he hunkered down and walked like a duck away from the cupcake truck.

Mel found two water bottles and put a rose in each one. The crowd outside had surged with the visit from the clown, and they were kept steadily busy for the rest of the morning.

Marty was the first to show up for the afternoon shift. He looked no worse for the wear, considering his condition last night. He climbed into the back of the van and started to tie on his apron when Mel noticed he was wearing something else on his hip.

"Marty! What the heck is that?" she asked.

"Oh, this?" he asked with a shrug. "It's nothing."

"What do you mean, 'nothing'?" she asked. "That is not 'nothing.'"

Angie turned from the window to see what was happening.

"Oh, my god, Marty Zelaznik, are you packing?" she asked.

Twenty-seven

"Aw, this little thing?" he asked as he pulled the gun out of its holster.

Both Mel and Angie fell to the floor. Mel folded her arms over her head, knowing that even her upper arm flab couldn't stop a bullet, and yet, her instincts screamed duck and cover, and she was incapable of lowering her arms.

"Marty, put that away!" she ordered. "Now!"

"It's not even loaded," he said, putting it back in its holster. "I already shot all of the bullets out of it."

"What?" Angie asked.

"When?" Mel demanded.

"Or should we ask who?" Angie said.

"No, no," Marty said. "Lily was giving me shooting lessons. She's a sharpshooter, you know."

"No, I didn't know," Angie said. She rose up from the ground and held out her hand. "Hand it over, cowboy."

Marty grumbled but he unstrapped his holster and handed it to Angie.

"New rule," Mel said. "No guns in the cupcake van."

"Aw, come on," Marty said. "What if we get robbed?"

"We're not going to get robbed," Mel said.

She pointed to the window, where a woman with two young girls was waiting. Marty gave a "humph" and stomped toward the window. She watched as Angie wrapped the belt around the holstered gun and looked around the van for a place to put it.

"Have all of our men completely lost their minds?" Mel asked.

"That's assuming any of them had a mind to lose," Angie said. "Which I'm beginning to doubt very much."

Mel shook her head. "Marty, I'm going to return the gun to Lily. Loaded or not, I don't want Oz anywhere near that thing."

"Fine," he said. He sounded as recalcitrant as a five-year-old, and Mel had to curb the urge to twist his ear.

"I'm starving," Angie said. "I'll go with you."

Mel glanced out of the van to see Oz making his way toward them, holding several enormous tubs. She quickly put the gun down and reached out of the open back of the van to take one of the tubs while Angie took the other.

"What's this?" she asked.

"Vegan cupcakes," he said. "Ruth let me use her kitchen again, so I spent the morning baking."

Mel beamed at him.

"Oz, have I ever told you how much I love your self-directedness?"

He bobbed his head. "Yes, but I never get tired of hearing it."

Angie grabbed the other tub, and Oz climbed into the van, taking up any available space. He took his tubs back and heaved a heavy sigh.

"Is something wrong, Oz?" Mel asked. He sounded melancholy, which was unusual for the even-tempered teenager.

He heaved an even deeper sigh. He seemed to consider telling her something, but then he shook his shaggy head.

"Nah, I'm fine," he said.

Mel and Angie exchanged a glance. Angie gave her a tiny headshake, which Mel understood to mean she should let it lie.

"All right," she said. "But if you change your mind and want to talk . . ."

Angie handed Mel the gun, and Oz jumped back, slamming into the freezers.

"What? Are you going to shoot it out of me?" he asked, putting his hands still holding the tubs of cupcakes in the air.

"No, this is Marty's," Mel said. "He fancies himself a sharpshooter now."

"I never said I was a sharpshooter," Marty protested. "But I did blow some nice holes in the target, thank you very much."

Angie rolled her eyes. "It belongs to Lily Hazard. We're going to return it, as we have a new rule: No guns in the cupcake van."

"That's cool with me," Oz said. "I'm all for peaceful resolutions."

"Yeah, you say that now, but just wait until someone defrosts all of our cupcakes again."

"We still wouldn't shoot them, Marty. Am I clear?" Mel said.

Marty looked pouty, but he agreed. "Fine."

Mel and Angie jumped out of the van.

"I have my phone; call me if you need backup," Mel said.

They acknowledged with a wave that had a bit of a buzz-off feel to it.

Mel looked at Angie and asked, "Do you think we're all getting a little sick of each other?"

"Oh, I don't know. Spending twenty-four/seven together in a place that smells of horse manure, handing out cupcakes and cake pops, while people are getting shot and gored by pitchforks . . . Yeah, that might strain the bonds of friendship just a bit."

Mel had to admit she was missing Joe and Captain Jack and her futon even more than she had expected. And she realized that one of the best things about getting away was discovering how much she loved home.

She tucked the gun under her arm and fell into step beside Angie.

"Whoa, look out! She's got a gun!" A shout sounded from the barbecue pit.

Mel looked over to see the Bubbas with their arms raised in mock surrender.

"Hey, we know we're beating you, but you don't have to get violent," Billy said.

Mel looked at Angie. "Maybe I was premature in taking this gun away from Marty."

"It is tempting," Angie said. Then she turned to the Bubbas, raised her voice, and shouted, "The gun isn't for shooting you; we just thought some of your customers might like us to put them out of their misery."

A few people in line laughed, and the Bubbas frowned.

"Hardy har har," Bob retorted.

"Then again, with a comeback like that, it might be considered a public service to put *you* out of our misery," Mel said.

Billy cuffed Bob upside the head, and they exchanged heated words.

"Hey," Angie called out, breaking up their tiff. "The closing ceremonies are tonight after the bronco busting. Are you two ready to tally up sales?"

The Bubbas exchanged a panicked look. But then Billy glared at her and said, "We compare total sales after the bronco busting. Then you can cram yourself into a pair of Daisy Dukes and schlep some barbecue."

"Oh, I don't know," Angie said. "I have a feeling you're going to be in the pink."

The Bubbas paled. Mel and Angie exchanged a grin and strode toward the road that would lead them to the ranch house. Even if Lily wasn't home, Mel felt better leaving the gun there than anywhere else.

The crowd surged around them, heading to the vendors' tent and the arena. Mel could hear the audience in the arena laughing, and she wondered if their clown was doing his show. She wished she had time to watch him.

The road was dusty, and it kicked up a fine brown dirt

that found its way into every crack and crevice of Mel's sneakers. She doubted even a run through the washing machine was going to save them.

Mel and Angie climbed the porch steps and knocked on the front door. Mel had no idea if anyone was home. She was hoping for Tammy, since that would alleviate an awkward scene between Angie and Lily. As the door was pulled open, she felt her phone vibrate in her pocket, and she fished it out.

She checked the display. It was Uncle Stan. She handed the gun to Angie and gestured for her to hand off the gun. She glanced up as she answered her call and saw Lily standing in the doorway.

Angie gave her an outraged look, but Mel shrugged and walked to the end of the porch. Angie was just going to have to be a big girl about this.

"Hi, Uncle Stan," she said. "What's the good word?"

She could hear Angie's voice behind her and hoped she was being civil, but really, there wasn't much Mel could do if she wasn't.

"I don't know that I would call it a good word," Uncle Stan said.

"Why not?" she asked.

"Well, I didn't find much on Shelby Hazard that you don't already know. I did do some digging into the rest of the family. It seems Hannah Hazard, Slim's sister, wasn't killed in a car accident," he said. "She died in childbirth."

"No, that can't be right. Lily was very clear that it was a car accident. Why would she tell me that?" Mel asked. She glanced over her shoulder and saw that the front door was closed, so Angie had obviously gone inside with Lily. Uh-oh.

"I don't know," Stan said. "The records are sealed, so there's no telling who adopted the baby."

"The father?" Mel asked.

"Not listed on the birth certificate," Stan said.

"Did you find out anything else about the family?" Mel asked.

"Slim is clean," he said. "No record for either him or his oldest daughter. His first wife died of cancer when she was fairly young. The second wife, Tammy, was a Texas beauty queen. She was married to an older man before Slim. He was very wealthy, oil money. He left her a nice inheritance, but the bulk of his money went to the kids from his first marriage. It seems she's really good at the second-wife thing."

"Indeed," Mel said.

"And then there's Shelby." Uncle Stan paused, and Mel could hear papers rustling in the background.

"Wild card?" she guessed.

"Yeah, helpful in a hand of poker, not so much in a person," he said. "She's had multiple arrests for driving under the influence, done time in rehab, stalked a Hollywood producer who she said was her boyfriend, although he denied it. She has been evicted from several apartments for disturbing the peace and non-payment of rent. Yeah, she's a real gem."

"So, bachelorette number three with the checkered past seems a likely suspect in the case of who stabbed Ty Stokes, given that she was seen with him right before he died and the fact that they were once involved," Mel said.

"Seems likely," Uncle Stan said. "Now, none of this proves anything, although it is interesting. I've already talked to Sheriff Dolan and let him know what I've found out."

"How did you manage that without him thinking you were stomping all over his case?" she asked.

"I told him I knew the Hazards from way back," he said.

"So, you lied."

"Yeah, but it was out of respect for his jurisdiction," Uncle Stan said. "Now, I expect you to uphold your end of our deal. The Shelby information is to help you keep Angie and Oz out of any more trouble by steering clear of her. As for the Hazard family history, that's just a little extra. I'd have to do a lot more digging to see if there's any relevance to what's happening now, and that is Sheriff Dolan's job."

"Well, I appreciate the info, Uncle Stan, and I will make sure we all keep a minimum distance of fifty feet from Ms. Shelby."

"That's my girl," Uncle Stan said. "Hey, I saw your boy last night at the retirement party for one of our detectives. He looked sad."

"Good," Mel said. Uncle Stan laughed.

"Call me if you need me," he said. "Love ya, kid."

"Love you, too," Mel said, and ended the call.

She didn't know what to make of all she'd learned but she'd bet dollars to doughnuts that Shelby Hazard was the killer.

A hoot of laughter sounded from the house, and Mel looked up in surprise. With Angie and Lily on their own, the last thing she'd expected to hear was the sound of merriment.

She hustled to the front door. She knocked but no one answered. She tried the knob. It turned, and she pushed it open. She supposed it was silly to be so concerned. Laughter was not indicative of Angie giving someone a smackdown.

Still, when she walked into the main room, she wasn't really prepared to see Angie and Lily doubled up and laughing.

She glanced between them and asked, "Good joke?"

"You have to see Lily's impression of Tate," Angie said. "It's spot-on."

Mel sank into one of the squashy leather seats and watched as Lily walked into the room, holding her head at the same particular angle that Tate always did. Mel had always gotten the sense Tate was listening to some far-off music that only he could hear.

Then she blinked at them in the exact way Tate did when he was taken by surprise. Finally, she ran her right hand through her hair just like he did when he was feeling utterly exasperated by a situation.

Mel had to laugh. It really was perfect. She looked at Angie questioningly, wondering what had made her have a change of heart about Lily, but Angie was avoiding her gaze.

"I'm sorry Marty brought his gun back to the cupcake van," Lily said. "I didn't think he'd do that. I thought he'd keep it in his room until we could do some more target practice."

"It's fine," Mel said. "I think he just got carried away."

She glanced over Lily's shoulder to the photos on the wall beyond her. It was on the tip of her tongue to ask Lily why she'd lied about Hannah's death. Then she thought about her promise to Uncle Stan and held her tongue. She was going to try to be good. Really, she was.

"We'd better get back to the cupcake van," Angie said.

"Yeah, I'd better go check on my dad," Lily said. "I'm worried he's been overdoing it. Ty's death really made the rodeo a PR nightmare for him, especially now that the media knows it wasn't the bull."

Angie was quiet for a second and then said, "I suppose it would have been better if I hadn't found the murder weapon."

"No, it's better that you found it," Lily said. "If there's a murderer out there, they need to be caught."

She was fretting her lower lip, and Mel could tell that she meant what she said and that she was clearly worried about who might be the murderer. In her place, Mel knew she'd feel the same.

Angie nodded. An awkward silence filled the room, and Mel rose from her seat, figuring they'd better go.

Angie followed her to the door, but before they left, Angie spun back and said, "Thanks for . . . you know."

Lily smiled at her. She was a pretty girl to begin with, but when she smiled she was beautiful. Given that she'd been palling around with Tate for days, Mel was stunned that Angie didn't want to run her through with a pitchfork herself.

As Angie closed the door behind them, Mel didn't even wait until they'd moved away to ask, "What was that all about?"

Twenty-eight

"Lily and I came to an understanding."

"So I gathered," Mel said. "Care to share?"

"I don't know that I can," Angie said.

Together they walked back to the rodeo. Mel tried not to badger her friend—really, she did—but Angie looked very happy, which made Mel anxious.

They reached the road that led back to the rodeo when Mel couldn't take it anymore.

"So, you're really not going to tell me, your best friend, why Lily Hazard is suddenly your buddy?" Mel asked.

Angie looked at her regretfully. "I can't. I promised."

"Fine," Mel said. She didn't know why she was feeling so irritated, but suddenly she wanted to get away from everyone and everything. "Listen, I've got some stuff to do. I'll meet you back at the van."

Angie raised her eyebrows in surprise, and Mel realized her tone had been a bit abrupt.

"I need to pick up a thank-you gift for my mom for watching Captain Jack," she said.

"Oh," Angie said. "All right. See you later, then?"

"Sure," Mel said. She headed off in the direction of the vendors' tent.

It was just as well she was irritated with her friends. She really had planned to get her mother something, since it had been awfully nice of her to take Captain Jack. Besides, although she hated shopping, she loved shopping for her mother.

Joyce was the world's best gift receiver. She liked everything, because she took all gifts in the spirit that they were given, meaning that she was just tickled that anyone ever thought to buy her anything.

Mel still remembered the year her dad, Charlie, had tried to hide Joyce's fifteenth wedding anniversary gift, tickets on a cruise to Greece, in a ceramic flamingo soap dispenser as a gag. Joyce had been delighted with the silly flamingo and proudly displayed it on the counter for all to see.

She had thought it was too charming for soap and refused to use it properly. Charlie had finally had to threaten to take it back if she didn't put some damn soap in it. Finally, she gave in, and when she opened it, she couldn't believe there was even more to her anniversary gift. Charlie had always said that giving Joyce gifts was one of the greatest joys of his life, because she was genuinely touched by even the smallest gesture.

Mel circled the vendors' tent and knew the perfect gift the minute she saw it. A pretty turquoise straw hat with a white flower tucked into the brim. Turquoise was Joyce's favorite color, and Mel knew she'd love wearing this hat poolside with her friend Ginny.

"Really? A cowboy hat? How pedestrian of you," a voice said behind Mel as she reached up to take the hat off the rack.

There was a mirror in front of her, and Mel used it to see whom the voice belonged to. It was Shelby. She was a bit surprised that Shelby wasn't otherwise occupied, say, at the police station, but she didn't say as much.

"Well, given that I've been walking everywhere since I got here, pedestrian is okay," Mel said. "Where are all of your little friends?"

"They have lives; they couldn't stay here all week," Shelby said. She sounded defensive.

"And you can't leave," Mel said. She tried on the hat, since she and Joyce shared the same-sized head. It was a perfect fit. She signaled to the vendor that she'd take it.

Shelby was giving her a nasty look, but she shook it off and forced a smile. "How's my little friend Oz?"

Mel knew she was only asking to get under Mel's skin. It worked, but she wasn't about to let it show.

"He's fine," she said. "Better, actually, now that he's changed the company he was keeping."

Shelby gave her pout. "I can't help it if men of all ages simply adore me."

"Sure you can," Mel said. "You just don't want to."

She paid the vendor and took the hat, which he had put in a box, and tucked it under her arm. As she started to leave, Shelby fell into step beside her.

"I'm not evil, you know," she said.

Mel didn't say anything. She was trying to stick to her agreement with Uncle Stan, but it really wasn't her fault that Shelby had found her and begun to talk.

"What do you mean?" she asked, knowing she shouldn't but doing it anyway.

"I know what they're saying about me," she said. "Everyone thinks I killed Ty just because we had a fling once. I didn't."

"Who's everyone?" Mel asked.

"Oh, you know, my dad, my wicked stepmother, and of course my perfect big sister," she said. Her voice had the acidic bite of a lifetime of bitterness. Mel glanced at her and felt repulsion for the whiny little brat beside her. Was she really as narcissistic as she seemed?

"Your family seems awfully nice," Mel said. "I find it hard to believe any of them would turn on you."

"Ha! That shows how little you know," Shelby sneered. "They're all just greedy and selfish. They don't care about me or my dreams. I could be a movie star if they'd just stop pulling me back here to live in this filth."

Shelby kicked at the road with her platform sandal, and brown dust flew up into the air. Mel looked out across the grassy pasture land that surrounded the rodeo, and even farther out to the ponderosa pines that hugged the surrounding hills. She didn't see how coming back to this gorgeous landscape once a year was a hardship.

Her thoughts drifted to Slim's sister, the one who had

gone to California and died in childbirth. Had she felt the same way about the ranch as her niece Shelby, or had it been hard for her to leave her home?

"Is Slim the last one of his generation?" she asked. "Or are there more Hazards out there?"

"He's it," Shelby said. "I think that's why Ty was trying to take the rodeo from him. With Lily and me as the only heirs, there really wouldn't be anyone but Lily to fight Ty, since I don't care. I'd have them buy me out, and I'd move to Hollywood and never look back."

They were headed down the road toward the cupcake van, and Mel didn't particularly want Shelby to get within one hundred feet of Oz. She slowed her pace, trying to think of a way to get rid of her.

"Didn't Slim have any siblings or cousins?" Mel asked.

"He had a little sister named Hannah, but she died before I was born," Shelby said. "I've been told I have her hair."

"I think I saw a picture of her at the house," Mel said. "She was a pretty girl. How did she die?"

Mel stopped breathing while she waited for Shelby's answer. If she knew how her aunt had died, it would change everything.

"She was killed in a car crash on a trip to California," Shelby said. "She was probably trying to escape."

Mel studied her face to see if she was lying, but she didn't see any sign that Shelby was telling her anything other than the truth. Frankly, Mel didn't think she was a good enough actress to pull off a lie that big.

"I'm sorry," Mel said. "That must have been very hard for Slim."

"It was," Shelby said. "From all of the stories I've heard, Dad doted on Hannah almost too much."

Mel had to wonder if that was why neither Lily nor Shelby knew the truth. Was Slim still protecting Hannah and her memory?

"I guess big brothers are like that with little sisters," Mel said.

"Well, it's too bad fathers aren't more like that with their daughters," Shelby said. Her voice had resumed its whiny pitch, and Mel felt her temples throb.

"Really, Shelby? Can you honestly tell me you feel neglected by your father?" Mel asked.

"Don't judge me," Shelby snapped. "You don't know anything about me."

"Fair enough," Mel said. "But I do know that my dad died over ten years ago, and there isn't a day that goes by that I don't miss him."

Shelby turned her face away, and Mel knew she'd hit her mark. She didn't waste her breath saying anything more but left Shelby where she stood as she crossed the dusty road and headed back to the cupcake van.

She knew she shouldn't have said anything, and she felt bad about being so harsh, but honestly, Shelby's mother was dead, and she was doing her level best to alienate her father and her sister. Where Mel came from, it was family first, even when they drove you bonkers, and she just couldn't stand to see someone with a perfectly nice family disregard it. Then again, it really was none of her business, and she should learn to keep her mouth shut.

She turned the corner around the side of the van and smacked into the solid form of a man. He instantly reached out to grab her and steady her, but one look into his familiar brown eyes and Mel felt herself get dizzy as all the blood rushed out of her head.

"Hey there, Cupcake," he said. Then he took a bite of the treat in his hand and said, "Or should I start calling you Cake Pop?"

Twenty-nine

"Joe!" she cried as she hugged him close. "What are you doing here?"

He finished his cake pop and planted a solid kiss on her. "I heard you were experimenting with the cupcakes, and I had to drive all the way up here to give them a taste test."

"And?" she asked. Given that Joe had a sweet tooth of mythic proportions, she valued his opinion above all others.

"I think I'm going to need another to be absolutely sure," he said.

She looked at the two sticks in his hand.

"Nice try. You've already had two," she said. "Now, what's the verdict?"

"I think I'm in love," he said. "Can I have one more? Pleeeease."

"Which ones haven't you tried?" she asked.

"The lemon and the vanilla," he said.

"Fine," she said. "Wait here."

She climbed into the back of the truck and saw Tate and Angie working the window together. She caught Angie giving Tate a wide smile, which left the poor man blinking and bewildered.

Mel gave her a chastising look, and she could tell that Angie was pretending not to see her.

She climbed out of the van with a shake of her head. Joe helped her jump to the ground, and she sat beside him on the bumper while he ate the two cake pops she offered.

"You're going to make yourself sick," she said.

He took one bite of the lemon and said, "It's worth it."

Mel waited until he took another bite and then she asked, "So, now that I've bribed you with sweets, you have to tell me the truth: Did my uncle Stan send you?"

Joe sputtered around his cake. "What makes you ask that?"

"Just a suspicion," she said. "Am I right?"

"He loves you, you know," Joe said.

"I know. I love him, too," she said. "I just hope he didn't convince you to come up here because he thinks I'm getting into trouble."

"Are you?" Joe asked. He gave her a look that said he suspected she was.

"No."

"Mel, it's me."

"Okay, maybe some odd things have happened," she said. "But I wouldn't call it trouble, not really."

"Oz calmed a bull by feeding it cupcakes," he said. "That's more than odd."

238

"Unusual, I'll give you that," she said.

"Angie found a bloody pitchfork."

"Again, a little out of the ordinary, I can admit that."

"Mel, I really think you should pack up the cupcake van and come home," he said.

Mel frowned at him. Was this Joe putting his foot down? Joe never did that. As the middle brother of the seven DeLaura boys, he was the negotiator, the peacemaker, the reasonable DeLaura.

She opened her mouth, then closed it. She wasn't sure what to say. Wait. Yes, she was.

"I don't think I can do that," she said. "I mean, business has been booming, and Angie and I are thinking of making cake pops a permanent thing at the bakery. Oz has made real innovations in the organic cupcake possibilities, and Marty might even have a new girlfriend. We can't just ditch. Besides, I don't think the sheriff would look too kindly upon us if we just bagged it and skedaddled."

"Did you just use the word *skedaddle*?" he asked.

"Yep," she said, making it a two-syllable word.

A slow smile crept over his face. "I didn't think you'd go for it, but it was worth a try."

Mel sagged against him with relief. She'd been hoping he wouldn't insist.

"Wait a minute," she said. "Are you just agreeing with me because you know the sheriff wouldn't like it?"

"Busted." He raised both hands, which now held empty cake pop sticks.

"Joseph DeLaura," she said. "What would you have done if I'd agreed with you and decided to leave?"

"I'd have hurried over to the sheriff's office and negotiated to get you out of here. I'd have convinced him that if he really needed any of you, I'd be able to get you back up here pronto."

"Do you think that would work?" Mel asked.

"I don't know," he said. "It helps that your uncle is PD and I'm a DA, but it really depends on where this case is going for the sheriff."

"There were a lot of people who didn't like Ty Stokes," she said. "Me, for one."

"Well, do me a favor and don't announce that too loudly to the world at large."

"So, do you want to take a quick tour?" she asked. "We could get you outfitted like Tate and have you in boots and a hat in no time."

Joe looked down at his khaki shorts and Margaritaville T-shirt. "What? This isn't cowboy enough?"

"Well, it is a nice departure from the suits," she said. She always thought casual Joe had a lot of appeal.

"Come on," she said. She took his hand and pulled him off the back of the van. Angie and Tate appeared to have things under control, and Mel wanted to spend some time with Joe before her next shift in the truck.

They poked around the vendors' tent. Joe had Mel in stitches as he tried on hats and strutted around like a cowboy. They ran into Slim and Tammy, and Mel introduced them to Joe.

"You've got a fine young lady, there," Slim said. He gave Joe a once-over that made him stand up a little straighter, and their handshake looked to be a test of character.

Tammy rolled her eyes, but as the men stepped back,

they were grinning at each other. They each must have passed the other's test.

"How's your arm, Slim?" Mel asked.

"As good as a twenty-year-old pitcher on opening day," he said. He leaned closer and whispered, "I'm just wearing the sling for the sympathy it gets me from the wife."

"I heard that," Tammy said. She tried to sound severe, but it was belied by her smile. "The doctor says you have to wear it for at least another week, and then you start therapy."

Slim looked grumpy, but he refrained from saying anything.

"Stop by the cupcake van," Mel said. "Sympathy will get you a free cake pop."

Slim cheered up immediately. He and Tammy said their good-byes, and Joe turned to Mel and said, "I like him."

"He's a good man," she said.

"I hear a *but* in there," he said.

Mel looped her arm through his, and they headed out to the bull pasture. She didn't want to talk badly of the Hazards, but there was definitely something that wasn't adding up.

She told Joe what Uncle Stan had found out about Slim's sister dying in childbirth and there being no record of what happened to the baby.

"Now, if that was your beloved sister," she said, "wouldn't you want to keep tabs on her baby?"

"That would not happen to my sister," he said.

Mel looked at him. He had that look on his face, the one that all of the DeLaura brothers wore when it came to Angie. It was called denial. As far as they were concerned, Angie would be forever twelve years old, and they treated her accordingly. The fact that she was in her thirties and dating a rock star was not discussed.

"Okay," Mel said. "Let me rephrase that."

"Please," he said.

"In a normal family," she said, "don't you think the family would know?"

Joe was silent for a moment. "Maybe they do."

Mel smacked her forehead with her hand. "Oh my God. Why didn't I see that? You're right. Slim probably does know what happened. He's probably been keeping tabs on the baby for years."

"It's possible," Joe said.

They were nearing the barn where the bulls were housed. Mel led Joe to the pen where Oz's new friend resided.

"Come on, you have to come and meet Buttercup," she said.

"Buttercup?" Joe asked.

"His real name is Thunderbolt, but Oz felt he would do better with a kinder and gentler moniker."

"I'm surprised the other bulls haven't beaten him up and stolen his lunch money," Joe said.

They stopped beside the bull's pen. He gave them an uninterested glance.

"Probably we should have brought him some cupcakes," Mel said.

Joe leaned on the top rail and gave a low whistle. "He is massive. You all could have been stomped to death."

"Angie and I were kept out of harm's way," Mel said. "Jake Morgan is Slim's right-hand man. He wouldn't let us near the bull. When I think about how close Oz was, I get a little weak in the knees."

"So do I," Joe said. He gave her a wobbly smile, and she grinned.

"For a while, it looked pretty grim for the bull," Mel said. "They were sure he had gored Ty Stokes, but then Angie found the pitchfork . . ."

Her voice trailed off and Joe looked at her. "What are you thinking?"

"Nothing, except . . ."

"Yes?"

"I just had a crazy thought. Do you think Ty Stokes could be Hannah's baby?"

"What?"

"Well, let's think about this," Mel said. "Lily told me that Ty came to Slim when he was a teenager. His grandparents had died and, well, Slim had some involvement with his father's death. I don't know what happened to his mother, but obviously she wasn't in the picture. But if it was Hannah Hazard, it would make sense that Slim would take in Ty. It would also be logical that he had issues with Caleb. After all, his beloved little sister had died giving birth to Caleb's son."

"But why wouldn't he claim Ty as his nephew?" Joe asked.

"Maybe Ty didn't know," she said, warming up to her idea.

"That's reaching," he said. "How could he not know?"

"The girls don't even know Hannah had a baby," Mel countered. "What if Ty didn't know he was Hannah's son until later? He would be furious at being denied his rightful inheritance."

"Didn't you say that Shelby and Ty had a fling?" Joe asked.

"Yeah," Mel said. They exchanged a look that said, "Ew." "And Slim was furious about it."

"Well, that would make sense if he knew that Ty was a blood relative."

They were quiet for a moment, each thinking over what they'd learned and what it meant.

"Joe, did I mention to you that Lily is a sharpshooter?"

"No," he said. "But since Ty was killed with a pitchfork, I don't see how it's relevant."

"Someone shot Slim," she said.

"You don't think it was Lily, do you? I mean, I thought she was the sister you liked," he said.

The bull passed by them with a snort, and Mel instinctively stepped back, not having the warm fuzzies for his intimidating girth like Oz did.

"She is, but this ranch is her life," Mel said. "If she found out that Ty had a claim to it, she might have felt utterly betrayed, angry enough with her father to shoot him and scared enough to stop Ty from trying to take what she sees as hers."

"I don't know, Mel," he said. "That's a lot of blood for one pair of hands."

"I know. Of the two, Shelby seems to be the one angry enough to shoot her father," she said. "But if Ty is her cousin and they were reacquainting themselves, as it were, it could very well be Slim who killed Ty."

"Except you said Slim was in the arena watching Lily compete," he said.

"He was," she agreed. "Still, do you think we should go and tell the sheriff what we're thinking?"

"It's all pretty circumstantial," he said.

"But worth following up on?" she asked.

"I'm sorry, Mel, but I can't let you do that," a voice said from behind them.

Mel spun around in surprise. "You!"

Thirty

"I'm sorry, Mel. I really am," Jake said. Then he pulled a gun from the holster at his hip and gestured for them to move away from the bull pen.

"Suddenly, I feel underdressed," Joe said.

"Jake, what are you doing?" Mel asked.

"No talking," he said. "Not here."

He pointed with the gun toward the door. Mel felt her stomach plummet to her feet. She glanced around the barn and realized that she and Joe were alone with Jake. Maybe if they walked slowly enough, someone would come.

A loud cheer from the arena seemed to mock her. Of course no one was going to come, not with the bronco busting event happening, which was to be followed by the closing ceremonies. How were they supposed to draw attention away from thousands of people watching a horse trying to buck a rider?

"Have you been following me?" Mel asked. "Wait! Are you the one who unplugged my freezers?"

Jake pushed them both ahead of him and out the door. "Yes and no."

"Explain," she said.

"Yes, I've been following you, and no, I didn't unplug your freezers."

"I don't really think the freezers are an issue right now, do you?" Joe asked.

Mel shrugged. "Sorry. I'm panicking."

"Understood," he said. "Um . . . who is this guy?"

"Jake Morgan, he works for the Hazards."

Jake pushed them through the door. Any hope Mel had been harboring that someone would be out here and stop this madness vanished.

Jake tossed his keys to Mel and said, "You know how to drive my truck. Get in."

"When did you drive his truck?" Joe asked.

"Getting cake pop supplies," Mel said. "Little did I know the opportunity would present itself again so soon and at gunpoint."

Jake wrenched the door open and had Joe sit in the middle with his hands on the dash where Jake could see them. Mel started the truck with shaking fingers.

"I know how much you care about the Hazard family, Jake," she said. "But this isn't the way to help them."

"Drive out of the rodeo, nice and slow, and act casual," he said.

Mel put the truck into gear. She could feel Joe pressed

against her side as he was wedged between her and Jake, and a landslide of guilt hit her when she realized he could be harmed, and it would be her fault. He was only here because he'd been worried about her. She couldn't let anything happen to him.

"Listen, Jake," she said. "I know what Lily did."

"No, Mel," Joe said. "Don't say anything."

Mel gave him a sharp look. What did he mean? Shouldn't they try to talk their way out of this?

"I'm sorry," Jake said. "I feel bad about this. I like you, Mel—you're good people—but you're too close."

"Too close to what?" she asked.

Jake shook his head, and Mel knew they wouldn't get any more information out of him. He was the original strong, silent type.

Joe must have come to the same conclusion, because he turned to Jake and said, "We know about Hannah's baby."

Jake's jaw tightened, but he didn't say anything. He was staring straight ahead while Mel drove along the jutted dirt road.

"Turn left here," he said.

Mel pulled the wheel to the left. She could see the rodeo in the rearview mirror. Would anyone in the van even notice that she hadn't shown up for her shift, or would they write it off because Joe was here?

"Jake, you can't protect her," she said. She saw Joe shake his head out of the corner of her eye, and she knew he was telling her to stop, but she kept going. "Was Ty trying to take away the ranch because he felt it was his rightful inheritance?"

"Mel, you've got it all wrong," Jake said.

She leaned over Joe and looked at him. What did she have

wrong? And then she saw it in his profile. He had Slim's nose and his jaw, and although his eyes were a different color, they were the same shape.

"You're Hannah's baby," she said. "Jake, you're a Hazard!"

"Stop here," he said.

Mel put on the brakes slowly, still reeling from the realization that Jake was the missing baby. How had she not seen it before?

"Get out of the truck and keep your hands where I can see them," he said.

Mel noticed that the sun had begun its downward descent. The shadow of the old, abandoned barn in front of them was long and ominous, like a boney hand reaching out to pull them into their grave.

Jake gestured for them to walk toward the ramshackle sliding door. It protested with a shriek when he slid it open, and Mel felt it slice all the way into her bones.

It was dark and dry and smelled musty. Broken farm equipment and rusty tools lay scattered along one wall like this was the crypt where old tools came to die in.

The only light came from the open door, and Mel felt her throat get dry as Jake led them to the center. She thought about running. She glanced at Joe to see if she could tell what he was thinking, and he turned and met her gaze with a small shake of his head.

"Stand back-to-back," Jake said.

He had brought a length of rope with him, and as Mel turned to stand with her back to Joe's, she wondered how Jake thought he was going to tie them and hold the gun on them at the same time.

There was the sound of a fist smacking flesh, and Joe fell against her back. She spun and tried to catch him before he fell.

"What the hell did you do that for?" she asked.

"If you run, I'll shoot him," he said.

Mel staggered under Joe's weight, easing him to the floor. With Joe unconscious, she suddenly felt very alone and very, very afraid.

"What are you going to do with us?" she asked.

"I don't know yet," he said.

If he hadn't been tying them up and holding a gun on them, Mel might have felt sorry for him. As it was, she just felt angry.

"Jake, think about what you're doing," she said. "It's not too late to turn it around."

"Yes, it is," he snapped. "Don't you get it? I killed Ty. Sit back-to-back. Now."

Mel turned her back to Joe's and propped him with her weight. She felt the bite of the rope as Jake tied her wrists and then Joe's, and then looped the last length of rope around their chests.

"Jake, what happened? What happened with you and Ty?" she asked. "If it was self-defense, you can do a deal. Everyone knows Ty was a mean and nasty drunk. You can get out of this, Jake."

"No, Mel, I can't," he said. "I'm really sorry."

He rose and left, leaving them sitting in the dirt of the old barn. When the sliding door squeaked shut, Mel began to shake so badly she was surprised Joe's teeth didn't rattle him awake.

A scuffle sounded in the corner, and her first thought

was that it was her imagination. Her second thought was that it was a rat. Her third thought was that it was a mountain lion, looking for dinner.

The only light came through the slits of the sun-dried, shrunken wood of the old barn walls. The fine cracks of light did nothing to illuminate the gloom, and Mel could feel her heart pounding in her throat.

The scuffle sounded again, and this time she was quite sure it was a rat. Mountain lions probably didn't make that much noise when they were stalking their dinner. Rats shouldn't, either, for that matter. What if it was a spider? She felt her skin crawl as she pictured a hairy tarantula scuttling on its eight legs toward her.

"Joe!" she hissed. "Joe, wake up."

She tried to jiggle him awake, but it was no use. He was deadweight against her back. She tried not to knock their heads together as she worked at the ropes. Since Jake had been less than forthcoming with his plans for them, she had no idea when he would be back or what he planned to do with them when he arrived.

The scuffling noise sounded closer, and Mel could feel her body break out into a panicked sweat. This was completely unacceptable. She stomped her feet against the floor. Whether it was in anger or just a grown woman's tantrum, she didn't know, but the scuffling noise stopped. In fact, she felt quite sure she heard it heading in the opposite direction now.

"That's more like it," she said. The sound of her voice in the closed, stale air gave her courage. She stomped on the floor again and again until she was quite sure that her ruckus had driven away any creepy-crawlies.

She twisted her wrists, trying to loosen the ropes, but managed only to give herself a scorching case of rope burn. She tried to wriggle out of the rope around her chest but only knocked her head against Joe's, giving herself a mild headache.

She had no idea how much time was passing, and she was worried that Jake had hit Joe so hard that he had a concussion. Her thoughts lingered on Jake. Why had he murdered Ty?

He was Hannah's son. He was a Hazard. Obviously, Shelby and Lily didn't know he was their cousin. They didn't even know they had a cousin. Did Slim know? If so, why hadn't he told anyone?

Why had Jake taken her and Joe out here? He said it was because she was too close to it. Too close to what? The truth? Which truth? The truth about him being a Hazard or the truth about him killing Ty Stokes?

Mel felt the dust tickle her nose, and she had a violent spell of sneezing, which was disgusting because, with her hands behind her back, she could hardly use them and had to wipe her nose on her shoulder. Ick.

"God bless you," Joe said.

"Joe! You're awake," she cried. "Thank goodness. Joe, we have to get out of here. I have no idea what Jake's planning or what he's up to, but it can't be good."

"Jake?" Joe's voice was groggy. "Did you remember to feed Captain Jack? I keep hearing him crying."

"I think you were dreaming, Joe," she said gently but insistently. "We're tied up in an old barn, and Captain Jack is home terrorizing my mother with his disappearing acts."

"Oh, yeah," Joe said with a chuckle. "He got stuck in your boot. I like that cat."

"Come on, Joe, catch up," she said.

"It's dark in here," he said. "And it smells like my aunt Carolyn's basement."

"It's a barn," she said with a sigh.

"Oh." He was quiet for a moment or two. "Mel, why are my hands tied behind my back?"

"We're in trouble, Joe," Mel said. "Big trouble."

"The last time I was in trouble with you, I was naked," he said.

"You're thinking about that now?" she asked.

"Then you launched a candle at him, and I got his gun," he said.

"Oh, you're thinking about *that*," she said.

She felt her cheeks grow warm in the dark. Joe had been thinking of the last time they had faced off with a killer, while she had been thinking he meant . . . Well, the word *naked* did bring certain moments to mind. She shook her head to clear it.

"Joe, how's your head? Are you woozy? Do you have a headache?" she asked. "I need you to help me think of a way out of here."

"You know, I'd rather be tied to you than any other woman I've ever known," he said. He leaned his head back so it rested on her right shoulder, and when she leaned her head back to do the same, she could just see the outline of his face.

"Oh, Joe," she sighed.

"Mel, will you marry me?" he asked.

Thirty-one

The door squealed in protest as it was forced open, and Mel wondered if it had been waiting for her answer. An answer that was wiped from her mind as she took in the figure of a man silhouetted in the doorway.

"Jake, you've reconsidered. Thank goodness," she said.

"I'm afraid not, Mel," he said. "You're going to have to come with me."

Mel wished she could see Joe's face to figure out what to do. Jake came over and hauled them up to their feet. He took off the rope that had them tied together, and Mel would have given anything to throw her arms around Joe. Instead, she circled around to the front of him, trying to see if his pupils were dilated. The light in the barn was dim, and his eyes were such a rich brown, she couldn't tell.

"Jake, I think you hit him too hard," she said. "I think he might have a concussion."

"I'm sorry about that," he said. He looked genuinely aggrieved, and Mel didn't doubt him, but it only added to the confusion that was swirling in her head.

"Into the truck," he said.

As they stepped out of the barn, Mel saw that he had parked his truck in front of the barn.

"Hey, nice truck!" Joe said. "Thanks for the lift. I really didn't want to have to walk back."

Jake frowned at him, and Mel tried to look into Joe's eyes again. Now that they were in the last bit of daylight, she could see that his pupils were just fine. Jake was standing on his left side, and Joe used the opportunity to wink at Mel with his right eye, the one Jake couldn't see.

"I really think he's gone wonky," Mel said. "He needs a doctor."

Jake shook his head. "A doctor can't help him now."

Mel and Joe exchanged an alarmed look. The despair in Jake's voice made her more afraid of what he was planning.

Jake pulled a long, lethal-looking knife out of a sheath on his hip, and he sliced through their bonds. Mel's arms ached with the release, and she rolled her shoulders, trying to stretch.

"Come on," Jake said. His voice was almost gentle when he said to Mel, "You'll need to drive."

"No problem. She's a great driver." Joe gave him a loopy look that Mel was glad she knew was a put-on, or she'd have been worried.

Joe strode to the truck as if he didn't have a care in the world.

"Where to, then?" he asked. He held open the driver's side door for Mel, and as she climbed in he made his way to the other side. "I'm hungry. Anyone else care for a nice, juicy steak?"

"Later, maybe," Jake said. He had his gun in hand, and he followed Joe into the truck cab.

Mel turned the key, and in a steady voice, she asked, "Where to, then?"

"Dead Man's Curve," Jake said.

"Is it a restaurant?" Joe asked. "Great name. It sounds like a restaurant with great steaks."

Mel felt her breathing get tight. She remembered her first encounter with Dead Man's Curve. The cupcake van had barely made it around the treacherous turns on their way here. She did not like the resigned feeling she was getting from Jake.

"Jake, what are you planning?" she asked.

"It's over," he said. "I have to go, and I have to take the only people who know who I really am with me."

"No, you don't . . ." Mel protested.

"Take a right," Jake told her. The conversation was clearly over as far as he was concerned.

Mel turned onto the road that Jake indicated. The truck was quiet. Mel was frantically trying to come up with an argument that might sway Jake, but she was at a loss. They were only miles away from the curve. Did Joe know what was ahead? Was there a way she could tell him?

"You know, I had an interesting case recently," Joe said. "You'll enjoy hearing about this, Mel."

She looked at him, trying to make him see her eyes, which were flashing "Really? Work talk now?"

He smiled and took one hand off the dashboard to pat her hand. "Seriously, it's a great case. You up for it, Jake?"

"Sure," he said.

"Well, we thought it was a slam dunk," Joe said. "We had a victim, we had the murder weapon, and we had who we thought was the killer."

Mel saw Jake inch closer to listen. He looked like a man being thrown a lifeline, and he was trying to decide whether or not to grab it.

"What happened?" he asked.

"Well, we didn't have the whole story," Joe said. "Turns out the guy had been trying to protect his sister from her abusive husband. The sister had been hiding out with him, but the husband found her. He broke into the house in the middle of the night and tried to kidnap his wife. The brother heard him and tried to stop him, but the husband grabbed him by the throat. He tried to choke him to death, but the brother had a knife tucked into his waistband, and he stabbed him."

"And that's considered self-defense?" Jake asked.

"Yes. But see, he was so freaked-out about killing someone that he didn't tell the police the whole story. He and his sister cooked up some crazy story about the guy tripping and falling on the knife."

"Seriously?" Mel asked.

Joe nodded. "By the time he told us the truth, so much time had passed, it really could have messed up his defense."

"I know what you're trying to do," Jake said. "And although I appreciate your good intentions, I'm not talking."

"But, Jake, don't you see?" Mel asked. "This is just going to make it worse."

"No, it won't," he argued. "Everyone will be free to continue their lives, and they won't ever have to know about what I did."

"Everyone but us?" Mel asked. "Because you're taking us with you, aren't you?"

Jake wouldn't meet her gaze. "I'm sorry, Mel. I really am. I wish I didn't have to do this."

"You don't have to," Joe said. "Jake, I'm an assistant DA. I know how the system works, and I can help you."

"Pull over here on the shoulder," Jake said.

Mel fell back in her seat, relief pounding through her. They weren't going to meet their end on Dead Man's Curve.

Mel hit the brakes, and they slid on the loose gravel toward the shoulder. Mel put the truck in park and went to switch the engine off.

"No, don't switch it off," Jake said. "Just climb out— both of you."

Mel and Joe exchanged an alarmed glance but hurried to do as he asked. Jake moved into the driver's seat, perched halfway out the open door and still holding the gun in his hand.

"I never planned to take you over the curve with me," he said. "I'm sorry if I scared you. I brought you out here because I want to confess to you, so you can tell everyone that I killed Ty."

Jake paused and looked out over the land, as if absorbing it one last time while he figured out exactly what he wanted to say.

"I killed him because he was going to kill Slim, and I couldn't let that happen, because Slim is my uncle and he's a good man. What happened with Ty's father was a freak accident, but if Ty had killed Slim, it would have been cold-blooded murder."

"Jake, please don't do this." Mel took a step forward, but Jake waved the gun at her.

"No, don't come any closer. I appreciate that you want to help, but there is no help for me now. There never has been."

He went to pull the door shut when a squeal of wheels made them all jump. Around the corner came the cupcake van with a crazy-eyed Oz at the wheel and Lily Hazard hanging out the passenger window, holding a rifle.

Joe grabbed Mel and jumped clear, covering her with his body. The rifle let out one blast, and Mel looked up to see Jake go down.

"She shot him!" she grunted from underneath Joe. "I can't believe she shot him!"

Joe rolled off Mel, checking her over for injuries while he helped her up.

The cupcake van skidded to a halt beside Jake's truck, kicking up a cloud of dust. The doors flew open, and the back hatch was yanked up, and out poured all of the Hazards as well as Angie and Tate.

Slim and Tammy hurried to Jake's side. He'd dropped his gun, and he was holding his leg and cursing.

Lily slid out of the passenger's door and lowered her shotgun. She looked pale and shaky, and Tate reached out and took the gun while Angie folded Lily into her arms.

Mel scanned the chaos around her and saw Oz still in the driver's seat. She squeezed Joe's arm and said, "Help Jake."

He nodded, and she hurried over to Oz.

"You okay?" she asked.

"I don't think I can let go of the steering wheel," he said.

He swiveled his head to look at her, and Mel noticed his bangs were blown back from his face, as if he'd run here and the wind had pushed his hair aside. His eyes were wide, but she wasn't sure if it was terror or just the surprise of not looking through his usual hank of hair.

"Let me help you," she said.

She reached into the vehicle and gently pried his fingers off the wheel. Oz let her. And once he was free, she reached over him and put the van in park and shut off the engine.

"Come on," she said. "You're okay now."

She stepped back and opened the door. She helped Oz out, and he doubled over, trying to catch his breath.

"I didn't think we were going to make it in time," he said. "Marty and Ms. Delia saw Jake holding a gun on you and Joe. They came and told us at the van. We knew something wasn't right, but then we couldn't find you. Luckily, Lily spotted Jake's truck at the old barn, so we all jumped in the van and followed him, thinking he'd lead us to you. And he did."

Mel ran her hand down his back, trying to offer comfort. His T-shirt was hot and wet and stuck to his skin. She knew he'd sweat through the cotton in an adrenaline rush that appeared to have left him dizzy.

"No worries," she said. "By the way, that was some sweet driving."

Oz eased his way upright and grinned. " 'My driving is rivaled only by the lightning bolts from the heavens!' "

Mel grinned. "*Cannonball Run*. Nice."

They tapped knuckles.

"Come on, let's check on the others," she said.

As they rounded the truck, she saw Lily propped be-tween Tate and Angie. A few days ago, Mel never would have believed that possible, but it seemed as if the three of them had reached some sort of understanding. She was go-ing to have to demand answers later.

Joe was kneeling with Tammy and Slim beside Jake. Tammy had taken off her Western shirt and was now in just a tank top. She was putting pressure on Jake's leg as Slim braced him. She looked very professional, and Mel won-dered what other skills the Texas beauty queen had.

"I need to call this in, Slim," Joe said.

Slim looked up at Mel as she joined their group. He looked older than Mel had ever seen him, even after he'd been shot and Ty had been stabbed. He gave Joe a nod, and Joe stepped away from the group with his phone.

"I don't understand, Jake. What were you thinking?" he asked.

"You need to tell him, Jake," Mel said.

Jake's face was screwed up in agony. He was huffing and puffing, as if trying to lasso the pain like it was a runaway bull. Finally, he drew in a shaky breath.

"I knew my cousin was a good shot," he said. "But I'd rather not be on the receiving end of her marksmanship."

Slim went very still. Tammy gasped. Lily, who had come forward and knelt beside Jake, looked bewildered.

"You're Hannah's . . ." Slim's voice cracked, and he didn't finish the sentence.

"Son," Jake said. "I'm Hannah Hazard's son."

Slim sat back in the dirt with a thump. Tears welled up

in his eyes as he studied the face in front of him that was so like his and his sister's.

"Why didn't you tell me?" he asked. "Do you have any idea how long I've looked for you?"

Jake looked surprised. "You did?"

Slim pressed his lips together and gave a sad nod. He cupped the back of Jake's head and pulled him close until they were forehead to forehead. Mel felt her own throat get tight, and Tammy began to silently weep.

"Daddy, what's going on?" Lily asked. She was looking from Jake to her father and back again, and Mel wondered if she was seeing the resemblance for the first time.

"My sister, Hannah, didn't die in a car accident," Slim said as he leaned away from his nephew. He didn't take his eyes off him, as if afraid he might disappear again. "My parents were ashamed, mortified really, that she'd gotten pregnant without being married. They sent her to California to have the baby. She was supposed to give it up for adoption, but she died giving birth."

Everyone was quiet, taking in the sad ending to a young woman's life.

"I never understood why my parents didn't adopt the baby themselves," Slim said. "I fought with them about it, but I couldn't budge them. The baby was put up for adoption. I'm so sorry, son. It shouldn't have gone that way."

Jake nodded. He understood that it had been out of Slim's hands.

"I tried to find you later, but the records were sealed. Did you have good parents? Did you have a good life?"

"I did," Jake said. "It was good, real good."

Mel wondered if she was the only one who could tell he was lying.

"Why didn't you tell me when you first came?" Slim asked.

Jake shrugged one shoulder in embarrassment. "I wanted to check you out first. Then when I got to know you and Tammy and the girls, well, I knew that I liked you, but it was too late. Lily and Shelby both thought my mom had died in an accident, and you never contradicted them, so I thought maybe that's what you believed, too. I wanted to tell you a million times. I just didn't know how."

"Aw, son." Slim shook his head.

Lily knelt down beside Jake and looked at him. "So, you're my cousin?"

He nodded. She sat back on her heels. "I just shot my cousin. Oh my God."

Mel reached out and patted her arm. "It was a good call, wasn't it, Jake?"

He lifted his head and met Mel's gaze. "I have to tell them, don't I?"

Joe was walking back to the group, and Mel nodded.

Jake closed his eyes as if gathering his courage. Now that the Hazards knew the truth about who he was, he seemed able to accept what had to be done.

"I stabbed Ty Stokes," he said.

Thirty-two

"What?" Slim, Tammy, and Lily said together.

"He was the one who shot you," Jake said. "It was supposed to kill you. He figured he'd be able to buy the rodeo from Tammy for a smoking good deal if you were dead, and then he'd rename it after his father."

"How do you know all of this?" Slim asked.

"He told me, right before I got him with the pitchfork," Jake said. His voice was so soft, Mel could barely hear him, and she saw a shudder run through him as he remembered the incident.

"Ty was drunk, and he had a gun. Since his first attempt at the parade failed, he was planning to shoot you again in the arena that night in front of everyone. He wanted you to die like his father did—with an audience."

Slim looked pained. "I knew he blamed me, but I had no idea."

The sound of approaching sirens could be heard in the distance. They were all silent for a moment, and then Slim rose to his feet and said, "We need to get you to the hospital."

"An ambulance is on the way," Joe said. "Hospital first, but he will need to speak to the police, too."

"Lily, get Tewkes on the phone," Slim said. Then he looked at Mel and the others and said, "Sam Tewkesbury, our lawyer."

"Good call," Joe said. "I've heard of him. He's excellent."

The ambulance arrived first. The paramedics took one look at Jake's leg and hustled him onto the stretcher and up into the back. Slim, Lily, and Tammy all got into Sheriff Dolan's car to follow it to the hospital.

Oz still looked shaky, so he climbed into Jake's pickup truck, which Mel drove, and sat on the bench seat in between Mel and Joe. Tate took the wheel of the cupcake van and drove Angie back to the rodeo.

After their mad dash in pursuit of Jake's truck, Mel was afraid to see what had happened to her cake pops and organic cupcakes. She imagined it would look like a train wreck but with cake.

She followed the van along the winding road and down the bumpy dirt road until they reached the rodeo, where Tate steered the big van back into its old spot, and Mel parked just beyond it.

When she got out of the truck, her jaw did a slow slide

open as she saw the Bubbas, Billy and Bob, wearing pink Fairy Tale Cupcake aprons and selling the remaining cake pops and Oz's organic cupcakes out of a small, hastily assembled booth. Marty sat beside them with his feet up, barking orders at them while they glowered at him.

Angie hopped out of the van and hurried over to Mel. "Oh, in all of the excitement, I forgot to mention we won the bet by a cake pop."

"No way!" Mel laughed and approached the Bubbas with her hand out. They both grudgingly shook her hand.

"Let it be noted," Bob said, "that barbecue men are men of their word."

"I think this color is picking up the red highlights in my beard," Billy said, and gave Mel a charming curtsy.

She laughed. "You know, if you hadn't sabotaged our freezers and defrosted all of our cupcakes, I wouldn't have had to make cake pops out of them, and you may have won the bet. The cake pops really put us over the top."

The Bubbas gave her a confused look. "We didn't sabotage your truck."

"Oh, come on," Angie chimed in. "You can admit it; it's cool. We won, so we won't be mad."

The Bubbas put their right hands over their hearts. "We're telling the truth. On our smoker's ability to turn out perfect brisket, we didn't mess with your van."

Mel and Angie exchanged a look as the Bubbas attended the line that had formed.

"So, it was just an accident?" Angie asked. "How crazy is that?"

"Almost as crazy as you being friends with Lily," Mel said. "So what gives?"

"Lily likes girls," Angie said in a low voice.

It took Mel a minute, and then she said, "Oh, so that's why Tate . . ."

"Yeah," Angie said. They both looked at their partner while he helped Joe, Marty, and Oz get the van ready for customers again. The Bubbas helped, too, and in no time the van was back in business.

"I broke up with Roach," Angie said. Mel snapped her head in Angie's direction. Angie turned and gave her a small smile. "Lily sort of made me see that I, well, you know. And no, I haven't told Tate yet, but I will. I promise I will."

"Wow." Mel didn't know what else to say. "How did he take it?"

"I don't think it was entirely unexpected," Angie said. "Now, what about you and Joe? Are you two okay? That had to be scary being carted off like that. I can't imagine what Jake was thinking."

"He wasn't thinking. Jake popped Joe in the temple, and he was unconscious for most of it," Mel said.

"Wow," Angie said. "That had to be scary."

"A little bit," Mel agreed.

She thought back to the barn and the scuffling noise and then remembered Joe's proposal. Had he meant it, or had he just been rocked from the shot he'd taken to the head? She didn't know. She certainly didn't think she could ask him. If he'd been deluded, that would be humiliating. She supposed she'd just have to wait and see.

"I don't know about you," Angie said, "but I think I'm

ready to go back to one hundred and fifteen degrees of normal."

"I hear that," Mel said. She looped her arm around Angie's shoulders and gave her a half hug. "So, shall we set the Bubbas free?"

"Let me just get a pic on my phone," Angie said. She snapped a quick one of the two men hanging out of the cupcake van holding cake pops, and together they ambled over to the van.

Mel looked up and saw Joe watching her. His gaze was warm, and she got a little dizzy at the impact of his grin. Was she always going to feel that way around Joe DeLaura? Somehow, she had a feeling she would. She grinned back at him and winked, and was pleased to see he looked as flustered as she felt. Maybe, if he asked again . . . well, maybe.

The Fairy Tale Cupcake crew spent the night and the next day packing up, saying good-bye to their new friends like Ruth and Delia and the Hazards in between their visits with the sheriff to give witness to everything they knew.

Mel asked Joe what the odds were that Jake would get off. He said he didn't know, but given that he had produced the gun that Ty had had that night in the stable, and that it matched the type of gun used to shoot Slim, things were not as bleak for him as they could have been.

Mel tried not to think about how different Jake's life

might have been if his grandparents had claimed him upon his mother's death. Despite what he'd done, she couldn't help but hope that he got a second chance.

When they were leaving, Mel decided to ride with Joe in his car. Even though they still had to get through Dead Man's Curve, she found she really couldn't face doing it in the van.

They were departing the rodeo grounds when a flash of pink caught her eye. Up ahead, parked on the side of the road, was Olivia Puckett's bakery van.

"What is she doing here?" Mel asked Joe, as if he could possibly give her an answer.

Mel pulled out her phone and quickly dialed Angie. She answered on the first ring.

"We see her," Angie said. Oz pulled the cupcake truck alongside Olivia's van.

"What is she—?" Mel began but Angie cut her off, "Hey, Puckett, you're a little out of your delivery area, aren't you?"

"I'm on vacation," Olivia yelled back. "You got a problem with that?"

"Yeah, I've got a problem with that," Angie yelled. "Especially when you sabotage our van. It was you! You unplugged our freezers and defrosted all of our cupcakes."

Olivia laughed and then sobered. "You can't prove anything."

Oz gunned the engine. Even from behind them, Mel could see Olivia grin.

"Oh, it's on!" Marty's voice came through her phone, and Mel gave Joe a look of alarm. He grabbed the phone out of her hand and said, "Angie! Don't do this! Do you hear me? Tate! Are you there?"

He dropped the phone in Mel's lap. "They hung up."

Mel glanced out the window just in time to see Oz and Olivia race down the dirt road.

"Idiots!" Joe said, and he stomped on the gas to follow.

They had gone only a half mile when there was a tremendous *bang*, and the pink van began to swerve. Olivia fought with the steering wheel but managed to get it to the side. A quick glance as they passed told Mel that she had managed to pop two tires.

She and Joe exchanged a look of relief, and then her phone rang.

"Did you see that?" Someone, it sounded like Tate, was yelling into the phone.

It was impossible to understand another word over all the whooping and cheering. "Apparently, they're fine," she said, and ended the call. "I can't believe Olivia drove all the way up here to sabotage our van."

"Really? Because she'd been so stable in the past?" Joe asked.

"Good point," Mel said.

She sank back into her seat. Even dealing with Olivia's kind of crazy felt more normal than the past few days, and although she had loved the gorgeous scenery and weather of northern Arizona, she was happy to be heading south.

"Let's go home, Joe," she said.

"We're on our way, Cupcake," he said.

Mel hadn't planned on falling asleep, but the stress and pressure of the past few days had left her exhausted. Without thinking about it, her eyelids drooped, and before they had even reached the grasslands, she was asleep.

⌇⌇

A change in the sound of the engine eased Mel out of her slumber. She had wedged herself against the seat and the door, and her neck was stiff from being at an odd angle for so long.

"Where are we?" she asked.

"Just passed Payson," Joe said.

Mel looked out the window to see that they were off the main road and on a dirt road that led into the desert. Joe drove a little ways down the road and pulled over. The sun was just setting, bathing the small canyon in front of them in a golden hue, a color that could only be found in nature. Mel gazed at it in awe.

"The brothers and I used to camp here. I thought it would be a good spot for us to stretch our legs," he said.

"Good idea," she said.

He shut off the engine, came around to her side of the car, and opened the door. Mel got out, grateful to stretch the kinks out of her legs and back. She paced a few steps down the deserted road and paused to glance up at the mountains in the distance.

The fireball of a summer sun slipped behind the ridge of the mountains and set the sky ablaze in the richest red she'd ever seen. She turned to point it out to Joe and saw him slowly sink to one knee.

"You never answered my question," he said.

Mel felt her heart slow down, pounding through her body like a mallet on a gong.

The hot desert air scorched her skin as it swirled past them in a dust devil, taking stray leaves and Mel's power of speech with it.

"I was telling you the truth in the barn when I said there was no one I'd rather be tied to for the rest of my life. It's you, Melanie Cooper. It's always been you. Will you marry me?"

Recipes

French Toast Cupcake

A vanilla cupcake with maple buttercream frosting and chopped bacon sprinkled on top.

Vanilla Cupcake

1¾ cups flour
1¼ teaspoons baking powder
½ teaspoon baking soda
¼ teaspoon salt
1½ sticks butter, unsalted
1 cup sugar
2 teaspoons vanilla extract
3 eggs

1½ tablespoons vegetable oil
⅔ cup milk

Preheat oven to 350 degrees. Put paper liners in cupcake pan. In a large bowl, sift flour, baking powder, baking soda, and salt. Set aside. With an electric mixer, cream the butter and sugar until light and fluffy. Add vanilla. Add eggs, one at a time. Add oil and milk. Slowly add the flour mixture and mix until just combined. Fill the cupcake liners about ⅔ full. Bake about 18–22 minutes or until a toothpick inserted in the middle comes out clean. Cool completely before frosting.

Maple Buttercream

½ cup shortening
½ cup butter, softened
2 tablespoons real maple syrup
4 cups powdered sugar
2 tablespoons milk
Chopped bacon for garnish

Cream together ½ cup shortening and ½ cup butter using an electric mixer. Add maple syrup. Gradually add powdered sugar and milk; beat until light and airy. Sprinkle with chopped bacon before frosting sets.

Vegan Chocolate Cupcake

A chocolate cupcake with a soy milk base and organic
chocolate frosting.

1 cup soy milk
1 teaspoon apple cider vinegar
2/3 cup agave nectar
1/3 cup canola oil
1 teaspoon vanilla extract
1/2 teaspoon almond extract
1 cup all-purpose organic flour
1/3 cup cocoa powder, unsweetened
3/4 teaspoon baking soda
1/2 teaspoon baking powder
1/4 teaspoon salt

Preheat oven to 350. Whisk together soy milk and vinegar
in a large bowl and set aside until it curdles. Add the agave
nectar, oil, vanilla extract, and almond extract to the soy
milk mixture and beat until foamy. In another bowl, sift together the flour, cocoa powder, baking soda, baking powder, and salt. Add to the wet ingredients and beat until no
lumps remain. Pour into cupcake liners until they are ¾ of
the way full. Bake 18–20 minutes until a knife inserted
comes out clean. Cool on wire racks.

Vegan Chocolate Frosting

1 cup cocoa powder, unsweetened
¾ cup organic margarine, softened
1 teaspoon vanilla
1 cup agave nectar

In a small bowl, mix together the cocoa powder, margarine, vanilla, and agave nectar. Beat until it is smooth. Spread on top of cupcake with a rubber spatula.

Vegan Vanilla Cupcake

A vanilla cupcake with a soy milk base and an organic vanilla frosting.

1 cup vanilla soy milk
1 teaspoon apple cider vinegar
²/₃ cup agave nectar
¹/₃ cup canola oil
2 teaspoons vanilla extract
1 cup all-purpose organic flour
¾ teaspoon baking soda
½ teaspoon baking powder
¼ teaspoon salt

Preheat oven to 350. Whisk together soy milk and vinegar in a large bowl and set aside until it curdles. Add the agave nectar, oil, and vanilla extract to the soy milk mixture and beat with an electric mixer until foamy. In another bowl, sift together the flour, baking soda, baking powder, and salt. Add to the wet ingredients and beat until no lumps remain. Pour into cupcake liners until they are $^2/_3$ of the way full. Bake 18–20 minutes until a knife inserted comes out clean. Cool on wire racks.

Vegan Vanilla Frosting

6 tablespoons vanilla soy milk
2 tablespoons Trader Joe's Vanilla Bean Paste
¼ cup organic margarine
1 16-ounce package organic powdered sugar, sifted

In a small bowl, mix together soy milk, vanilla bean paste, and margarine. Slowly beat in the sugar until frosting is smooth. Spread on top of cupcake with a rubber spatula.

Cake Pops

A cake and frosting confection dipped in candy coating
and served on a stick.

1 cake (9 x 13) or 18 cupcakes (out of liners)
2 cups buttercream or cream cheese frosting
2 packages of candy melts
30 lollipop sticks (large thick ones)
1 large foam block

In a large bowl, crumble up the cake into very small pieces. Using a rubber spatula, stir in the frosting until it is well mixed; it should be the consistency of truffles. Roll the cake frosting mixture into walnut-sized balls and place on a cookie sheet coated with wax paper.

Once all the cake has been rolled, put it in the fridge to harden a bit. Melt the candy in a double boiler or a microwave according to the manufacturer's instructions.

Take the cake balls out of the fridge and dip the end of a lollipop stick into the melted candy. Slide a cake ball about half an inch down onto the candy-tipped stick. Now dip the whole cake ball into the melted candy, tapping it very gently on the side of the bowl to get rid of the excess.

Stand the cake pop up by pushing the non-cake end into the foam block. If you're decorating with sprinkles, sugars, or coconut, now is the time to do it, as the candy will harden fairly quickly. Repeat until you're out of cake balls and melted candy.

Turn the page for a preview of Jenn McKinlay's
next book in the Cupcake Mysteries...

Going, Going, Ganache

Coming soon from Berkley Prime Crime!

"No, I'm not feeling it," Amy Pierson said. "Do it again and this time try to give it that southwestern city-girl flare. This photo shoot is for *Southwest Style* magazine, after all."

Angie DeLaura looked at Melanie Cooper as if to ask if she could please hurl a cupcake at the bossy butt in the couture suit. Mel gave a slight shake of her blond head in the negative. She didn't want to move too much and have Amy yell at her again.

It was mid-October in Scottsdale, Arizona, and although the sun was hot, the breeze was cool, keeping the inordinate amount of make-up Mel had on from melting off her face. She and Angie were outside their bakery in the small patio area, posing for a picture to run alongside the piece that had been written about them for an upcoming issue of *South-*

west Style, the premiere magazine about urban living in the desert.

What Mel had assumed would be a staff photographer snapping a picture of them behind the counter in the bakery had turned into a full-on spread, featuring Mel and Angie in poofy retro fifties skirts, with crinolines, and starched cotton blouses with pearls.

Because Scottsdale's heyday had been the fifties and because the bakery was decorated in a retro fifties style, Amy Pierson, the magazine's art director, had decided to run with the fifties theme, and thus Mel and Angie found themselves outfitted like June Cleaver on stilettos.

The make-up artist had teased Angie's long brown hair into an updo a la Audrey Hepburn, while Mel's short blond locks had been styled in waves reminiscent of Marilyn Monroe. They were tricked out in an ultrafeminine chic that made them positively unrecognizable.

"My head itches," Angie whispered.

"My feet hurt," Mel returned. The high heels they had put them in were arch crampers, and Mel longed for her beat-up Keds, her comfy jeans, and a simple T-shirt.

"Okay, ladies, let's see those smiles," the photographer said. He was a young guy named Chad, who happily snapped away while Mel and Angie stood frozen, trying to look like they were having the time of their lives, surrounded by tiers and trays of cupcakes.

Fairy Tale Cupcakes, their bakery in Old Town Scottsdale, was in the heart of the tourist district, which was one of the many reasons for their success. They did loads of special orders but their walk-in traffic kept them steadily busy with drop-ins who wanted to fortify themselves with a cupcake or two before, during, and after a day of doing the tourist thing.

Mel observed the crowd gathering to watch and hoped that Marty Zelaznik and Oz Ruiz, her two bakery employees, were inside preparing for the crush once the magazine people departed.

The magazine had asked Mel to design cupcakes that would reflect the Southwest, so she had used bright fondant to create cupcakes devoted to cactus flower blossoms. Each cupcake sported a flower, so magenta prickly pear blooms blended with white and yellow saguaro flowers in several tiers of cupcakes that were festive and lovely and very southwestern.

Mel wasn't entirely comfortable with the look she and Angie were using to represent the bakery. But given that the magazine had a national subscription rate of several hundred thousand, she was determined to do whatever it took to get in print. The coverage would go a long way toward making Fairy Tale Cupcakes the place to buy cupcakes in the Valley of the Sun.

Chad snapped away, stepping closer and then backing away, dropping to one knee and then climbing on a chair, all to get the shots he wanted. Mel smiled until her face hurt and her eyes began to cross. Angie was making small whimperlike noises in the back of her throat as Chad paused in front of them. *Snap. Snap. Snap.*

"No!" Amy said, peering over his shoulder to study them. "I'm still not feeling it. Chad, let's discuss. Maybe it's the lighting."

"Relax, ladies, but don't move too far," Chad said as he went to confer with Amy.

" 'Every girl on every page of *Quality* has grace, elegance, and pizzazz. Now what's wrong with bringing out a girl who has character, spirit, and intelligence?' " Angie muttered to Mel.

Classic movie buffs, they had played this game with their friend Tate Harper since they were kids. Mel was about to identify the movie when a voice from nearby said, " 'That certainly would be novel in a fashion magazine.' "

Mel and Angie both turned to look at the man.

"*Funny Girl* with Audrey Hepburn and Fred Astaire," he said. "Good one."

"Looks like we found a new member of our tribe," Mel said. She held out her hand to him. "Melanie Cooper."

"Angie DeLaura," Angie said as she did the same.

The tall, red-haired man smiled as he shook each of their hands. He was dressed all in black and had the chiseled good looks of a male model. Mel noticed that his hand was soft to the touch and his fingernails were neatly trimmed and buffed. She sighed. She couldn't remember the last time she'd had a professional manicure.

"Travis Freehold," he said. "Creative director for *SWS*."

"Is it just me, Travis?" Angie asked. "Or do there seem to be an awful lot of chefs in this photo shoot kitchen?"

"Nice mixed metaphor," Mel said. "But she's right, who are all of these people?"

Travis scanned the crowd.

"Good question," he said. "Pretty much anyone with their name on the masthead is here and that's why."

He jerked his head in the direction of a man standing apart. He was tall and fit, but looked to be somewhere in his fifties, as his dark hair was giving way to silver. He had laugh lines that creased the corners of his eyes but he also sported a hard jaw that made Mel think he was accustomed to making tough decisions.

"That would be our new leader, Ian Hannigan," Travis said. "He just bought the magazine and saved it from an untimely death. Everyone is determined to shine under his ever-watchful gaze."

"So that's why this went from a 'say cheese' to a 'strike a pose' layout," Angie said. "I suppose in the end it will be better for the bakery, but when we get done, I may just shave my head. Honestly, feel this."

She raised her right hand and patted her head. It didn't move. Curious, Mel touched the loaf of hair on Angie's head. Yep, it was as crusty on the outside as a baguette.

"Wow," she said.

"More like ow," Angie retorted.

Travis squinted into the crowd. "I know most everyone here, except for her. Does she work for you?"

Mel followed the line of his gaze. Striding through the crowd, with her stocky frame wedged into a polka dot blouse and a black poodle skirt with a pink poodle on it and wearing black and white saddle shoes, was Olivia Puckett. She was also hoisting a tray of brightly colored cupcakes over her head.

"Please tell me I'm hallucinating," Angie said.

"Okay, but you have to do the same for me," Mel said.

Olivia owned the rival bakery called Confections and for reasons unknown to Mel, she had developed a pathological competitiveness with Mel and Angie. It seemed if there was baking attention to be had, Olivia wanted all of it.

"Oh, yoo hoo, magazine people," Olivia called. "If

you're having a hard time photographing these two, I'd be happy to fill in."

"Is she for real?" Angie snapped. "I did not let them do this to me," she pointed to her head, "so that woman could march in here in that ridiculous skirt and take over our photo shoot."

"I'll take care of this," Travis said. "I can't imagine Amy would do a switch-up like this in the eleventh hour."

Mel watched as Travis approached Amy and Chad and the silver-haired Ian Hannigan. They huddled together like players on a football team, and Mel was alarmed when she saw Amy's head break out of the circle and stare at Olivia with a considering look.

"This is unbelievable," Angie said.

"What's the holdup?" a cranky voice asked from behind Mel. "How long does it take to snap a few pictures?"

Mel turned to find Marty and Oz had slipped out the front door to join them.

"What's she doing here?" Oz asked. He did not have to specify that he was talking about Olivia.

"Trying to horn in on our photo shoot," Mel said. "Apparently, Angie and I are so unphotogenic that they're actually considering it."

"Aw, what's the matter, Princess?" Olivia sneered as she ambled over to the patio. "You don't really think you're model material do you?"

Mel heaved a sigh. She was pretty sure she was developing a bunion on her right foot, and the last thing she needed was a battle with Olivia.

"How did you find out about this?" she asked.

Olivia shrugged. "I have my ways."

Her eyes shifted away, however, and the piercing truth hit Mel like a dart in a bull's-eye.

"You have a spy!"

"What? No, I don't!"

"Oh, my god, look at her face!" Oz said. "She's totally lying."

"I am not," Olivia huffed.

"Then how did you know to dress in that getup?" Marty asked as he moved in front of Mel and Angie as if to protect them. "Someone tipped you off that they were doing a fifties theme."

"Listen, old man," Olivia said.

"Who are you calling old, gray beard?" Marty interrupted.

"Ah!" Olivia took one hand off the tray of cupcakes she was still holding to feel her chin for errant whiskers.

Feeling none, she snarled at Marty, grabbed a vivid pink cupcake off of her tray, and lobbed it at him.

Marty ducked and it landed in Angie's hair and got wedged there like a bird in a nest. Angie wobbled on her feet; obviously the weight of the cupcake in her already heavy hair had knocked her off balance.

"Ha! How'd you like that, Princess?" Olivia cackled. "I've got one with your name on it, too."

"Stop calling me Princess!" Mel snapped, trying to steady Angie as she listed to one side.

"No?" Olivia asked. "How about I call you b—?"

A white cactus flower cupcake landed with smack dab precision right in Olivia's pie hole. Mel whipped her head around and saw Marty looking at her with an innocent expression.

"What?" he asked. "I slipped."

"Nice," Oz said, and the two exchanged a knuckle bump. "Pitcher?"

"All-American," Marty said. "You know, back in the day."

Mel propped Angie against the table. Angie gave Marty an impressed thumbs-up, but Mel knew retaliation—

Smack! A cupcake slammed into the side of her head. The cupcake thudded to the ground, but she could feel the frosting ooze down her face as it slid out of her short blond hair and landed on her shoulder.

Now she was mad. Mel forgot about Ian Hannigan the owner of the magazine. She forgot that they were supposed to be here to showcase their shop with a happy, peppy photo shoot. Without thinking of the consequences of her actions, Mel snatched the spotlighted extra large cupcake in the center of the table and charged at Olivia with a roar reminiscent of Mel Gibson's character in *Braveheart*.

FROM *NEW YORK TIMES* BESTSELLING AUTHOR

JENN MCKINLAY

~~~

THE CUPCAKE BAKERY MYSTERIES

Sprinkle with Murder
Buttercream Bump Off
Death by the Dozen
Red Velvet Revenge
Going, Going, Ganache

INCLUDES SCRUMPTIOUS RECIPES!

~~~

Praise for the Cupcake Bakery Mysteries

"Delectable . . . A real treat."
—Julie Hyzy, national bestselling author
of the White House Chef Mysteries

"A tender cozy full of warm and likable characters
and...tasty concoctions."
—*Publishers Weekly* (starred review)

jennmckinlay.com
facebook.com/JennMcKinlaysBooks
facebook.com/TheCrimeSceneBooks
penguin.com

M1212AS1112

FROM *NEW YORK TIMES* BESTSELLING AUTHOR

JENN MCKINLAY

-The Library Lover's Mysteries-

BOOKS CAN BE DECEIVING
DUE OR DIE
BOOK, LINE, AND SINKER

Praise for the Library Lover's Mysteries

"[An] appealing new mystery series."
—Kate Carlisle, *New York Times* bestselling author

"A sparkling setting, lovely characters, books, knitting, and chowder! What more could any reader ask?"
—Lorna Barrett, *New York Times* bestselling author

"Sure to charm cozy readers everywhere."
—Ellery Adams, author of the Books by the Bay Mysteries

facebook.com/TheCrimeSceneBooks
penguin.com